A month after her adventures trying to track down the killer of her friend Charles Latimer, Emmeline finds herself in a car that has crashed on a lonely country road in Kent with a dead man as her companion. How did she come to find herself in this predicament? It all started with a man named Ambrose Trent, the fiancé of her friend Claire Sedgwick. But there's something not quite right about Ambrose. When he ends up dead, Emmeline believes she knows who the killer is. But as new evidence comes to light, she realizes she's dead wrong—and only Gregory can save her.

KUDOS for *Deadly Legacy*

"Stolen diamonds, revenge, and murder are served up at a cracking pace as Emmeline unites with Gregory once again in this intriguing second installment of Daniella Bernett's mystery series." ~ Tessa Arlen, author of the *Lady Montfort* series and Agatha Award finalist

"Melding mystery and romance with fast-paced action and spine-tingling suspense, the author has crafted a story that will appeal to mystery and romance fans alike." ~ Taylor Jones, Reviewer

"Emmeline and Gregory's new adventure is a delightful blend of mystery and romance, filled with dazzling twists and turns, unexpected dangers, and old and new tensions in their relationship." ~ Tracy Grant, author of *London Gambit*

Deadly Legacy is a well-written tale of love, murder, greed, and the determination to do the right thing, even in the face of harsh opposition. Once you pick it up, you won't want to put it down until the end. ~ Regan Murphy, Reviewer

ACKNOWLEDGEMENTS

My continued gratitude to the Mystery Writers of America New York Chapter for its support, particularly Sheila and Gerald Levine, Richie Narvaez, and Nina Mansfield.

I also would like to thank bestselling authors Tracy Grant, Tessa Arlen, and Susan Elia MacNeal for their kindness and for believing in me.

DEADLY

LEGACY

An Emmeline Kirby/
Gregory Longdon Mystery

Daniella Bernett

A Black Opal Books Publication

To my parents and my sister Vivian with love.
I am so lucky to have you.

PREFACE

The noise came from a long way off. Angry, persistent. It rattled round and round the outer edges of Emmeline's consciousness. A despicable pain throbbed mercilessly as it slowly slithered up from the base of her skull all the way to her temples. Surely her head was going to explode at any moment. She couldn't see. The menacing blackness was everywhere. Taunting her, clawing at her. She suffocated in its embrace.

Gradually, she realized that her eyes were closed. She shifted slightly, groaning as her head rebelled against the thousand needles of pain the movement caused. Something was holding her back. What was it? She opened one eye tentatively and then the other. It was still dark. With a supreme effort that made her wish she were dead, she managed to lift her head. Beads of perspiration moistened her brow from the exertion. Trying to catch her breath, she focused on her surroundings. She was in a car. Her eyes fluttered closed again. The seat belt was cutting into her ribcage. Her clumsy fingers fumbled to open it. After the third attempt, she was free.

Emmeline opened her eyes once more, squinting hard to channel her disjointed thoughts. The noise that had plucked her from the inky depths of oblivion was rain. Not a pleasant spring rain, but rather a seething torrent that lashed against the windows and sent an icy tremor of fear down her spine. *Where was she? What was she doing here?*

Before she could answer these questions, she passed out.

When she came round, there was another sound mingling with the tempest outside her window. It was…violins. *Violins? In the middle of nowhere?* She thought she had become delirious. Her ears strained toward the music. Yes, it *was* violins mimicking the rain. *The Four Seasons…Summer…*Vivaldi. It was the radio. She wasn't losing her mind after all. She sighed with relief. But Vivaldi reminded her of her recent trip to Venice, which, in turn, led to thoughts of Gregory. She squeezed her eyes tightly shut, hoping to push away these unsettling ramblings. However, her eyes snapped open as a searing white flash scorched the night sky. Then thunder cracked its vicious whip.

In that instant, when the lightning illuminated everything as if it were daytime, Emmeline saw that she wasn't alone in the car. There was a man in the driver's seat and he was quite dead. *A dead man*, just like Venice. The pounding in her head and the music were converging in a crescendo, but, despite her revulsion, she made a concerted effort to look at him. It was Ambrose Trent.

She could feel herself slipping from consciousness. *He was right. I did kill him. But you can't kill a man who never existed. Can you?*

Emmeline was dead wrong.

CHAPTER 1

London, March 2010:

It wasn't the mizzle—a particularly noisome cross between mist and drizzle—that made Emmeline hurry along the pavement toward the teashop. It was the wind that whipped everything into a frenzy and helped the chilly dampness to burrow deep into the marrow of her bones. She longed for sunshine and the caress of a gentle spring breeze. It wasn't too much to ask for, was it? It was the end of March, after all. Her umbrella was useless against the onslaught, so she dug her hands into her coat pockets and leaned into the wind. She was determined to come out the victor in this battle of wills.

At Queen's Gate, she turned right onto Cromwell Road. She already could see the Victoria and Albert Museum. It was not far now to Miss Charlotte's Tea Room—a quaint relic of a gentile era that she and Maggie had stumbled upon one autumn afternoon when they were at university together. They both had fallen instantly in love with the place—delighting in its dusky rose walls, mismatched porcelain cups and saucers, lace tablecloths, and quiet charm. On that first day, Emmeline and Maggie had made a pact to meet at Miss Charlotte's once a month, no matter what else was going on in their respective lives. The two friends had kept their vow, religiously meeting on the third Thursday of every month.

The teashop was the kind of place that encouraged cozy

chats and where one's cares seemed to melt away the moment
one set foot inside. Today, Emmeline could hardly wait to
wrap her numb fingers around a steaming cup of Earl Grey and
to tuck into a slice of Miss Charlotte's decadent chocolate
brandy torte. Mmm. Sheer heaven. She sighed and let her
tongue roll around her lips in anticipation. And to catch up
with Maggie, *of course*. But the hot tea first. She quickened
her pace.

At last, Emmeline reached Miss Charlotte's. She put out
her hand and turned the doorknob. In that instant, a gust of
wind bore down on her and flung back the door. It shuddered
on its hinges. A tall, slim man in a beige trench coat was hovering just inside in the doorway and blocked her path. The
wind snatched a small piece of paper from his hand. They both
watched its precarious flight down the street, until it had disappeared from view.

The man, whose tousled fair hair clung damply to his
scalp, turned a pair of cornflower-blue eyes upon her. He said
nothing for a long moment, incredulity spreading over his
squared features. Incredulity and something else—*fear*. Emmeline could almost taste it. The muscle in his jaw twitched.
There was a restless, hunted look in his eyes as they darted to
the right and left. This sent a frisson slithering down her spine.

"Oh, pardon me," she mumbled softly as she tried to step
around him.

"Pardon you? *Pardon you?* Do you know what you've
just done?"

"Well, I—"

"You've just killed me. That's all," he announced melodramatically. "I hope you'll be able to sleep at night knowing
what you've done."

He pushed past her without a second glance, the door
slamming angrily behind him. Emmeline felt it as surely as if
he had slapped her across the face.

She stood there on the threshold—her mouth gaping
open—and stared after him. She was stunned by the entire odd
incident.

"Emmeline. *Emmeline.* Over here." Maggie's stage whisper pulled her from her contemplation of the strange young man. Seated at a corner table in the back and waving furiously to attract her attention was Maggie Acheson.

Emmeline waved back and made her way across the L-shaped tea room. She bent down and kissed her dearest friend on both cheeks with genuine affection. "Sorry, Maggie."

"Who was that chap you were chatting with?"

"I've absolutely no idea." Emmeline shrugged out of her coat and plopped down onto the peach-velvet-cushioned chair. "I've never seen him before in my life." Her eyes drifted toward the door again and the whole scene replayed itself inside her head. "It was all rather bizarre." And then, she told Maggie about the contretemps that had been over in a flash.

"Positively intriguing. You do run into the oddest characters. How delicious."

Maggie was warming to her subject. Emmeline recognized the gleam in her friend's sparkling green eyes. She had to put an end to this right now or who knows where it might lead and she didn't want to think about that man any longer.

"Well, we'll never see him again so let's not dwell on the incident. How are the twins?"

Maggie's lovely mouth drooped at this abrupt turn in the conversation. She looped a long strand of reddish-gold hair around her ear and rolled her eyes. "They are a pair of little monsters. I never thought two five-year-old boys could get up to such mischief. But they do. If there's a way to make something dirty or to break it, they always manage it. Sometimes I lie awake at night wondering what Philip and I have done to deserve such punishment."

Emmeline laughed because she knew her friend did not mean a single word of what she was saying. "But you love them anyway and you wouldn't have it any other way."

The corner of Maggie's eyes crinkled as she rested her chin on her hand and joined in Emmeline's laughter. "You're right, of course. You know me too well. How many years have we known each other now?"

"Ten."

"Ten years? My God, I can't believe it. I was only twen-

ty-one and you were a spry twenty. I remember the day we
first met in Prof. Winthrop's Medieval Literature class at Oxford. I don't think I would have survived, if it hadn't been for
you."

"Rubbish. I seem to remember you were the class star."

"That's only because we studied together. You made it all
seem so easy."

Emmeline shook her head. "That's not true. You would
have done perfectly well on your own. Your natural drive and
intelligence will see you through anything that stands in your
path. Look at the way you started your company from scratch.
That took a lot of determination and raw courage."

Indeed, Maggie was president of one the most prestigious
public relations firms in London. Although she came from a
wealthy and well-connected investment banking family and
had lived a privileged life from the day she was born, Maggie
refused to accept any money from her father. She wanted to do
things on her own terms. Perhaps being the youngest, and a
girl, had driven her. Her two older brothers had followed their
father into the bank, but Maggie had no desire to join the family business.

"Oh, go on." She waved a hand dismissively in the air.
"You'll make me blush. And what about you, miss? You told
all of us on the university newspaper that one day you'd be a
reporter at *The Times of London*, not some piddling little rag,
but the THE *Times*. Not an ambition for the faint of heart. And
look at you now. Not only are you at *The Times*, but you're the
paper's top investigative correspondent with a string of awards
to your name. Back at Oxford, we all knew you would succeed
because you were better at it than any of us ever hoped to be.
For us, playing at journalists was a bit of fun, a way to pass the
time. But for you, it was a passion. We could see it in your
eyes. Mix in a heaping spoonful of talent and poof—" Maggie
snapped her fingers in the air. "—and you've got the highly-
respected Emmeline Kirby, whom I'm privileged to call my
best friend."

Emmeline felt tears prick her eyelids. She reached out and
squeezed Maggie's hand. "Thank you. You know I love you

like a sister. Until the day I die, I will be grateful to that literature class."

They were both teary-eyed and giggly at the same time. Maggie gave Emmeline a quick hug. "Look at us," she said as one of her elegant hands wiped at her moist lashes. "What a soppy pair we make. It's a good thing Philip's not here. I can just see him rolling his eyes and trying to pretend he doesn't know us."

The waitress appeared with their tea and cake. Maggie knew exactly what her friend would order so she hadn't waited until Emmeline arrived. The waitress's fussing with the plates and saucers gave Emmeline time to arrange a neutral expression on her features. The mention of Maggie's husband had sobered her mood.

"How is Philip?" she asked tentatively.

"Oh, you know my husband," Maggie said with another wave of her hand. "He never lets anything get him down. True stiff upper lip. That's my Philip. But I can tell you that it scared the life out of me when he came home that night a month ago and told me he had been shot in the arm by a would-be mugger. 'It's just a graze, Maggie love. The doctor said it's nothing to worry about.' Just like that. Calm as you please. Can you imagine? Men. Hmph. I'll never understand them."

Emmeline looked down and made a show of stirring her tea with her spoon. She didn't like keeping things from Maggie. They had never lied to each other before. However, she couldn't explain how Philip had really managed to get shot because she was now bound by the Official Secrets Act. Everything that had happened that night was locked away somewhere in MI5's files. There were only a handful of people who knew the ugly events leading up to the shooting in St. James's Park on that foggy February night. This little group included Philip, of course, herself, Chief Inspector Burnell, Detective Sergeant Finch, and Gregory.

She tilted her head slightly and looked at Maggie, who was babbling on about something or other. Emmeline wondered if the guilt she felt was reflected in her eyes. But she couldn't tell Maggie that her husband had been shot by a Russian spy and that he really worked—had always worked, in fact—for MI5, Britain's counterintelligence agency, and not the Foreign Office's Directorate of Defense and Intelligence as everyone believed. No, she couldn't do that.

"So I told the boys—Emmeline, I get the distinct impression that you haven't been listening to a word I've been saying."

Emmeline shook her head, trying to physically toss away her troubled thoughts. "No, I have."

"Right. So what have I been talking about for the last ten minutes?"

Emmeline took a sip of tea to stall, but she burned her tongue with the scalding amber liquid. It served her right for keeping secrets. "You were talking about your wonderful, darling twins."

"Uh, huh. What was I talking about *exactly*?"

"Exactly?" Emmeline hedged and squirmed slightly under that unwavering stare. Now, she understood what the twins must feel like when they had been caught out doing something naughty.

"Yes, exactly."

Emmeline sighed and threw her hands up in surrender. "It's no good. You were right. My mind was somewhere else."

"I could have told you that much. You've also got a funny expression on your face. It doesn't do to lie to me, miss. I can always tell when something's wrong or you're hiding something."

Emmeline shifted in her seat and touched a hand to her cheek. It felt warm. "Hiding something? What makes you say that?" Her voice cracked slightly.

Maggie's cool green eyes locked with her own dark ones and for a long moment neither of them said a word. Maggie was the first to break the silence. "Fine. Have it your way."

"Honestly, Mags, nothing's the matter." Emmeline heard the little bell above the door tinkle and this prompted her to say, "I suppose the incident with that strange young man disturbed me more than I initially thought."

"Well, you should forget about it. He's not important. Let's talk about something more pleasant. Claire's wedding. It's only a week away now. I've never seen her so frazzled."

"Ooh, yes. She rang me the other day and was quite incoherent. Would you ever in your wildest dreams have imagined that the always poised, always in control Claire Sedgwick would fall apart like this?"

"Never. It's a bit amusing to watch." They both giggled.

"Seriously, though," Maggie continued, "I think this calls for strong action. We must step in and help the poor girl."

Emmeline popped a heavenly bite of the chocolate-brandy cake into her mouth and swallowed a bracing sip of Earl Grey. "I thought, as we're her two oldest friends, we should take her out to dinner one night before the wedding to help settle her nerves. Claire's mother has made it perfectly clear that she is arranging the reception and the rehearsal dinner. That's why I thought it might be nice for just the three of us to sneak away for a quiet meal together."

"That's a lovely idea. Philip will watch the twins. I'm meeting Claire tomorrow for lunch and I'll broach the subject then. She was supposed to join us this afternoon, but she rang a little while ago to say she had to cry off because she had a million and one things to do for the wedding."

"What do you know about her mysterious fiancé...what's his name?"

"Ambrose. Ambrose Trent."

"Claire's kept me in the dark about him. I was in Venice last month when the engagement was announced. Don't you think it's a bit odd that she hasn't introduced him to us?"

"I agree. *Distinctly* odd. But then, the only ones who have met him have been her parents."

Emmeline frowned. "That's not like Claire. What's wrong with him?"

Maggie laughed. "You're always trying to see problems where there are none. I don't know that there's anything 'wrong' with him."

"But?" Emmeline prompted as she leaned in closer.

"What do you mean?"

"There was a distinct *but* left hanging in the air at the end of that sentence. So out with it."

"Well, this whole whirlwind romance of Claire's. It's not like her at all. We both know her. Everything always has to be planned to the minutest detail. Then suddenly, she comes home from her Mediterranean cruise and announces that she's fallen madly in love with the 'most handsome, most dashing, most charming man' in the whole world *and* she's engaged. Oh, and by the way, the wedding will be in a month's time. But where's her fiancé? He's gone back to Switzerland. Why? Because he's in the midst of relocating his business to London and can't get away. No, if you ask me, it's all a bit dodgy." Maggie speared her fork into the defenseless apple tart in front of her.

"Hmm." Emmeline nodded with pursed lips as she took another sip of tea. "He's Swiss then?"

"No, he's as English as you and I. But he moved to Geneva about ten years ago to start his company."

"And what sort of company is it? What does he do?"

Maggie spread her hands wide and shrugged. "I wish I knew."

"What did her parents think of him?"

"Claire's father was furious with her. That's not really surprising. They've always had an uneasy relationship. Under no circumstances was he going to allow his daughter, a descendent of the noble family of Sedgwick, to marry some chap she had only known for a fortnight. Needless to say, this led to a major row. Claire is past the age of consent and, short of imprisoning her in the family dungeon, there was not much her father could really do about the matter except cut off her money. Although her mother was far from happy about the situation, in the end she stepped in and acted as peacemaker. Since Claire was determined to go through with the marriage, no matter what they said, her mother insisted that they fly out to Geneva to meet their future son-in-law before the wedding."

"What happened?"

"Apparently, darling Ambrose was all deferential charm and he won them over. Now, her parents are as smitten with

him as Claire is, at least from all outward appearances. I ran
into Lady Sedgwick last week, and she couldn't stop gushing
over *dear Ambrose.* Such a 'nice boy.' The 'boy' is all of thirty-five or so. She still thinks of all of us as children. 'But what
does he actually do, Lady Vanessa?' I asked. 'Oh, he owns
some sort of import-export business. I couldn't actually get the
gist of it all,' she said vaguely. And *this* is what she wants for
Claire?"

Emmeline stared off into space as she mulled over
Claire's new fiancé. "Something does not feel right. I don't
like the sound of this mystery man."

The bell above the door tinkled again. Emmeline had her
back toward the front of the parlor, but Maggie glanced up as
the newcomer entered. "Speaking of mysterious men," she
mumbled under her breath.

"What was that?" Emmeline asked as she turned her gaze
back to her friend.

"Nothing." Maggie glanced at her watch and took a hurried gulp of her tea. "I just realized the time. Must dash. I have
an…appointment. Yes, an important appointment."

Emmeline blinked in bewilderment. "But we've hardly
seen one another. You didn't mention anything about an appointment earlier."

"I forgot…and now I've just remembered." Maggie's
chair scraped against the polished parquet floor and there was
a soft swish of her navy skirt as she sprang to her feet. She
thrust her arms into her raincoat, scooped up her handbag and
umbrella, and gave Emmeline a quick peck on the cheek. "I'll
ring you tomorrow after I've seen Claire. Oh, and look who's
here. I won't feel guilty leaving you. You won't be alone after
all. Bye." She waved and was gone.

Emmeline turned around to find herself looking up into
Gregory's handsome, smiling face.

CHAPTER 2

Gregory Longdon—her former lover, former fiancé, *and* a professional jewel thief—bent down and kissed her cheek. "Hello, love." Then he proceeded to take his coat off and drape it over the back of the chair Maggie had just vacated. As always, he exuded a masculine grace. It was something that couldn't be learned. One was simply born with it. This impression was only enhanced by his selection of a double-breasted charcoal suit, crisp white shirt of the finest Egyptian cotton and cobalt-blue silk tie. Not a wrinkle could be discerned anywhere.

"I didn't ask you to join me," Emmeline retorted acidly, crossing her arms over her chest as Gregory lowered himself into the dainty chair anyway.

"Didn't you, darling? Well, I'm a magnanimous chap and I'll overlook your lapse in manners this time. By the way, that's a lovely frock." He cast an admiring glance over her turtleneck knit dress, especially the way it clung to her curves. "Red was always your color. It brings out your fiery spirit."

For a moment, Emmeline's lips twitched into a smile and her cheeks suffused with heat. The dress was new—and he had noticed. She sat up straighter in her chair. Then she remembered who she was talking to. She balled her hands into tight fists as his cinnamon-brown eyes twinkled with amusement. "What are you doing here?"

"Doing here, darling? I stepped in out of the rain for a bit of shelter and a soothing cup of tea. It is a free country, you know."

"Yes, it is a free country," she agreed through gritted teeth. "But how did you decide to step into *this* particular tea room *today*?"

He leaned back in his chair and waved a large, elegant hand in the air to attract the waitress's attention. Raindrops glistened in his dark wavy hair, which was graying slightly at the temples. At forty-two, he was more dashing than ever, if that was possible. "It's a funny thing."

"Is it?" Her tone dripped ice. The two tiny words were like bullets fired at a moving target.

"Yes, it is. I just happened to be walking by—"

She glowered at him, in no mood for levity. "Just *happened* to be walking by?"

"—and I said to myself—" he continued as if she hadn't spoken.

"I see. Now, you talk to yourself as well."

"'—Self,' I said. We're on intimate terms, you see."

Emmeline rolled her eyes.

"'Self, it's chilly out here. Why don't we find a nice little tea shop to warm up?' And there before my eyes, like an oasis appearing before a dying man in the desert, was Miss Charlotte's Tea Room. The heavens were indeed smiling down upon me today," he ended with a cheeky grin.

"Uh huh. You got to Maggie somehow. She told you we would be meeting here."

"Maggie? Was that Maggie who left just now? I didn't recognize her."

Emmeline let out a snort of disbelief. "Rubbish. You know very well that it was. I have a feeling Maggie has been talking to Gran and the two of them—at your behest—are conspiring against me. How is it that women simply fall at your feet? What spell—or rather, I should say, curse—do you cast over them?

"Take Gran and Maggie. Two perfectly sane, intelligent women. Then you appear and they become like schoolgirls. I don't know." She leaned forward and wagged her forefinger at him. "I'll tell you again, as I did in Venice, we are not getting back together."

Gregory folded her hand in his larger one and turned it over to place a warm kiss in the center of her palm. "Manners again, Emmy. It's quite rude to point."

The kiss sent a shiver up her spine and a series of confusing thoughts shooting through her brain. Ooh, the sheer bloody gall of the man. He always knew which buttons to press to turn her into emotional jelly. She was just starting to heal from the loss of the baby and his running out on her the day before their wedding two years ago.

Then last month, Gregory reappeared—out of the blue and just in time to swoop in to save her from two men who had been trying to kill her. All the old feelings she thought she had buried deep, deep down had come bubbling to the surface, and now she didn't know up from down anymore. Maggie and Gran had a lot to answer for.

She snatched her hand away as she became aware of the waitress at her elbow. "Ah, there you are, miss. I'll have," Gregory peered into her cup, "a pot of Earl Grey and a slice of that nice seed cake I glimpsed over there on the counter."

"Don't forget a liberal dollop of strychnine on the cake."

The waitress cocked an eyebrow. "Sorry, miss?"

"Never mind her," Gregory said in a patient, almost cooing, tone as he jerked his head toward Emmeline. "They just released her from the mental asylum this morning and she's trying to adjust to life on the outside. As you can imagine, it must be rather difficult after being locked up for nine years."

The waitress took a step backward. "Locked up? Mental asylum?"

Her blue eyes flickered to the knife resting beside Emmeline's hand. She was new and Emmeline had never seen her in the tea room before.

"It's all right, though," Gregory tried to reassure her. "The doctors say she's cured and no longer a danger to society."

"I'll get your tea. I won't be but a moment." The waitress bumped into a chair at the next table in her haste to get away.

Laughter burst forth with a rumbling snort, as if he'd been storing it in the back of his throat.

Emmeline leaned across the table and swatted his arm.

"Ouch. That hurt." He made a show of rubbing the spot where she had hit him. "I bet a bruise is forming already."

"You are a beast."

Before she had a chance to say anything else, Gregory grabbed her wrist and pulled her toward him. He pressed a firm but gentle kiss on her lips. If she was honest with herself, she had to admit that it had been rather nice. But she was not going to give him the satisfaction of knowing that.

They stared at each other for a moment before he released her wrist and gave her a soft push backward. "Now, sit down like a good girl."

Ooh, there were times—like now—that she simply wanted to throttle him. She resumed her seat and, instead, glared at him, her fingers drumming on the table, until his tea and cake arrived. "What are you doing here today? What do you want?"

"Absolutely nothing, Emmy love. As I was telling you earlier, it is a mere coincidence that our paths crossed in Miss Charlotte's charming establishment today."

"I don't believe you." She raised a hand to stop any protest. "Have you nothing better to do than to hound me relentlessly? Aren't there some jewels you can go out and steal?"

Gregory took a sip of tea and smoothed the corners of his mustache. "*Steal* is such an ugly word. I'm surprised at you, darling." He clucked his tongue in disapproval. "As a journalist, you should take more care. We have very stiff libel and slander laws in this country. For your information, what I do is liberate jewels from their cold, loveless existence and find them a warm new home. It is a very noble and worthy calling, if you think about it."

Tea spluttered from Emmeline's lips as she choked on these last words. "*Noble calling?*"

He flashed a row of white teeth at her. "Yes."

"I think Chief Inspector Burnell would heartily disagree with you. You're a thief. He knows it. Interpol knows it. MI5 knows it. I was the only naïve fool who didn't see it."

"First, I take exception to 'thief.' Second, you are far from being a fool. And third, what the police *think* and what they can actually *prove* are two totally different matters. Besides, imagine how dull old Oliver's life would be if he didn't have me to chase around now and then. You must admit he is getting a little rotund around the middle and could do with the exercise."

She had to laugh. She was certain Chief Inspector Burnell did not view their little cat-and-mouse tussles with quite the same bemused irreverence. But then, nobody viewed things the way Gregory did. She sighed as she watched him over the rim of her cup. Sometimes she wished—*No*, she didn't wish anything, she told herself firmly. She sat up straighter and squared her shoulders.

"You and Maggie looked quite serious when I walked in. Is anything the matter?"

"I thought you said you didn't recognize Maggie. Oh, never mind." She shook her head to prevent another poor excuse from trespassing his lips. "Something is troubling us, yes." She put her cup down on the saucer and leaned closer to him.

"What is it, Emmy?"

"We're terribly worried about Claire and her impending marriage. There's something...*wrong* about the whole thing."

"In what way?"

His humor vanished. He could hear the concern in her voice and didn't like the way her eyebrows knit together. He was quite familiar with that look and hoped she was not being dragged into something dangerous again in a bid to help a friend. Her loyalty to her friend Charles Latimer had embroiled her in an international intrigue that had nearly gotten her killed, *twice*. He reached his hand across the table and squeezed her smaller one, hard. He was not going to let anything like that happen to her again.

"Ow, Gregory. You're hurting me."

He let go abruptly. "Sorry, love. But I know you, and the tone of your voice just now reminded me of you hot on the trail of Latimer's murderer."

She flexed her sore hand open and closed a few times to get the circulation going again. The imprint of her bracelet could be seen on the skin of her wrist. *The gold bracelet Gregory had given to her.* She pushed this errant thought from her mind. "We were not discussing Charles."

"No, but I do not want the same thing repeated. Ever."

"Don't be so melodramatic. Nothing like that is involved here."

"I sincerely hope not, Emmy. So what's the problem?"

She sighed and threw up her hands in surrender. It was useless to argue with him and perhaps a man's point of view would be useful in the current situation. "Claire's wedding is in a week's time."

"Yes, I know."

"How do *you* know?"

"Aside from the fact that you've just told me, I've been invited."

She blinked in surprise. "What do you mean you've been invited?"

"It works this way. A stiff, buff-colored card with engraved lettering was popped into the post requesting my presence at the forthcoming nuptials of Claire Sedgwick and Ambrose Trent. As I didn't have anything to do that day, I thought it might be a jolly nice way to pass the afternoon."

"Why?"

He shook his head as if the answer should have been obvious to anyone. "Because weddings tend to be happy and festive occasions, darling."

"No, I mean why were you invited?"

"Oh, I see. I suppose it's because Ambrose Trent and I are old friends."

CHAPTER 3

W hat? *You* know Ambrose Trent?"
Emmeline was stunned at this unexpected piece of
news. As close as she and Gregory were—*had been*,
she corrected herself—she knew virtually nothing about his
past. All she had managed to wangle out of him when they had
been together was that he had been out on his own in the world
since the age of seventeen. He never spoke about his family or
his friends or anything before the night they met on Regent's
Street, when they had sheltered in the same doorway to get out
of the rain. She had never wanted to press him, assuming there
must be something too painful in his past, and she didn't want
to intrude. He was entitled to his privacy, after all. When he
was ready, he would tell her. But now, with Claire about to tie
herself to a virtual stranger—but a friend of his—it was time
for Gregory to answer a few questions.

He sat there, calmly sipping tea, as Emmeline cocked her
head to one side and fixed him with her shrewd journalist's
eye, assessing his reliability as a source. As there was no one
else who could help her at the moment, she decided to plunge
ahead. "How long have you known Ambrose Trent?"

"Oh, years." He leaned back in his chair and smoothed his
mustache. His brow furrowed in concentration, as if trying to
remember. "I don't know. It must be about ten or so. Something like that. However, it's been ages since I've seen him.
Ambrose was always a bit of a nomad. Always restless. Never

content to settle down in one place for very long. He was seized by wanderlust when he was very young and was always roaming the globe in search of a new adventure. That's why I was surprised when I received the wedding invitation. The last I heard he was somewhere in Switzerland."

"I see. From your description of him, it's not surprising the two of you became such bosom pals. You have so much in common. Restless, turning your back on your responsibilities, running out on people who love—" She bit off what she had been about to say. *Fool*, she chided herself. *He means nothing to you anymore. Nothing. This is about preventing Claire from making a mistake she will regret for the rest of her life. This is* not *about you and Gregory. There is* no *you and Gregory. That's in the past.*

Is it really? a niggling little voice at the back of her mind asked. *Yes*, Emmeline answered with a determined nod. *Yes, it is.*

Gregory watched in fascination as a range of emotions flickered over her pretty features and in her dark eyes. "Emmy, darling, is there something matter?"

"What? I—" He had interrupted her internal dialogue and the disturbing thoughts that it had provoked. She once again focused on the matter at hand but self-consciously fingered her bracelet. "What sort of work does your friend do? And *how* can he possibly support a wife if he's always wandering hither and thither?"

"Ambrose is a clever chap. He can turn his hand to virtually anything and, in an instant, it's a gold mine. As for your second question, I'd like to point out that Claire Sedgwick is not short of a bob or two. What's this third degree about anyway?"

Emmeline put her elbows on the table and leaned toward him. "What this is about," she hissed, "is the fact that Claire became engaged to this *wonderful* chap after a whirlwind romance on a two-week Mediterranean cruise. She knows nothing about him. None of us have met him. Maggie and I don't like it. There's something not quite right about the whole thing."

"Now, now, love. It doesn't do to make snap judgments. Aren't you forgetting that journalists are supposed to be objective?"

"You don't have to teach me my job. I'm going to find out what *your* friend's secret is, before he hurts *my* friend. That's a promise."

"What makes you so certain that he's hiding something?"

She looked him directly in the eye. "Instinct. Everyone is hiding something and lies always have a way of coming out."

Gregory had to turn away. Her last remark touched a nerve.

ℯↄℯↄ

The young man's nerves were so frayed that his hands trembled violently as he tried to light a cigarette. Someone had been following him ever since he left the tea parlor. He wasn't sure at first, but he was certain of it now. The hairs on the back of his neck prickled with the knowledge. His heart hammering against his chest told him so. His strangled breathing whispered it. He didn't know who it was. Was it one person? Two? He didn't dare to turn around. Walking along Brompton Road, he quickened his pace. His stalker's footfalls echoed in his ears as the young man weaved his way through the crowd in front of Harrods. He could feel the beads of perspiration dotting his brow. He checked his watch. Five-thirty. Rush hour. At least there were a lot of people about—queuing for buses, hurrying along the pavement, descending into the Underground. Although it was March, the afternoon's lingering malaise of gray rain had hastened the gloaming's appearance.

The young man ran a hand distractedly through his still-damp hair. He was nearing Hyde Park Corner. Should he turn up Park Lane? Should he continue straight on along Piccadilly? *Oh, God, please help.* If anyone was ever in an hour of need, it was certainly him at this very moment. He rued that fateful day when he had entered the casino in Monte Carlo and found himself sitting next to the fair-haired chap at the roulette table.

He could have been looking in a mirror. The bloke had the same coloring—except for the eyes—and they were virtually the same height and build. The chap had murmured a few sympathetic words when the young man had lost the £5,000 on a turn of the wheel. He had seemed so friendly when he had invited him to have a drink later on that evening. He could picture it all, as if it were happening before his eyes at this very moment. The other man was savoring a glass of Calvados when he had broached his offer in that smooth, plummy voice. Whatever had possessed him to accept? However, he already knew the answer to this question. *The money.* More money than he could ever hope to make in his lifetime. It had seemed like such a lark at first. A harmless masquerade. A bit of fun. Who could get hurt? He shuddered at this thought. He quickly discovered that it was no game. He wanted out, but it was too late. He knew too much. And now they believed he had gone to the press. All because of that bloody journalist. Not just any journalist, but Emmeline Kirby. Why did she have to pick that particular tea room? The footsteps were getting closer. Park Lane or Piccadilly? Which way would lead to a dead end?

දාදා

It was dark by the time Emmeline and Gregory left Miss Charlotte's. They stopped on the pavement outside. "I'll hail a taxi for you." He stepped to the edge of the curb.

"I'll walk, thank you. It's a fine evening," she said primly as she unfurled her umbrella and took a few steps down the block.

"What? In this weather?" He peered up at the murky, charcoal sky and pulled up the collar of his trench coat. The rain had gotten harder as the afternoon wore on. "Don't be daft," he called after her. "You'll catch your death of cold and then where will I be? I'll tell you where. I'll have Helen banging on my door, demanding satisfaction."

Emmeline turned around and walked back toward him. She had to laugh at this image of her grandmother as an avenging angel. "Gran is too good-natured and even-tempered. Besides, she adores you for some unfathomable reason."

"That's because she has excellent taste. Unlike others I know...Ahem." He cleared his throat and looked down at her pointedly. "But Helen isn't very forgiving if something happens to her little chick. So, won't you please indulge me and take a taxi? My honor is at stake here. Look, if you won't do it for me, then think of England." He wrung his hands together in mock anxiety and stared at her with the doleful gaze of a lost puppy.

She laughed again and gave him a little shove. "Oh, get on with you. What a lot of blather. I'll take the taxi. It'll make things easier in the long run."

He wiped his brow melodramatically. "Oh, thank you, ever so much, Miss Kirby. You don't know how it eases my mind."

They were still engaged in this playful banter when a silver Mercedes came barreling down Cromwell Road, picking up speed as it went along. It nearly sheared off the passenger-side mirror of a parked Opel. People on the pavement screamed and scattered for cover. The lunatic was headed directly toward them.

Emmeline was standing at the curb with her back toward the street. Gregory saw the car before she did. "*Look out.*"

In one swift movement, he lunged toward her and grabbed her arm. This sent them teetering off balance and they tumbled to the pavement together. It was a hard, jarring fall that rattled their bones. The Mercedes continued on and was lost to view when it rounded the corner at Queen's Gate.

Gregory was the first to recover. His eyes were filled with concern. "Emmy, are you all right?"

She groaned as she rolled onto her side. "I think so."

"Can you sit up?" She nodded mutely. "Here, let me help you," he said.

Emmeline was grateful for the strong arm supporting her, as she first sat up and then unsteadily got to her feet. Her legs felt like water.

She took a deep lungful of air. "Thanks. It seems I owe you my life, *again.* That's twice now that you've snatched me from the jaws of death."

"Three times, actually, if you want to be technical about it. I don't mind playing the role of the hero. With my chiseled good looks, I think the mantle rather suits me. But I sincerely hope you will not make a habit of putting yourself in harm's way." He pulled her toward him and she gratefully melted into his embrace. His lips placed a warm kiss against her temple. As always, she felt safe in his arms. Suddenly, she pushed herself away. *No, that was the past.*

"Emmy?" His voice rose at her brusque movement.

However, neither of them had a chance to say anything else. A middle-aged man in a crumpled tweed hat came running up to them and asked a little breathlessly, "Are you all right? I saw the whole thing. But I'm afraid it all happened so quickly that I didn't get his license. The chap must have been drunk or on drugs the way he was weaving about."

"I wonder," Gregory said slowly. "I wonder."

Emmeline's ears pricked up at the odd tone in his voice. She shot him a probing look. "What do you mean?"

"Nothing, love. Come on." He took her elbow and extended a hand to the gentleman. "Thank you, sir. We're fine."

"Well, that's all right then." The man's face relaxed. "You have to be so careful these days, don't you?"

"Yes, you do." Gregory's brows knit together and his eyes darkened with some unreadable thought. "You do, indeed."

CHAPTER 4

Every evening, no matter the weather, Alice Grimshaw and Reggie could be seen taking a stroll through Hyde Park. Reggie was a happy-go-lucky golden retriever, who was staunchly protective of his blind mistress. Any stranger would have to answer to him before getting within ten feet of Alice—a petite woman of "mature" years with fine silver hair and pale green eyes. She never admitted her age, but those who knew her speculated that she must be about eighty.

Alice had lost both her husband and her sight about three years earlier. However, she didn't allow her impairment to slow her down. She still volunteered at the charity shop twice a week, and she attended the monthly meetings of the book club. Although nowadays, a couple of students from the local school would come to her flat and read to her in the afternoons. Alice would tell her friends she was too old—more likely too set in her ways—to bother learning braille. The real reason, however, was that she longed for someone to talk to for a little while. She enjoyed fussing over the students. They were lovely, and she liked to listen to their big plans and dreams. But once they went home, it was time for Alice and Reggie to quietly mull over the day's events together. This was done most pleasantly by strolling through the park, which was not far from Alice's flat in South Kensington. Their route was always the same. They would enter through Palace Gate, turn right down Flower Walk, and continue straight on until they reached the Serpentine. They would amble along the water as they headed toward the Italian Fountains. After a little break for Reggie to chase the ducks, it was time to slowly make their way home.

"Come on, Reggie," Alice called as she tapped her cane. The dog barked once and wandered over to his mistress. He took a last, mournful glance back at the ducks, which were quacking noisily at his welcome departure.

"Never mind, Reggie," Alice said sympathetically. "Tomorrow's another day."

A smile crossed her lips as Reggie barked in answer. She stopped for a moment and bent down to give his head a scratch. "Good dog. Come on."

She chatted amiably with Reggie as they turned down the avenue of horse chestnut trees, which was lined with benches on either side. How she and her late husband Edward loved to wander down this peaceful avenue hand in hand and listen to the birds singing merrily in the branches high above. She sighed. Overcome by a flood of memories, she stopped and drew a handkerchief from her pocket to wipe away the salty tears moistening her cheeks. "Sentimental old fool," she murmured as she blew her nose.

Reggie suddenly started barking and ran off up ahead. Then he came back to Alice's side and ran off again, barking even louder this time. "Reggie, come back here. What's gotten into you? Reggie?"

The dog just kept barking. If anything, he was becoming more agitated.

"What the devil is the matter? Oh, all right. I'm coming."

Tap, tap, tap. Her cane scraped along the gravel walk as the soft drizzle became a steadier rain. Once she sorted out Reggie, they would have to hurry home.

Finally, she reached the dog's side. "Now, what's all this in aid of, eh, lad? You're making enough noise to wake the dead."

He kept barking. She felt his tail brush the back of her knees as he circled around her. He tugged at the hem of her skirt, his teeth pulling her forward a few inches. He had never behaved this way before.

"Reggie, what's wrong?"

He growled as he pulled harder on her skirt.

All of a sudden, her cane bumped against something. She probed cautiously. It was something immovable. It was...*a foot?* She tapped higher to make sure. Yes, a foot attached to a trousered leg. A man.

"Oh, I beg your pardon, sir. Please forgive my dog. He's not normally so agitated. He's really quite friendly." She turned back and snapped, "Hush, Reggie. You're disturbing this gentleman, who's trying to have a quiet sit down."

In the rain? Who would be sitting in the rain, in the dark? All at once, Alice felt very cold.

"Sir?" she asked meekly. "Are you all right?" There was no response. "*Sir?*" With trembling fingers, Alice reached out until her hand came in contact with a hard shoulder. She shook him lightly. "Sir?"

Alice screamed as he slumped over and her hand came away moist and sticky. Bile rose in her throat when she realized that it was blood. *Good Lord. He's dead.*

Reggie finally stopped barking.

ഇഇഇ

Chief Inspector Oliver Burnell and Detective Sergeant Jack Finch pulled up outside Lancaster Gate on Bayswater Road. There was already a swarm of police constables on the scene. Some were trying to keep the curious from entering the park. Meanwhile, others could be seen walking along the paths, their torches flashing about wildly as they searched for clues. Burnell and Finch showed their badges and were waved through.

The chief inspector pulled up the collar of his coat against the rain that had started trickling down the back of his neck. "Filthy night," he grumbled. "Why do murderers always choose to dispatch their victims when it's raining like an Indian monsoon, eh, Finch? Why not a sunny afternoon in June? Can you tell me that?"

The sergeant suppressed a smile. "I'm sure I don't know,

sir. Shall I nip back to the car get an umbrella?"

"No, I'm sure we won't melt, but it's damned unpleasant."

"Yes, sir. There I must agree with you."

"Come along, lad. Let's see what mess is awaiting us down there."

They made their way to the tree-lined avenue, which was already cordoned off with yellow DO NOT CROSS tape. Several huge flood lamps had been brought in. The forensic team was hard at work, carefully scouring the immediate vicinity of the bench in its quest to find any shred of evidence that might lead to the killer. These efforts were being hampered by the rain, which was slanting sideways in unforgiving pellets.

As Burnell and Finch got closer, they could see the body slumped over. His blue eyes were frozen open.

A young man. The chief inspector judged that the victim must have been in his mid-thirties. There was no sign of the medical examiner.

"PC Davenport," he called to a woman police constable, who was a little farther down the path. "Has Dr. Meadows been called?"

"Yes, sir. He's on his way. He should be here any minute."

"Good. What can you tell me about what happened?"

"Not a lot, I'm afraid, sir. It appears that he was shot in the chest at close range."

"Any identification on him?"

"Yes, sir. A wallet. His name was Ambrose Trent from Geneva."

Burnell thoughtfully stroked his neatly trimmed white beard. "From Geneva, you say? And why did Mr. Ambrose Trent from Geneva travel all the way to London to get himself killed?"

"I think I can answer that question for you. Not about the murder bit. Just about why he was in London."

"You can, can you?" The chief inspector said, astonished. "By all means, go ahead and enlighten us. We're all ears."

"There was an announcement in *The Times* a couple of

weeks ago. He is—was—going to marry Claire Sedgwick,
Lord Douglas Sedgwick's daughter. The wedding is Friday
next, if I remember correctly."

Burnell's bright blue eyes widened in surprise. "Bloody
hell. All we need is to have one of the country's most preemi-
nent barristers and a leading member of the Conservative Party
hounding our every move. Damn and blast." The chief inspector thrust his fists deep into his pockets and scowled at the
dead man as he began pacing in front of the bench. "He's not
the only one who will be hounding us. This is a gift to the
press, served on a silver salver and tied with a red ribbon. And
of course, we can't forget our ever-charming Superintendent
Fenton, who will be breathing down our necks when he finds
out that Lord Sedgwick's future son-in-law was murdered. I
can't think of a more perfect way to end my day."

Both Sergeant Finch and PC Davenport remained silent
during this tirade. Finch knew better than to interrupt and the
constable…well, she could see the lay of the land. She tried to
slip away quietly, but Burnell waylaid her. "Who found the
body?"

"A Mrs. Alice Grimshaw. Widow. About eighty. Has a
flat nearby and takes a walk in the park every evening with her
dog, Reggie. That dog is a terror, I can tell you. We had the
devil of a time when we arrived. He wouldn't let us get near
her, barked his head off, he did. Mrs. Grimshaw is over there
in one of the cars. PC Wilkins is seeing to her. The whole
thing has been a bit of a shock. I suggest you go easy on her,
sir. She's a bit fragile."

"Thank you for the advice, Davenport, but I think by now
I know how to conduct an interview."

The constable blushed. "Yes, sir. Of course. Sorry, sir."
She hurried off before she could put her foot any deeper into
her mouth.

Finch watched her shoulders hunch forward as she tried to
put as much distance between herself and Burnell as possible.
"Sir, I don't think she meant to overstep her position. I think
she was just concerned about the old woman."

Burnell was staring at Ambrose Trent's lifeless body.

"What are you driveling on about, Finch?" he said as he turned his attention back to his sergeant.

"I was talking about PC Davenport. I don't think that she meant anything—"

But Burnell cut him off with a dismissive wave of his hand. Everything was already forgotten. "Never mind all that. Let's go have a chat with Mrs. Grimshaw."

Alice, her unseeing eyes staring out the window, was huddled in a corner in the backseat of the police car. PC Wilkins had been kind enough to find a blanket for her, but she was shivering, although the temperature was mild. Probably the shock.

"Are you feeling better, Mrs. Grimshaw?"

"Yes," she lied, as she tugged the blanket more tightly around her shoulders. Burnell could see from her huddled posture she didn't want to be a nuisance, knew the police had their work to do. "Yes, I'm fine. Thank you."

"I'm ever so glad," PC Wilkins said, smiling although the woman couldn't see him.

"Uh, Mrs. Grimshaw." His tone changed slightly. There was an undercurrent of nervousness in his voice now. "Do you think you're strong enough to answer a few questions? Chief Inspector Burnell and Sergeant Finch are here and they'd like to speak with you."

Reggie's low pitched growl told the chief inspector the retriever did not like the look of the two new arrivals.

Alice sat up straighter. "Certainly, Constable Wilkins. Please tell them I am at their service. And tell Reggie to mind his manners."

Wilkins clearly hid a smile as he popped out of the car. "Right. Sir," he called.

There was a brief interval of silence as someone took Reggie away. Burnell opened the back door and sat beside Alice, his bulk adjusted by the shock absorbers. Finch opened the front passenger door and slid into the car.

"Chief Inspector Burnell and…" Alice said.

"Sergeant Finch, Mrs. Grimshaw."

"Of course." Alice extended her hand toward Burnell and

then thrust it in the general direction of where Finch sat. Burnell and the sergeant exchanged surprised glances when they realized she was blind. No one had bothered to tell them.

"I'm sorry to trouble you, Mrs. Grimshaw. It must have been a terrible shock to come upon the body like that, but you must understand that we are conducting a murder inquiry."

"Yes, I do understand, Chief Inspector. I am prepared to help in any way I can. But I must warn you I do not know more than what I told that nice Constable Wilkins."

"Well, let us be the judge of that. Since Sergeant Finch and I were not here when you gave your statement to Wilkins, I'd appreciate it if you could go over it again. Take your time. Perhaps you've remembered something in the interim."

"I very much doubt it, but I will endeavor to do my best," she said briskly.

"That's all we can ask, Mrs. Grimshaw."

Alice carefully went over everything from the moment she and Reggie left the flat, until they found the body. She had been right. There seemed to be nothing that could help them.

"And you didn't see anyone suspicious—Oh, forgive me, Mrs. Grimshaw. That was rather stupid of me."

Alice reached out a blue-veined hand and patted Burnell's arm. "Don't be silly, Chief Inspector. I do not view—Ha! You see? I do it as well—my blindness as something to be ashamed of. You were asking a perfectly natural question. I use my other senses to compensate for my blindness. However, I still cannot help you. There was no one else about when we found—when we discovered—that man. It must have happened before we came upon him. Otherwise, Reggie would have chased the murderer until he caught him. And I don't mind telling you—" She leaned in closer. "—the chap is quite fortunate that did not occur. Reggie is the most loving dog anyone could ever ask for, but he is very protective."

"Yes," Burnell murmured, "we did see that."

Finch appeared to be stifling a smile. Burnell scowled. Reggie had growled at him as if he were Jack the Ripper.

"Thank you, Mrs. Grimshaw. I'll have Wilkins take you and Reggie home now."

"That's very kind of you, Chief Inspector."

⚜

Dr. Meadows was bent over the body, examining the wound, when Burnell and Finch walked up behind him. "Oliver, I can feel you breathing. Now, move off and give me some room to work."

"How did you know I was here, John?" the chief inspector asked his old friend. "We were as quiet as two little mice in a field."

"Mice in a field. Hmph," Meadows mumbled under his breath, but without the slightest trace of rancor. This was typical of the genial banter that he and Burnell regularly engaged in. They had been friends for over twenty years. They knew one another as well as a person could know a fellow human being. Burnell was the one person Meadows could always count on. God knows, if it hadn't been for the chief inspector he would never have been able to get through that awful time after his wife Sarah was killed by a drunk driver five years ago.

It had finally stopped raining. Meadows's knees creaked as he stood up. He was feeling his sixty years more and more lately. "Ooh, I'm getting too old for these calls," he said as he peeled off his surgical gloves.

"Nonsense. You're a stripling." Burnell, five years his junior and twenty pounds heavier, clapped him on the shoulder. "Now, what can you tell us, John?"

"He knew the murderer because he was shot at close range. Two bullets. The first hit him in the shoulder. The impact must have knocked him backward onto the bench. The second pierced his heart. Went clear through and out his back. I found it lodged in the slat of the bench. The second bullet is what killed him."

"I see. About what time would you say he died?"

Dr. Meadows pushed his tweed hat off his forehead and glanced at his watch. "Let's see. It's eight-thirty now. I'd estimate he's been dead about two, two and a half hours. No more than three. However, I'll know better once I do the autopsy."

"Fine. When can I expect the results?"

"I'm backed up at the moment. In a few days. Possibly the end of next week."

Burnell put his arm around the doctor's shoulders again. "John, I'd appreciate it if you could give this top priority."

Meadows raised his eyebrows and fixed his slate-gray gaze upon the chief inspector's weary face. They said nothing for a moment. Burnell wouldn't ask him to expedite the autopsy unless it was important. He snapped his black bag shut. "Oliver, you're a slave driver. I'll see what I can do."

Burnell smiled and thrust out his hand. "Thanks, John. I'll walk you to your car." They went up the gravel path with Sergeant Finch following a few steps behind.

The doctor jerked his head back in the direction of the bench, where the late Ambrose Trent was being zipped into a black body bag. "I take it you already know who he is."

The chief inspector nodded grimly and his eyes narrowed. "Unfortunately, yes. He was Claire Sedgwick's fiancé. Lord Douglas Sedgwick's future son-in-law."

Meadows stopped and stared at his friend. A low whistle escaped his lips. "My sympathies, Oliver. I don't envy you. It's times like these I'm glad I didn't follow in my father's footsteps and become a policeman. I don't have the necessary social skills to juggle all the nasty types you come into contact with every day. Not to mention having to deal with the press. At least the people I meet are already dead and cannot do me any harm."

Burnell scowled and said more to himself than anyone in particular, "I have a feeling that if we don't tread carefully, this dead man's tale will haunt us to the grave."

CHAPTER 5

It was midnight, when the shrill peal of the telephone shattered the somnolent stillness in Emmeline's darkened bedroom. She whimpered and reached out a hand from under the sheet. The phone kept up its rude ringing as she fumbled around blindly on her bedside table until her fingers finally came in contact with the receiver. She pulled it toward the bed, heedless of anything that she might knock off the table in the process.

"Hello." Her voice was a hoarse whisper heavily laced with sleep.

"Emmeline, did I wake you?"

She groaned. It was her editor, James Sloane. She rolled over onto her back. Her eyes were still closed. "No, James, you didn't wake me. I was just sitting here contemplating the universe. It's what I usually do at midnight. Of course, you woke me, you silly man. What's so urgent?"

"Sorry. I didn't realize the time. But I thought you'd want to know, seeing as Claire Sedgwick's your friend."

She sat up and flicked on the lamp, her chest tightening with fear. She was wide awake now. "Has something happened to Claire?"

"No, but her fiancé was found murdered in Hyde Park tonight. He was shot twice."

She gasped, stunned. "Oh, poor Claire. I must go to her at once. Thanks for ringing, James."

She flung the bedclothes off and stood up, the receiver wedged between her neck and shoulder. She grabbed a pair of jeans and a yellow sweater that were draped on the back of a chair.

"Emmeline, don't be so hasty. I wouldn't rush off in the middle of the night," James hissed in her ear.

She stopped, one leg in the jeans and one still bare. "No, I suppose you're right. Her parents are probably with her. I'll pop over in the morning. I'm sorry, James, but I'll be a little late getting into the office. I hope you understand."

"Of course. That's why I rang you actually. I'm putting a small article in the morning edition with whatever we have now, which is not much. But if you promise not to engage in the same kind of dangerous antics you did with the Charles Latimer murder, I'd like you to cover this story from here on out. You know the family. They like you. I think they might appreciate it if a friend of Miss Sedgwick's was telling the story with sensitivity."

"Uh huh. I don't believe a word of this drivel. You're afraid of Lord Douglas Sedgwick and you think having me cover the story might prevent him from quashing it. Isn't that so, my dear James?"

A brief silence followed at the other end of the line. "Listen, Emmeline. You're my best reporter. I would have given you the story, even if you didn't know the family. But since you do—"

"It doesn't hurt. Right?"

"Well—"

She could hear the smile in his voice. "Oh, James, you are so transparent. You should have become a politician. You know how to manipulate people with the best of them."

"I take great exception to that. Politics is a dirty game and I'd never want to soil my lily-white hands with it. It's the lust for power that corrupts a person's soul. No, thank you. Politics is definitely not my cup of tea."

She never realized that he felt so strongly about it. She admired his convictions. They mirrored her own. "Well, you needn't have worried. I would have done the story anyway."

"I know. Your instincts wouldn't allow you to pass up such an intriguing mystery."

She imagined he was smiling again and felt her own lips twitch in response. "Now," She plopped back down on the bed, shrugging her leg out of the jeans, and reached for the pad and pen by the phone. "What can you tell me?"

"Not much, I'm afraid. The details are still very sketchy. He was found on a bench in Hyde Park with two bullet holes in him."

"Well, who's the officer in charge of the case? Surely, you must know that at least."

"It's your old friend Chief Inspector Oliver Burnell. That's another reason why I put you on the story."

"I see." Everything seemed to be converging, like with Charles. Pretty soon, Gregory would get involved, too. What was she saying? He was already involved. Ambrose Trent is—was—his friend. "I'll go see Claire in the morning and then I'll pay a visit to Chief Inspector Burnell. I may already have a source for information on Ambrose Trent."

"Amazing. It's midnight and she's already pulling sources out of the ether. Care to tell me who this might be? I'm only your editor, after all."

"No. Now, let me get some sleep. I'll check in with you later tomorrow—" She glanced at the clock on the night table. The little red numbers flashed 12:30. "Rather, I should say later this afternoon."

"Just remember, if this starts to get dangerous, you're off the story. Do I make myself clear?"

"Yes, boss. Crystal clear. I wouldn't have it any other way."

"*Emmeline.*"

She recognized the lecturing tone of his voice. Now, why didn't her assurance give him a sense of comfort? Perhaps he knew her too well. She gave an exaggerated yawn, stifling her chuckle. "Is that the time? James, I simply must get some sleep or I'll be no use tomorrow. You do want me to have all my wits about me, don't you?" He sighed and she imagined him throwing up his hands as he always did when he got frustrated.

"I'm a grown woman," she told him, forestalling another lecture. "And there is only so much you can do to protect me. But I do promise to be careful."

"I just wish I believed you." Another weary sigh. "Good night, Emmeline."

❧❧❧

After breakfasting on toast and marmalade, Emmeline lingered over a second cup of coffee in the cozy kitchen of her townhouse in Holland Park. She seemed to do her best thinking in this room, which was always filled with light. The buttery cream walls were decorated with various tiles. There were little Dutch scenes with windmills and children in wooden clogs, as well as others with flowers and vegetables.

Today, Mother Nature seemed to be mocking last night's tragedy. She had chased away all of the dreary grayness of yesterday and, in its wake, left a beautiful cerulean sky without a trace of clouds.

Emmeline could hear little birds cheerfully singing outside in the garden.

She was mulling over the murder of the mysterious Ambrose Trent, when the doorbell rang. She glanced at her watch. Eight-thirty. Who would be calling on her at this time of the morning? Taking a last swallow of coffee, she pushed her chair back from the table.

The bell rang a second time. "Just a minute. I'm coming," she called as she walked down the corridor. "Honestly," she mumbled under breath. "It's rather rude to be so demanding at this hour of the morning." She turned the bolt, opened the door, and rolled her eyes. "I should have known it would be you."

Gregory was standing on her doorstep—flashing one of his most engaging smiles and oozing charm. "I must say, Emmy darling, I've had warmer welcomes in my day."

For a brief instant, she caught a whiff of his aftershave when he bent down to kiss her, his mustache brushing her cheek. She pulled away and looked up into his face, drowning in that intense cinnamon-brown gaze. Her knees suddenly felt as if they would buckle beneath her weight. She grew warm, memories assailing her—the feel of his skin against her own, his fingers in her hair, their lips hungrily seeking out one another.

She closed her eyes, slammed the door shut on the past, and shook her head. "No."

"No what, love?"

Her eyes flew open. She hadn't realized she had spoken aloud. "Nothing. Nothing at all." Her voice was a hoarse whisper. She cleared her throat and straightened her shoulders in a bid to collect her wits. "Are you going to stand there on the doorstep all day, gathering dust, or are you going to come inside?"

"I thought you'd never ask." Gregory stepped over the threshold and pushed the door shut behind him.

Emmeline wished she could wipe that puckish grin off his face. He always took great pleasure in setting her off kilter. "Yes, well. I'm actually glad you're here. I was going to ring you later, but you saved me the trouble."

"Music to my ears, Emmy darling. You're an intelligent woman. I knew you'd see sense in the end and realize what a capital fellow I am."

She shot a withering look at him and groaned. "Oh, shut up and come to the kitchen for some coffee."

He bowed deeply. "Your wish is my command. Lead on, dear lady."

"You forget that I know you. These theatrics don't impress me and they certainly don't suit you."

She turned on her heel and left him in the middle of the corridor. The unmistakable sound of his chuckling floated upon the air as he straightened up and followed her.

Gregory slipped into a chair at the blond wood table in the center of the kitchen and waited patiently as she poured him a cup of steaming coffee. A couple of birds had settled on the window ledge and were singing merrily. "Ah, a serenade just for us. How lovely."

Emmeline placed the cup before him and sat down. She

folded her hands over one another and looked directly at him. "I have something to tell you. I don't know whether you will have heard yet."

The smile vanished from his lips and he sat up in his chair. "What's happened?" Gregory reached out and squeezed her hands. "Are you in some sort of trouble, love?"

Her heart softened. She was touched at the concern she saw reflected in his eyes. "I'm fine." One of his eyebrows quirked upward. She shook her head. "Really. I'm fine."

His shoulders relaxed and he gave her hands another squeeze. "Right. Then, what is it?"

She took a deep swallow. "James Sloane, my editor, rang me at midnight." Gregory said nothing, waiting for her to tell the story in her own time. The words came out in a rush. "Last night, Ambrose Trent was found murdered in Hyde Park. Apparently, he was shot twice."

Gregory sucked in his breath and slumped back in his chair, disbelief clearly etched on his handsome features. "Good God."

"I'm sorry. I know he was your friend." She touched his arm lightly. "I thought it best just to tell you straight out."

"What?" It took a second for Gregory's eyes to focus on her. "Yes. Yes, of course. Thank you, darling," he said absentmindedly. "Very kind of you. It's the last thing I expected to hear."

"Are you all right?" She searched his face. The lines on either side of his mouth seemed deeper all of a sudden and his brow was furrowed.

He smiled and reached out for her hands again. "It's my turn to say I'm fine. Ambrose and I were friends, yes, but I never felt I really knew him. I always had the feeling—"

"Yes?" There was an eagerness that she could not keep out of her voice.

"Well, that he was not quite what he seemed."

"You would certainly know about that. You're an expert at pretending to be something you're not." She slipped her hands out from his grasp and crossed her arms over chest defensively.

He wagged a finger at her. "Now, now, love. I thought we were going to play nice today."

"Hmph. So Ambrose Trent was keeping secrets—which if you'll recall I said in the tea room but you dismissed my concerns. And this is the type of man you were going to allow Claire to marry?"

"Emmy, it's not my place—nor is it yours, for that matter—to interfere. They're both adults and can make their own decisions. They don't need, and likely wouldn't appreciate it, if we held their hands."

"But—"

"There are no buts. You know I'm right." His eyes locked with hers and a momentary stare-down ensued.

In the end, Emmeline sighed. "Much as I hate to admit it, you're right," she conceded.

"Ah, there speaks the second wisest woman I know."

She glared at him. "Second?"

His lips curled into a grin. "Darling, surely you must know that Helen will always hold the top honor in my heart."

"Gran, of course. How can I possibly compete with Gran?" Emmeline returned his smile as she thought of her grandmother, who had raised her from the age of five after her parents had been killed covering a story in the Middle East. Her parents, Aaron and Jacqueline, had been journalists like herself.

"Mind you," Gregory took a sip of his coffee, "you come in a close second."

"Thanks. That's very generous of you."

"What can I say? I'm the epitome of chivalry and charm."

Coffee spluttered from her lips. "You also have one of the biggest egos I know."

He leaned back and hooked one elbow around the back of the chair. "I've never been one for false modesty."

"No, I agree. No one could ever accuse you of that. Other crimes, yes. But false modesty, definitely not."

"Ah, there you go again hurling unsubstantiated accusations about. Darling, I detect Oliver's influence in these scurrilous—and, if we're honest—slanderous comments. I can see that you've been spending far too much time around the good chief inspector."

"Ha. We could go on like this all morning and the end result would still be the same. You're a thief. Ah, ah." She raised a hand to forestall any further argument. "But I don't have the time today to engage in a mental test of wills. I must go and see Claire and Chief Inspector Burnell. James has assigned me to the Ambrose Trent murder. He thought that, as Claire and I are old friends, it might be easier for me to get the story."

"You mean Lord Sedgwick might be a bit more malleable about access."

She slid a sidelong glance in his direction. "Something like that. In any case, even if I didn't know Claire, I would have pushed to do the story. Who wouldn't jump at such a chance? It has all the right elements—intrigue, glamour, politics and *murder*."

Gregory didn't like the gleam in her dark eyes. It was the same look of determination that had nearly gotten her killed—*twice*—when she was trying to find out who murdered Charles Latimer. "Emmy."

"Don't look at me like that. I don't need a lecture. Certainly not from you. This is my job."

"Fine. Then I'm coming with you."

"That's silly. I don't need a chaperone—or a bodyguard."

"Nevertheless, I'm coming with you. I'd like to pay my respects to Claire and to have a quiet word with Oliver."

"But—"

"I will brook no arguments. Either we go together, or I'll meet you on Claire's doorstep."

"Ooh." She balled her fists on the table. Sometimes he was like a piece of granite and nothing could move him. "This is absurd. I'm not a child. I don't need you to hold my hand. Besides, what can happen to me?"

"After that little episode with the car yesterday afternoon, I would rather not wait around to find out."

Emmeline's head snapped up. "What do you mean? That was just a drunk driver."

He shook his head. "No, love. I'm afraid that was no accident. He knew exactly what he was doing. The question now is: who was he trying to kill? You or me?"

CHAPTER 6

Lord Douglas Sedgwick gazed down at the crush of reporters and cameras camped in Cliveden Place outside his daughter's two-bedroom Belgravia flat in an immaculate building of classical design. He let the lace curtain drop back into place at the sash window, disgusted. "Ghouls," he muttered under his breath as he paced in front of the mantelpiece. It was eight-thirty in the morning, for God's sake.

At sixty-two, he was still lean and handsome. Not a strand of his thick, snowy hair was ever out of place, and his emerald eyes were always alight with keen intelligence. He was a seasoned politician and distinguished Queen's Counsel, or QC—a barrister who was appointed by a nine-member panel comprised of barristers, solicitors, a judge and non-lawyers—and had the right to appear in the higher courts of the realm. Sedgwick was a darling of all the news programs. Not a day could go by without his face flashing on some television screen somewhere across England because his all-important opinion had been sought.

He snatched up a tapestry pillow from the sand-colored sofa and began to pummel it between with his fists as he continued his pacing. "Bloody Ambrose Trent. Nothing but trouble."

The door opened. He turned to find his wife Vanessa precariously balancing the tea tray, while trying to close the door. "Doug, no matter what you felt about Ambrose, I wouldn't let Claire hear you speaking that way about him."

"Allow me, dear." Sedgwick crossed the room in two strides and took the tray from his wife. He set it down on the coffee table and then wearily plunked himself down beside her on the sofa. For a moment, he leaned back and pressed his fingers to his eyes.

"Darling." He opened his eyes again as Vanessa handed him a cup of tea. Sedgwick splashed a little milk into the steaming amber liquid and gave it quick stir with his spoon. He took a careful sip before speaking.

"How's Claire?"

"As well as can be expected under the circumstances. She's absolutely devastated, but the doctor gave her something and she finally managed to fall asleep around two o'clock. I'll go look in on her in a bit."

Sedgwick gave Vanessa's hand a squeeze. They had been married for thirty-five years and were still as much in love as that first day when they started their life together. Thirty-five years. Sometimes he could hardly believe that it had been so long. Sedgwick's gaze skimmed over his wife's face. Her porcelain skin was marked with a few more wrinkles these days and her rich chestnut hair was now threaded with silver, but at sixty she was still as lovely as ever. Her warm brown eyes always danced with amusement as her silvery laughter filled the room. But most of all, his dear Vanessa listened with her heart and was always there when he needed her.

They were quiet for a time, content simply to be in each other's company. Sedgwick sighed and put his cup and saucer on the table. "Why did she have to get mixed up with the chap?" He searched his wife's eyes as if the answer could be found there. "What did she see in him? That's what I don't understand. He was a good-for-nothing, lying scoundrel."

Vanessa gently traced a finger along his taut jaw. She could feel the muscle twitching. "Doug, she loved him," she said softly. "Surely, you can understand that nothing else mattered."

Sedgwick took her hand and pressed it to his lips. "Yes, but why him? What a cliché." He got up and started pacing again. "She goes on a two-week Mediterranean cruise and comes home engaged. Darling, it's too much. Couldn't she see that he was—"

"We can't choose who we fall in love with. It just happens."

"You never liked Ambrose. Neither of you." Sedgwick and his wife turned abruptly at the sound of their daughter's voice. They hadn't heard her come in.

Vanessa got up and put her arm around Claire. "Come, darling. Come sit next to me and have a cup of tea. It will buck you up."

Claire shook off her mother's arm. "I don't want a cup of tea, Mum. I don't want to 'buck up.' I want—" She choked on a sob. Her throat was thick with tears. Her chest tightened and she couldn't breathe. She collapsed onto the sofa and dropped her head between her hands. "I want Ambrose." The words were muffled. "I want Ambrose."

Vanessa and Sedgwick exchanged concerned looks over their daughter's head as she wept. Vanessa came and sat next to her. She smoothed back Claire's golden hair. "I know, my darling. I *know*."

"Oh, Mum." Claire suddenly threw herself into her mother's arms just as she used to do as a child. "Mum, I loved him so much. Why did this happen? Why my Ambrose? *Why?*" She lifted her tear-ravaged face to look at her mother.

The pain Vanessa saw in her daughter's emerald eyes tore at her heart. She felt tears sting her own eyes. She took Claire's face between her hands and brushed away the salty wetness on her cheeks. She placed a gentle kiss on Claire's forehead. "I don't know why this happened, love. It was quite senseless, but Ambrose is gone. You must come to terms with that. What I'm most concerned about at the moment is *you*. All this worry is not good for you. I'm here, darling. There's nothing for you to worry about. Not anymore. Do you understand?"

Mother and daughter looked at one another for long moment without speaking. "But how can I go on without him? I don't know what I'll do." Claire buried her face against Vanessa's neck and wrapped her arms around her waist. "I don't know what I'll do."

Her mother felt every shudder of Claire's body.

The doorbell buzzed. Sedgwick scowled. "You stay here with Claire. I'll sort it out. It's probably just the bloody press, anyway."

Preoccupied about his daughter's state of mind, he flung open the door. "Now look here, my daughter isn't speaking to the press at this time, so you can take your intrusive questions—" Sedgwick stopped abruptly. "Emmeline?"

"Hello, Lord Sedgwick. I'm sorry if I'm—" She cast a quick sidelong glance at Gregory. "—if we're intruding. I heard about—about Ambrose and came to see if there's anything I—we—can do. I'm terribly worried about Claire. How is she?"

For a moment, Sedgwick said nothing. He simply stared at Gregory. He had never taken to him and didn't understand what a sensible girl like Emmeline was doing with such a chap. Besides, didn't Claire say it was all over between them? Apparently not. However, Sedgwick opened the door wider and allowed them to step into the corridor. "Come in, Emmeline, Longdon."

When he had slipped the bolt back into place, he turned to them and lowered his voice. "Claire's in the living room with Vanessa. She's still in shock. As all of us are."

"Naturally. Perhaps we should leave. We certainly don't want to intrude." Emmeline put a hand on the doorknob.

"No, don't be silly. Claire will be glad to see *you*."

Although Sedgwick spoke to Emmeline, Gregory understood that the words were being directed at him. Their meaning was crystal clear—*he* was not welcome here. Well, the pompous lord of the realm would just have to lump it.

Gregory smiled and took Emmeline's elbow. "Yes, darling. Claire needs her friends at a time like this. She'd be so disappointed to hear you had popped by and then left without seeing her. Isn't that so, Lord Sedgwick?"

Emmeline blushed, while Sedgwick fumed inwardly. The insolence of the chap was astounding. However, ever the politician, he tamped down his anger and said through gritted teeth, "Yes, Claire would be extremely disappointed. Please come in."

They followed him down the corridor. Emmeline poked Gregory in the ribs and hissed out of the corner of her mouth. "Why do you always have to rub people the wrong way? You know it only makes the situation worse, when you say things like that."

Gregory whispered back without moving his lips. "But it wouldn't be half as interesting, would it?"

Emmeline tilted her head toward the ceiling and muttered under her breath. They didn't have time to say more. Sedgwick led them into the living room. Vanessa smiled when she saw Emmeline. "Claire darling, look who's here."

Claire disentangled herself from her mother's arms and turned around. Her blonde hair was all mussed and her normally bright green eyes were bloodshot, but her lips curved into a smile. "Emmeline." She stood up and held out her hands to her old friend.

Emmeline crossed the room and gave her a warm hug. They made a funny pair—Claire, all willowy limbs and long blonde hair. And Emmeline, in her tailored navy trouser suit, was petite with short dark curls that framed her round face. She only came up to Claire's shoulder.

"Thank you for coming," Claire said as they settled themselves on the sofa. "It's times like these that you know who you can lean on." She squeezed Emmeline's hand hard as tears welled up in her eyes again.

"You know that I'm always here for you. And Maggie, too. I rang her this morning to tell—to let her know. She wanted to come at once, but she has a big meeting with a client and can't reschedule. She said she'll pop by as soon as it's over."

"That's nice. We were supposed to have lunch today to discuss a few things about the wedding—*the wedding*—which will never happen now because Ambrose is—gone. Emmeline, what I'm going to do without him? I loved him so much."

Emmeline looked over at Claire's mother, who was sitting on her other side. Vanessa shook her head and gave a small helpless shrug.

Emmeline put her arm around Claire's thin shoulders. "Of course, you'll go on. You have to. You can't just stop living."

"But that's just it. I feel numb—dead inside. There is no life for me without Ambrose."

"Don't be silly, Claire. I'm not saying it will be easy. It will likely be difficult for a long time. It's never easy to lose someone you love." For a second, Emmeline hesitated as the memory of the baby she'd lost came unbidden to her mind. But she pushed this thought away and said in a stronger, more determined voice, "You just need time. To grieve. To heal. Things are too fresh right now."

"Darling, listen to Emmeline. She's right."

"Mum, don't you understand? Things will never be all right again," Claire snapped.

Vanessa sighed and stood up. "I will get some more tea."

Emmeline started to rise. "Please let me do that, Lady Sedgwick."

"No, you stay with Claire." Vanessa picked up the tea tray. As she brushed past Emmeline, she mouthed, "Talk to her."

Emmeline nodded.

"May I help you, Lady Sedgwick?" Gregory asked. This was the first time he had spoken since they entered the room.

Vanessa shook her head. "Thank you, Gregory. That's very kind of you. I can manage. By the way, it's very nice to see you again. It's been a long time." She smiled warmly at him.

"Likewise, Lady Sedgwick. Allow me to get the door for you."

"No, it's all right. My husband can do that. Doug, perhaps you could come help me with the tea?"

Lord Sedgwick nodded with stiffness, telegraphing his dislike of having Gregory Longdon in his daughter's flat.

"Doug?" There was a hint of impatience in his wife's tone.

"I'm coming."

Gregory was impervious to the withering glance Lord Sedgwick shot in his direction as he pulled the door closed. He despised men like Sedgwick, who thought their position, their rank, or wealth made them better than everyone else. Wasn't it funny how these same men *always* had something to hide?

"Gregory? I didn't realize that you were here as well. It's been ages since I've seen you." The sound of Claire's voice pulled him from his contemplation of her father.

He walked over to the sofa and bent down to kiss her on the cheek. "I came with Emmy. I'm sorry for your loss."

"Thanks," she said softly as she wiped away a stray tear with the back of her hand. Claire swallowed hard and tried to get her emotions under control. She turned back to Emmeline. "I didn't realize that the two of you were back together. When did this happen?"

Emmeline felt heat suffuse her cheeks. She didn't dare look at Gregory. "We came here today together, but we're not *back together.*"

"Aren't you? But—" Claire's green gaze flickered from one to the other in confusion.

"We are *not* back together," Emmeline stressed more firmly.

"*At the moment.* But you never know about the future. The possibilities are endless." Gregory winked at Claire.

She smiled back, probably the first genuine smile since she learned of her fiancé's murder. She liked him. They had always gotten on well. She whispered back, "I hope so."

"What was that, Claire?" Emmeline asked suspiciously.

"Nothing." Claire exchanged a conspiratorial look with Gregory. "Nothing at all. Here Gregory." She patted the sofa. "Come sit next to me."

Emmeline sighed. He'd done it again. Damn. He'd gained another ally. First it was, Gran and Maggie. Admittedly, he didn't have to do too much arm-twisting with those two. And now Claire. How did all these women succumb to his charms? What she conveniently chose to forget, though, was that not only did she herself succumb to those same charms once, she nearly married him. But if Emmeline recognized this fact, she'd have to acknowledge a number of other thoughts that were roiling through her head. Or was it her heart? She shook her head to banish this dangerous stream of consciousness.

"Claire, I'm here today as your friend. But I want to let you know that I've been assigned to—the story about Ambrose's—about Ambrose. I wanted to tell you from the outset so there are no misunderstandings or recriminations between us. It's my job."

Claire closed her eyes for a moment and a faint smile crossed her lips. "I'm glad," she said with relief as she opened her eyes and squeezed Emmeline's hand. "Truly. At least I know you'll be objective. Not like the rest of that lot out there." She jerked her head in the direction of the street.

"Well, I'm glad that's out in the open."

"And of course, you'll find out who did this and make sure they pay."

Gregory frowned at this remark. It only encouraged Emmeline to put herself in harm's way. Again. She needed very little encouragement as it was.

"Now that we've gotten all that out of the way—" Emmeline dug into her handbag and pulled out her pad. "—do you mind if I take notes?" She searched Claire's face. Her friend seemed to be a little calmer, more in control of her emotions.

Claire cleared her throat and straightened her shoulders. "No, of course not. Please go ahead. Ask anything you like. I have no secrets."

With her pen poised in the air, Emmeline thought, *You might not have secrets, but what about Ambrose?* However, aloud she said, "What can you tell me about Ambrose? About his family? His background? His business?"

"Well—" Claire twisted and untwisted the tissue between her fingers in her lap, "—actually—You see—Ambrose was a very private person and didn't really like to talk about his past. So I didn't press him."

For a second, Emmeline didn't know what to say. She looked over at Gregory on Claire's other side. His eyes narrowed. He seemed to share her misgivings. Emmeline tried to frame her next question cautiously. "Didn't you find that a little...odd? I mean here was the man you were on the verge of marrying and you didn't know anything about him."

"It was enough that he loved me." Claire thrust out her chin, daring Emmeline to criticize Ambrose.

"I see. Well, of course, you knew him best."

"Yes, I did. You have no right to judge him."

Emmeline sought to diffuse the anger smoldering in her friend's green eyes. "I'm not judging anyone, Claire. How could I? I never even met Ambrose. I'm just trying to find the truth, but I need your help. Will you help me?"

This seemed to mollify Claire a bit and she nodded.

"Good," Emmeline said. "Now what—"

The doorbell rang at this point. Gregory stood up. "I'll answer it."

But Vanessa was quicker. They heard her in the hall. There was some shuffling followed by a brief murmur of voices.

Gregory's face broke out into a smile. "If I'm not mistaken, I do believe—"

Vanessa opened the door and two gentlemen entered the living room.

"Yes. It is. Oliver, old chap, what a pleasure to see you again."

"*Longdon?*" Chief Inspector Burnell's eyes widened in disbelief. "What are *you* doing here?"

Sergeant Finch simply stared down at his feet and shook his reddish-brown head. Emmeline thought she heard him mumble, "Here we go again."

Gregory was in his element now. There was nothing like needling his old nemesis to brighten the day. "Oliver, is that any way to greet an old friend?"

"*Chief Inspector Burnell.* And we are not, nor will we ever be, friends."

"Oh, *Oliver*, you wound me. Truly you do." Gregory put a hand over his heart and puckered his lips into a pout. "Even after everything we've been through lately?"

Burnell remembered the night a month ago, when Longdon shoved him out of the way of a killer's bullet. A split second later and he would have been dead. Unbidden, Burnell felt his head move in an infinitesimal nod and Longdon smiled in response. Then the moment was gone and they reverted to their usual sniping.

The chief inspector pushed past Gregory. "I don't have time for your nonsense today, Longdon." He turned to the sofa and noticed Emmeline for the first time. He inclined his head and took a step forward. He extended a hand and she returned his grasp. "Miss Kirby, forgive me. I was distracted by Longdon there." His gaze strayed for a second in Longdon's direction as Burnell silently speculated on why they were here together.

As if Emmeline could read his thoughts, she said, "Claire and I are old friends and I came as soon as I heard about— about her fiancé. Coincidentally, Gregory happens to be—was an old friend of Ambrose Trent's so he came with me today. He also knows Claire and wanted to pay his respects." She gave Claire's shoulders a quick squeeze.

Burnell straightened up after he shook Claire's hand. "Is that so?" He stroked his chin as was his wont when in thought and glanced over at Longdon, who was standing next to Vanessa. "I don't like coincidences."

"Don't you, Oliver? What can I say? I have a very large and eclectic group of friends," Gregory replied smoothly as he flashed a grin at the chief inspector.

A gurgling sound came from Sergeant Finch, who had quietly slipped into a deep armchair and sat with his pen poised over his notebook.

"Mmph." It was the only reaction that Gregory's comment deserved.

"Chief Inspector?" Emmeline sought to change the direction that this conversation was headed.

"Yes, Miss Kirby?"

"I also want to let you know I have been assigned to this story. That means you'll be seeing a lot of me. Therefore, I would appreciate it tremendously if you could share any information you may have thus far on the investigation."

Burnell sighed. He was getting too old for this. "It's not you I mind. It's others who might try to interfere with the investigation who bother me."

He meant Longdon, but at that moment Lord Sedgwick came back into the room.

"What's going on here?" Sedgwick demanded.

"It's all right, Doug," Lady Vanessa answered. "This is Chief Inspector Burnell and Detective Sergeant Finch from Scotland Yard. They're investigating Ambrose's murder. Chief inspector, my husband, Lord Sedgwick."

Sergeant Finch got to his feet as Burnell went over to shake his lordship's hand. "Sir, my condolences. I'm sorry to intrude at a time like this, but you understand we have to interview everyone who knew the victim."

Sedgwick's eyes narrowed and became the color of a rolling green sea as a storm approaches. "See you don't bother my daughter. I don't want Claire harassed by your lot. It's bad enough that half the London press corps is camped outside her door like vultures waiting to pounce—present company excepted, Emmeline." Her cheeks reddened. Sedgwick took a step toward Burnell. He was several inches taller, which only seemed to magnify the smug superiority reflected in his eyes as he looked down his long nose at the chief inspector. "Tread carefully, Burnell. One false step and, not only will you be taken off this case, you'll find yourself out of a job. Do I make myself clear?"

Burnell seethed at this public dressing down. His fists clenched and unclenched at his sides. Longdon bounced on his toes as if he, too, wanted to land a punch right in the middle of Sedgwick's patrician nose.

"Doug, really," Lady Vanessa chided. "That's quite enough." She stepped between them. "Just let Chief Inspector Burnell get on with his job. I'm terribly sorry. You must forgive my husband. We're all upset. It's the strain, compounded by lack of sleep."

The chief inspector swallowed hard. "Of course, Lady Sedgwick, I do understand. We will do our best not to inconvenience those involved, but in the end my duty is to find out who killed Ambrose Trent—regardless of whose secrets are exposed in the process." Although he spoke to Lady Vanessa, his eyes challenged Lord Sedgwick.

Sedgwick took a half-step forward. "What are you insinuating, you insolent bastard?"

Vanessa blanched. An involuntary shiver sent a frisson up her spine. She put a restraining hand on her husband's arm, but he shook it off. "Doug, *please.*"

"Don't interfere, dear." This was a command, not a request. Sedgwick was within a hair's breadth of Burnell now. His eyes were aflame with emerald fire. "I'd watch my step, if I were in your shoes. You have no idea with whom you're toying."

The chief inspector could feel Sedgwick's warm breath upon his cheek. "I don't play games, Lord Sedgwick. Personally, I despise politics. It's rife with corrupt scoundrels. I'm a simple policeman, and all I'm looking for is the truth. I would think that you would want that for your daughter. To find out who killed her fiancé."

"Of course, it is. That's what we all want, Chief Inspector," Vanessa said quickly, hoping to diffuse the tension. "Isn't that right, Doug? *Doug?*"

An uncomfortable silence fell as everyone watched the test of wills taking place in the middle of the room.

"No, it isn't, Mum. Dad wouldn't care if Ambrose's killer is never found." All eyes fell on Claire, whom they had all forgotten about in the heated exchange between her father and Burnell. "I'm right, Dad. Aren't I? You never liked him. Nor you, Mum, for that matter. Please don't." She put up a hand to forestall any false denials from her parents' lips. "Please don't insult my intelligence by pretending otherwise."

"Claire, darling, you're overwrought. I think you should go back to bed." Concern was etched in every line of her mother's face.

There was something else as well, Emmeline thought. What was it? Fear?

"I don't want to go back to bed, Mum. I don't want to hide. That's not going to solve anything. What I want is Ambrose." Claire's voice cracked as she plunked down onto the sofa and buried her head in her hands. "But he's never going to come back to me and not one of you gives a damn. Not one of you." She lifted her tear-stained face to accuse them all with one sweeping look of her swollen, red-rimmed eyes.

"Claire, that's not true. We love you." Vanessa hurried forward and put an arm around her daughter, who by turns trembled with grief and anger. Her mother rocked her back and forth for few moments as the others looked on helplessly.

Emmeline joined them on the sofa. She put a hand on her friend's shoulder. "Claire, we all want the truth. We all want to see Ambrose's murderer brought to justice. I promise you that."

Claire tore herself from the cocoon of her mother's protective embrace and turned on her friend so violently that Emmeline shrank back. "I don't want justice. What good does justice do me? I want Ambrose's killer to rot in hell for taking everything away from me," she hissed.

"Chief Inspector Burnell and Sergeant Finch will find him. Trust me. You do trust me, don't you, Claire?" Emmeline asked, so softly that she could barely be heard.

They all seemed to be holding their breath as Claire stared at Emmeline for an agonizing moment. "Yes. Yes, I do trust you," Claire replied at last.

Emmeline smiled. "Well, I'm relieved to hear it. Now, do you think that you're up to answering a few questions for Chief Inspector Burnell?"

"Will you stay? You and Gregory. Please," Claire implored.

Emmeline reached out for her friend's hand. "Yes, of course we'll stay."

"Of course," Gregory echoed from his corner.

"Thanks. Then I'm ready to help you in any way I can, Chief Inspector." Claire gave him a watery smile. Then, she turned to Vanessa. "Mum, I think you and Dad should leave now. I'll give you a ring later."

"But, darling—"

"It's all right, Lady Sedgwick," Emmeline assured her. "I'll take care of Claire. Plus, Maggie said she'd pop over as soon as her meeting is over. So you see, Claire will be in good hands."

Vanessa smoothed Claire's golden hair from her face and stood up uncertainly. "Well, if you're sure—"

Emmeline nodded. "Yes, it will be all right. Don't worry."

Lady Sedgwick bent down to place a kiss on her cheek and gave her shoulder a squeeze. "You're a good girl. My daughter is lucky to have such a good friend. Take care of her."

Emmeline patted her hand. "I will. I promise."

Lady Sedgwick smiled. "Then, it's time for us to go, Doug."

"Vanessa, you can't be serious," Lord Sedgwick blustered.

"I am. Now, let's go. We must allow Chief Inspector Burnell and Sergeant Finch to get on with their job." She took her husband firmly by the arm and propelled him out the door.

Heated whispers and shuffling could be heard in the corridor for a few minutes. Then the door opened and closed and Claire's parents were gone.

Burnell cleared his throat and smiled down at Claire. "Thank you for your cooperation, Miss Sedgwick."

Sergeant Finch resumed his place in the armchair opposite and opened his notebook again.

"I just want Ambrose's killer found." Nervously, she touched the teapot on the tray. "Oh, it's gone cold. Would all of you like some tea? I could go make a fresh pot."

"No, thank you, Miss Sedgwick. I assure you we're fine."

"Emmeline? Gregory?"

"No," they said in unison.

Claire's long, tapered fingers twisted nervously in her lap. "Well, then, I suppose you should start, Chief Inspector."

"Right." Burnell paced in front of the fireplace as her father had been doing earlier. "Do you know of anyone who would want to harm your fiancé?"

"No. Ambrose was the sweetest, kindest man. I don't understand why anyone would want to do this."

"Yes, Miss Sedgwick," the chief inspector said. She would need to be handled with kid gloves. "But he must have had enemies. Everyone has enemies."

"That's quite impossible. I told you," Claire responded tersely.

Burnell sighed. *God grant me patience—right now!* "Yes, I know. 'He was the sweetest, kindest man.' All right. What can you tell me about his friends?"

"Not much. Nothing, in fact. I didn't even know that he and Gregory were friends."

Burnell looked over at Finch and raised an eyebrow. Emmeline put an arm around Claire's shoulders and gave them a quick squeeze. Defensiveness in a witness usually meant lying, or willful blindness.

"Chief inspector, if I may say something."

"By all means, Miss Kirby. If you know of anything that could shed light on this case, I'm all ears."

"I don't have any direct knowledge I'm afraid. I just wanted to clarify something." Burnell waited. "Although Claire and Ambrose had been planning to marry next week, they'd only known each other for a very short time. A month, in fact." Emmeline avoided looking at Claire. The subject was a sensitive one that required tact. "They met on a cruise in the Mediterranean. It was love at first sight and they decided to get married right away."

"Ah, I see." Burnell leaned his elbow against the mantelpiece.

"You see nothing. You sound just like my father," Claire spat. "Simply because we hadn't known each other for years and years doesn't mean that we didn't know what we were doing."

"Of course not, Claire. No one meant to imply such a thing. I just wanted to explain things to Chief Inspector Burnell so that he could understand why you couldn't answer questions about Ambrose's friends."

Claire stood. Clearly, this was the wrong thing to say. "I can't believe it. You're on their side. Aren't you?"

"If I'm on anybody's side, it's yours, Claire. You must know that," Emmeline said quietly.

"No, you're not. You're on theirs."

"Claire, listen to me—"

Claire flew halfway across the room. Burnell and Emmeline exchanged worried glances. Gregory shrugged his shoulders.

"Here, look." Claire came back and thrust a framed photograph in Emmeline's hand. "Does that look like the face of a man who had anything to hide?"

Emmeline's dark eyes widened as she looked down at the photo. "Is *this* Ambrose?"

"Who do you think it is? The Prince of Wales."

"I know this man."

"What do you mean?" Claire asked, surprised.

All eyes in the room turned to Emmeline. "I don't know him *personally*, but this is the man who nearly knocked me down yesterday afternoon when I went to meet Maggie."

Gregory leaned forward to glance over Emmeline's shoulder. "Darling, there's a problem."

She glanced up at him. "You mean aside from the fact that Ambrose Trent is dead?"

"The problem is that's *not* Ambrose Trent."

CHAPTER 7

Emmeline opened her mouth to say something, but changed her mind. She was too stunned.

"Longdon, what the devil are you playing at?" Burnell snapped.

"Oliver, old man, it's very simple. I don't know who that man is, but he is not Ambrose Trent. At least, he is not the man who *I* know as Ambrose Trent."

Claire took the photo from Emmeline and smoothed her hand over the smiling face of the man who had been her fiancé. "I don't understand," she whispered hoarsely. "What do you mean?"

Gregory came around the sofa and bent down on his haunches before Claire. He took her hands in his larger ones. "I don't know what's going on here. I'm as much in the dark as the rest of you. I'm sorry, Claire, but it seems someone has been lying to you. That man is not Ambrose Trent."

Emmeline finally found her voice. "Then, *who* is he?"

"That's a very good question. A matter for the police, I believe. Isn't that so, Oliver?"

"Naturally, Longdon. I intend to get to the bottom of this mystery," the chief inspector asserted, as he stroked his neatly trimmed white beard and mulled over this new wrinkle.

"You'll pardon me for mentioning it, sir." Sergeant Finch interrupted their thoughts. "But there's another question that's just as important."

"And what's that, Finch?"

"If the dead man is not Ambrose Trent, then *where* is the real Ambrose Trent?"

ↄ৵ঌ৵ↄ

Emmeline and Gregory walked in silence along Piccadilly. They had left Claire's flat ten minutes earlier. Maggie had swooped in and started fussing like a mother hen. There wasn't much more that they could do. And frankly, Emmeline had been happy to finally get away. The morning's revelations had left her with a lot of work to do. But where to start?

Gregory took her by the elbow. "How about a cup of coffee?"

"Hmm? No thanks. I have to get to the paper. I have to talk to James."

"Your editor can wait. How about if we walk in the park for a bit?"

Emmeline saw that they had reached the eastern side of Green Park. She looked up at the sky. It was a glorious shade of blue with a smattering of wispy clouds floating above the still bare branches of the planetrees. The park looked terribly inviting after last night's rain. "Oh, what difference could another few minutes make?"

Gregory smiled and threaded her arm through his as he guided them down Queen's Walk, where honeyed stands of sunlight danced along the gravel path. "That's my girl."

Emmeline stopped and withdrew her arm. "I am not your girl. Not anymore."

He sighed. "Darling, it is too early in the day to start this argument all over again." He pulled her toward him and pressed a soft kiss on her lips. When she opened her eyes, she saw that he was smiling down at her with bemused fondness. "Now, come on." She didn't resist when he tucked her arm through his elbow this time.

What was wrong with her? Were her defenses beginning to crumble? No, she couldn't have it. She cast a quick sidelong glance at Gregory from under her eyelashes. No, she couldn't go back to all that pain. And yet—and yet, it wasn't all bad. She had to admit there were happy times too. Many happy times. But that was before he disappeared and she found out that he was a jewel thief. *Before the baby.* She crushed this thought before it could take hold. No, a voice inside her head said more firmly, things are definitely over. Unequivocally. Irrevocably. *Forever.*

Gregory was saying something, but she had missed what it was. "Pardon."

"Emmy, you haven't heard a word I've said."

She felt her face flush. "Sorry, I was thinking about poor Claire and your bombshell about Ambrose Trent," she fibbed. "It was bad enough that her fiancé was murdered. But now, to learn that he wasn't who he purported to be. I simply can't imagine what she must be going through. Her mind must be reeling."

"Yes," Gregory said. "So many questions are running through my head. Like where is the real Ambrose? Did he know that this chap was impersonating him? And, most disturbing of all, who was the intended target—the real Ambrose or the impostor?"

ᴇꙅᴇꙅ

The first person Burnell and Sergeant Finch saw when the lift doors opened was Sally Harper, Superintendent Fenton's officious secretary.

"Bloody hell," the chief inspector mumbled under his breath. "Pandora and her box of plagues out to greet the world."

Finch coughed to cover the laughter bubbling in his throat.

Out loud, the chief inspector said, "Good morning, Sally. What a vision of loveliness you are. Isn't it a beautiful day?"

She would have been a good-looking woman, if she didn't have that scowl permanently plastered on her face. He pitied her poor husband.

"I wouldn't know about that. I've been cooped up in here

since eight o'clock this morning with a stack of reports for Superintendent Fenton."

"Have you? What a shame. Well, I hope the rest of your day gets better. If you'll excuse us, we're busy with a new case. See you later, Sally. Come along, Finch."

Burnell took the sergeant by the elbow and propelled him past her. She was left standing in the middle of the corridor, bristling with indignation. Sally angrily pushed back a strand of brown hair that had come loose. Her brown eyes narrowed. "Chief Inspector Burnell," she called after him.

He felt the force of every word as surely as if a knife had been plunged between his shoulder blades.

"I knew that was too easy," he whispered out of the corner his mouth to Finch. "Go on. No need for the two of us to be put through the ringer. Start digging into Trent's past."

"Right, sir." Finch scooted along before he could come within her sights.

"Yes, Sally?" Burnell turned round to face her. "Was there something you wanted particularly?" he asked sweetly.

The smile that he flashed was lost on the woman. She didn't have an ounce of human kindness in her thin body.

"Superintendent Fenton would like to see you *immediately.*"

Damn and blast. This had Sedgwick's fingerprints all over it. "Does he, really?" Burnell took a few steps toward her. "Can't it wait until this afternoon? You see, just at the moment we're—"

"What part of immediately don't you understand, Chief Inspector?"

"Aha. Well, if it's that important."

"Chief Inspector Burnell, must I continually remind you that Superintendent Fenton's time is precious. With his crowded schedule, he doesn't have time to dance attendance on you. Therefore, it behooves you to see him at once."

"But can he spare the time, Sally, what with his schedule being full? That's the real question. I wouldn't want to disturb the great man." Burnell choked on these words. Perhaps he was laying it on too thick.

"Naturally, he has the time to see you. He asked for you, didn't he?"

Burnell snapped his fingers and ventured another smile. "So he did. Thank you for pointing out that fact to me. It had slipped my mind."

"Hmm," was all Sally said as she fixed him with her cold, brown stare, like a witch conjuring an evil spell.

"Yes, well, I'd be delighted to spend a few moments chatting with the superintendent. Shall I follow you, then?"

"That would be the best course of action, if I were you."

"Thank you for being concerned about my well-being."

The frosty look she gave him over her shoulder told him that she cared naught about his well-being. Somehow this did not come as a great surprise. The feeling was mutual.

"Please wait there a moment, while I tell Superintendent Fenton you're here. At last." She pointed toward two chairs outside her boss's office.

"Certainly. It would be my pleasure," Burnell responded facetiously.

After a moment, she placed the phone's receiver back in its cradle. "Superintendent Fenton will see you now, but mind you don't keep him chatting too long. He has a very full schedule today."

Chatting? With Fenton? That was not Burnell's idea of a pleasant way to while a few minutes of his time. He sighed and heaved his bulk out of the uncomfortable chair. "I feel honored that the great man could manage to squeeze me in."

Sally sniffed dismissively as she turned her attention back to her computer.

Burnell knocked.

"Come in," his chief barked. "Ah, Burnell, there you are. Glad that you could drop by." Fenton said the same thing every time he summoned Burnell for an audience. As if the chief inspector had any choice in the matter.

The superintendent was seated behind his huge oak desk, designed to make him look imposing. He took off his designer glasses with an elegant sweep of his manicured hand and waved Burnell toward a chair. Fenton was a man in his late fifties with salt-and-pepper hair and light brown eyes. Women of all ages found him attractive. He was what they called distinguished *and* he had pots of money to boot. His wife's money, but money nevertheless. This allowed Fenton to wear designer Italian suits—like the charcoal one with pinstripes he had on at the moment—and to hobnob with actors, politicians, and others who moved in the upper echelons of "society."

The superintendent was not dumb. But rather than using his intelligence for police work, he preferred to wield it against those he believed were plotting against him. Like all weak men, Fenton resorted to demeaning those with real talent and capabilities, simply to demonstrate that he was in control. And the one who threatened him the most was Chief Inspector Burnell. He was terrified that Burnell was angling to push him out of his job. For this reason, Fenton continually called the chief inspector in for these "little chats."

"Sir, you wanted to see me?"

Fenton leaned back in his high-backed swivel chair and steepled his fingers over his flat stomach, which came from running twelve miles every day and playing tennis. "I think you know what this is about, don't you?"

"No, sir, I can't say that I do," Burnell replied, fighting to maintain an innocent expression.

"Don't you?" Fenton's brown eyes were thoughtful as he studied Burnell's face closely. "Well, never mind. The reason I sent for you was that Lord Sedgwick was on to me this morning to complain about you and how you're handling the investigation into his son-in-law—almost son-in-law's—murder."

"Really, sir? Most disturbing. Obviously the poor man is still reeling from the shock."

"Mmm," was all his superior said.

"How else can you explain it? Sergeant Finch and I have just started our inquiries."

"It is clear that something you said or did rubbed Lord Sedgwick the wrong way."

Burnell lowered his head in what would appear to be an appropriate show of contrition. "I'm truly sorry if that's the case."

"Mmm." Fenton leaned forward and folded his hands on the desk in front of him. "Steer clear of him. Sedgwick's out of your league. He's not a man to cross. If you're not careful, he'll crush you like a gnat."

"Right. Point taken, sir. I'll mind my step." Burnell stood to go.

"See that you do. I did all I could to protect you—this time. I can't answer for the consequences if another incident occurs. Understood?"

Protect me? Not bloody likely. "Yes, sir. Message received and understood."

"Good. Send Sally in on your way out." The interview was at an end, and Burnell was being dismissed like an errant schoolboy. Fenton put his glasses back on and picked up a sheaf of papers. He had already lost interest in the chief inspector.

With his hand on the doorknob, Burnell turned back to his boss. "Sir?"

"Mmm," Fenton replied, without looking up.

"I was just wondering."

"Yes?" There was a hint of impatience in the superintendent's voice.

"If Lord Sedgwick has nothing to hide, why is he so determined to get me off this case when I've barely scratched the surface? It's something to think about, anyway. Isn't it, sir?"

Burnell left before the superintendent had a chance to say anything.

CHAPTER 8

Gregory and Emmeline had resolved nothing on their ramble through Green Park. They just came up with more questions, whose answers remained elusive. It was getting on to ten-thirty and Emmeline wanted to get to *The Times* to discuss the story with James. Gregory said he "knew a chap" who might be able to help shed some light on their little conundrum. Emmeline's journalistic antennae went up.

"'A chap?' Anyone I should meet?"

Gregory kissed the top of her head and flashed her a smile that was intended to charm so that you forgot what you had been thinking. "No, darling. Now, off you go. Your editor is waiting. If I learn anything, you'll be the first to know." He gave her a tiny shove toward the Green Park Underground station. "I'll collect you at eight for dinner."

"I don't recall making any plans with you."

Gregory pulled her back to the top of the staircase as they were blocking the path of those wishing to enter the station. "Oh, you silly girl. We have to meet to discuss what we've both discovered, don't we? And we have to eat, don't we? This way we can kill two birds with one stone."

"There are telephones."

"Bah, telephones," Gregory said, with a disgusted wave of his hands. "Such cold, sterile things."

"Jolly useful things, though. A perfect medium for communication."

"It will be much more pleasant my way. Remember eight o'clock." He kissed her again and started walking down Piccadilly.

"Gregory, come back here. We have not finished this discussion," she called after him. "I will not be at home. You'll be having dinner on your own."

He simply raised a hand in the air and waved back without turning around.

"Ooh." Emmeline clenched her fists into tight balls, her nails digging into her palms "Of all the insufferable, egotistical men," she mumbled as she descended into the station. "I will not be home. You can drop by, but I will not be home."

People started to give her strange looks. She could see that they were trying to determine whether she was drunk or simply unhinged. Let them think whatever they liked. She didn't care.

The man on the beige Vespa across the street had watched the argument between Gregory and Emmeline from a safe distance. The question was who should he follow? Which one was the bigger threat?

℮౨℮౨

Chief Inspector Burnell took off his navy blazer and hung it neatly on the hanger on the back of his office door. He loosened his blue-gray tie and rolled up his shirtsleeves as he paced in front of the window. His seventh-floor office in the steel-and-glass office tower faced onto Broadway. He could see the famous revolving sign down below that told all and sundry they had reached New Scotland Yard, the headquarters of the Metropolitan Police. If he craned his neck to the right, he could just see the St. James's Park tube station.

But none of this interested him. The question running through his mind was why did Lord Sedgwick feel threatened by him? Beneath the bluster and smug superiority, Burnell had seen real fear in his lordship's eyes. Now what or who could be responsible for that? Sedgwick had done little to cover his lack of remorse over Ambrose Trent's death. Then why was he allowing his only daughter to marry a man that he so evidently despised? The chief inspector turned it over and over in his mind. Blackmail was the only thing that made any sort of sense. But what on earth could be so damaging that he was willing to sacrifice everything? Burnell was determined to find out what Sedgwick was hiding.

A tap on the door broke his train of thought.

"Come," he yelled.

Finch entered the office. He was carrying a folder. "Sir, I thought you should see this. Interpol just faxed it over."

Burnell turned away from the window and held out his hand. He walked over to his desk and put his glasses on the bridge of his nose. He hated wearing the damn things, but lately he needed them more and more for reading. His chair groaned as he sat down. He waved Finch to a seat opposite.

Finch said nothing as his boss read the contents of the file.

"So our victim has a name after all—well, another name. Born Kenneth Armitage in Burford in 1976. Aka Kenneth Waters. Aka Douglas Greville-Jones. Aka Kenneth Douglas. Aka Kenneth Greville-Jones. And now, Ambrose Trent. My, my. Our boy seems to have had a multiple personality disorder. What else do we have here? Ah, quite a pedigree. Embezzlement. Grand larceny. Mostly worked in the South of France and Spain. Specialty: relieving wealthy women of their money. The old story. Why am I not surprised?" Burnell pursed his lips and shook his head. "Not a nice chap, would you say, Finch?"

"No, sir, definitely not a nice chap."

Burnell closed the folder and leaned his elbows on the desk. He took off his glasses and wagged them at the sergeant. "But why was Armitage murdered? In my experience, wealthy women who are foolish enough to give their money to a bloke they barely know are too embarrassed when they see the lay of the land. They're afraid the truth will come out and would rather hush up how easily they'd been manipulated."

"I would have to agree with you on that point, sir."

"Then who did our friend Armitage cross? And what did he find out that he had to be silenced?"

Finch cleared his throat. "Sir?"

Burnell's blue eyes fixed intently on the sergeant's face. "Yes, what is it?"

"Lord Sedgwick—"

"What about Lord Sedgwick?"

"Well, sir," Finch's brown gaze met his boss's with confidence, "it strikes me that he would have a great deal to lose, if someone chose to blackmail him."

Burnell leaned back in his chair and smiled at the sergeant as he steepled his fingers over his growing stomach. He remembered Fenton's slim physique. Perhaps, it was time he went on a diet. Meadows had been badgering him about it for a long time. Tomorrow. He would start the diet tomorrow. He was too busy at the moment with the matter at hand. "Ah, Finch. I knew there was a reason why I liked you. The same thought occurred to me. But what could Sedgwick possibly be hiding? And another thing, how's the real Ambrose Trent mixed up in all this?"

"I don't know what Lord Sedgwick is hiding, but I discovered some information about Ambrose Trent that I thought you might find interesting. It's in the file too."

"Is it? I must have missed it." Burnell shoved his glasses on again and pulled the file toward him.

"It's at the back. After the Interpol information on Armitage."

The chief inspector flipped through the first few pages. "Ah, here it is. I did miss it before. Now, let's see." He scanned the single paragraph. "What?" He read it a second time, shook his head, slammed the folder closed, and snatched off his glasses. "Finch, I knew this was going to be a devil of a case."

"I thought you'd want to know immediately."

"You're bloody right."

The sergeant held his tongue. He'd learned long ago that it was best to do so when a tirade was simmering. Better to let the fuse fizzle out of its own accord.

"I don't like intrigues, Finch. And this—" The chief inspector tapped the file angrily with his forefinger. "—is like the vicious and unexpected sting of a scorpion."

He opened the file again and read out aloud, "No birth certificate on record. *Anywhere.* No photographs on file. *Anywhere.* Nothing on Ambrose Trent before he surfaced in Paris in 1995. And he seems to have gone to ground completely about a year ago."

"That's all that I could find out. I tried to dig deeper, but there simply wasn't anything."

"Why, Finch? Who *is* this Ambrose Trent? There has to be something on him, *somewhere.* I don't like it at all." He tapped the paper again. "It doesn't smell right."

"I'm as baffled as you are, sir. But there is one person who might be able to shed some light on all this."

"Is there? Yes, of course, you're right." A feline smile curled across Burnell's lips. "How could I have forgotten? His good friend Longdon. Get Longdon in here. *Now.* I want to have a little chat with him."

ന്ദ്രന

Not long after he left Emmeline at the Green Park Underground station, Gregory caught a glimpse of the chap on the beige Vespa. He couldn't see his face because the visor of his black helmet was down. Gregory continued walking along Piccadilly for a bit, stopping from time to time to take a look in the shop windows. When he saw the No. 38 bus approaching from the opposite direction, he made sure that the Vespa was several car lengths behind. He waited until the light turned red and then made a dash across the street. Gregory hopped onto the back of the bus, just as it was pulling away from the curb. His stalker was trapped. He had no choice but to continue with the traffic flow on his side of the street. Gregory couldn't resist. He smiled and gave the chap a cheeky little salute.

He got off at the first stop and crossed the street again. He hailed a taxi to Charing Cross Station. There, Gregory got out and paid the fare. He waited until the taxi had disappeared into the line of midday traffic, before turning right up the Strand, where shops, offices, banks, hotels, and theaters all rubbed shoulders in a lively mix of nineteenth- and twentieth-century buildings. He passed the Adelphi Theater. When he reached the Savoy Hotel, Gregory ducked inside and took a turn about the lobby just to make sure he wasn't being followed. It was all clear. He walked back out into the sunshine and headed east toward the Temple area and Fleet Street.

In no time at all, Gregory found himself in front of The George, a lovely little pub in a black-and-white Tudor-style house that faced directly onto the Royal Courts of Justice—the home of the Court of Appeal and the High Court of England and Wales since the late nineteenth century. Gregory slipped into the pub. It was twelve-thirty and already the lunch crowd had started to gather. However, he squeezed past two barristers and triumphantly claimed a small table in the front along the window. He ordered a beer and sat back to soak in the ambience. He hadn't been here in ages, but he had always found the place warm and inviting. It had character. The color scheme probably had a lot to do with it. Everything was awash in red—the walls, the leather banquettes, and the chairs. A number of ornate portraits, light fittings, and stained-glass decorated the walls and wooden partitions. Oak beams ran across the ceiling giving The George an historic air. The pub opened out toward the back, where there was a cozy seating area and a fireplace—a perfect place to escape to on a rainy autumn afternoon or a chilly winter evening.

The dull murmur of conversation thrummed all around him. He took a sip of his beer and decided to order a beef sandwich from the carvery. As he waited for his lunch to arrive, he turned his body slightly so that he could watch the people scurrying along the pavement and into and out of the courts. He rested one elbow on the banquette and took another swig of beer, as he quietly admired the magnificent Victorian Gothic architecture of the imposing gray stone edifice across the street. The courts building, resplendent with various carvings and spires, was designed by George Edmund Street, a solicitor turned architect. It took eight years to construct and was opened by Queen Victoria in 1882.

"Here you go, sir," the pretty waitress with long gold hair

and pale blue eyes said as she placed the plate down in front of
him.

Gregory turned around. "Ta, love. That looks just the
ticket. I'm famished."

"Would you like another beer?"

"No, I'm fine for the moment."

"Then I'll leave you to tuck in. Give a shout if you want
another beer or anything else." She gave him a wink and a
smile that left no doubts in his mind. It was a good thing that
Emmeline was not here. She tended to get a bit jealous, despite
her protests to the contrary.

"I will. Thanks," he replied as he watched the waitress
thread her way back toward the bar. Gregory began to devour
his sandwich. He was hungrier than he had thought.

He was about to order another beer when, out of the corner of his eye, he caught a glimpse of a man entering the pub.
It must have been at least five years since he had last seen him,
but the man hadn't changed. He was a little grayer and his
shoulders stooped forward slightly, but otherwise it was as if
time had stood still. The man was small, not more than five-
foot-five, and rail thin. His once sandy hair had faded to ash.
He looked like a weary professor or accountant. Only he
wasn't.

He took a few steps into the pub and, as was his habit,
nervously pushed his glasses up the bridge of his nose. His
gray eyes flickered over the patrons. He froze suddenly. All
the color drained from his cheeks when his gaze at last came to
rest on Gregory.

The man licked his lips. He cast a glance right and left,
trying to gauge the most expedient way to flee. Gregory had
anticipated such a move and was across the room in two
strides. He clapped the fellow hard on the shoulder. "Nick, old
man. It's been ages. Won't you join me for a drink? We can
reminisce about old times."

"Greg, fancy meeting you after all these years. You're
looking well. I'd love to stay and chat but—" He shot the cuff
of his shirt and glanced at his watch. "I'm already late for an
appointment." He tried to shake off Gregory's arm and make a

dash for the door. A foolish move since Gregory was taller and stronger.

"Nonsense," Gregory said with forced cheerfulness and gripped the man's arm even tighter. "Surely you have time for one drink with an old chum. My table's over there. You can keep me company, while I finish my lunch. I hate to eat alone."

Lingering in Gregory's presence for one second longer was the last thing Nick wanted to do. The little man slid a sideways glance at the door. The desire to run as far and as fast as he could away from the pub was overwhelming. But he was trapped. Gregory was guiding him firmly by the elbow through the crowd toward the table.

Gregory shoved him down hard into the chair and resumed his own seat on the banquette. He signaled to the waitress. "Two beers, love."

"I'll have them for you in a tick."

"Thanks, but nothing for me, Greg," Nick said as he half stood to go.

Gregory reached out casually and pressed a sensitive spot between Nick's shoulder and neck, forcing him to sit down once again. "Sit down. Now, then," he said as he picked up his sandwich, "we have a lot of catching up to do, don't we, Nick?"

A thin line of sweat appeared on Nick's upper lip. "It wasn't me, Greg."

"What wasn't you, Nick?" Gregory's voice was as smooth as silk, but he knew his eyes were as hard as granite and held a challenge. "That sounds like a guilty conscience, if ever I heard one."

"I didn't grass on you to Burnell that night. Honest. It wasn't me. You've got to believe me."

That night two years ago—the night before Gregory was supposed to marry Emmeline—when someone tipped off the police that he may have, *may* being the operative word, entrusted into his own keeping the Hamilton diamond. That tip and something else that he had discovered that night had forced Gregory to run, leaving Emmeline behind—and shattering her dreams. Chief Inspector Burnell had been the one to gleefully inform Emmeline that her fiancé was a notorious jewel thief, though he had never been caught.

To his dying day, Gregory would regret the decision he made that night. With the wisdom of hindsight, he should have stayed and told Emmeline everything. Maybe she wouldn't have lost the baby. On the other hand, maybe she would have left him if she knew the truth. Even now, he wondered whether it wouldn't be better—better for Emmeline, certainly not for him—if he simply disappeared again. But after seeing her again in Venice and going through all that business last month with Charles Latimer's murder and the Russian spy, Gregory knew that he couldn't. He loved her and he could see that she still loved him, despite her stubborn protests to the contrary. He knew he was being selfish, but because of what he saw in her eyes he would rather stay and spend what little time they had together before the truth came crashing down around him. Which it would, eventually—he had no doubt on that score.

Gregory put the sandwich down and brushed crumbs off his fingers. He didn't say anything as the waitress put down the beers. He leaned back against the banquette and smoothed down the corners of his mustache. All this made Nick appear even more jittery, as if he had seen the wheels turning in Gregory's mind and didn't like it one bit.

"I don't see why I should believe you," Gregory said at last. "Your word has never counted for very much in the past. So why should it start now?"

"Greg, on my dear granny's grave, I didn't grass on you."

Gregory only stared at him in response. He took a sip of beer and rolled it around his tongue before letting it slide down his throat. "We'll let that pass, *for the moment.* There's something else I wanted to ask you about."

"Is there?" Nick tried to sound casual, but his hand shook as he picked up his beer and took a deep gulp. Some sloshed onto the table when he put the pint back down. "I don't know anything about anything. So it would be no good asking me any questions. Especially if it has to do with Ambrose. I haven't seen him."

He knew that he had made a mistake the minute the words came out of his mouth.

Gregory's eyebrow arched upward. "Ambrose? I didn't say anything about Ambrose, but it's funny that you should mention him."

"Didn't you mention him? I could have sworn you did just now."

Gregory shook his head gravely and leaned forward. He clamped his hand down hard, pinning Nick's to the table. His voice was barely above a whisper. "Now, *my friend*, you're going to tell me what you know about Ambrose or I'll make sure that a certain Scotland Yard chief inspector whom we both know and love receives an anonymous tip about the little sideline you run out of the back of your quiet bookshop. Burnell will be fascinated no end to learn that amid the leafy streets of Chelsea you do a brisk business as a purveyor of stolen goods."

"Oh, Greg, I'm just a hard-working entrepreneur. You wouldn't do that to me."

"Wouldn't I? Give me one good reason why I shouldn't."

"Well, out of professional courtesy for a start."

Gregory had to laugh at this. "Professional courtesy?"

Nick was backed into a corner and he was still trying to con his way out. "Naturally, professional courtesy. Haven't you heard about honor among thieves?"

"I draw the line at murder."

Nick swallowed hard. Gregory could feel the dampness of the man's hand beneath his own. "The papers said Ambrose was killed in Hyde Park last night, so what do you possibly want to know about him? Let the poor bloke rest in peace."

"Because," Gregory hissed through clenched teeth, "you and I both know the man was *not* Ambrose Trent."

"But the papers said—"

"Forget the bloody papers. You can't believe everything you read in the papers. They often get the wrong end of the stick. Now, where's Ambrose?"

"Why are you asking me? How should I know where he is? He's *your* friend."

Gregory released Nick's hand and sat back, disgusted. Nick flexed his fingers quickly several times to get the circulation going again. "He's not who I thought he was."

"Which of us is, old darling? We're all playing a part. You never really know anybody in this world," Nick replied derisively.

I know Emmeline. There was never a more honest person in this world. She opened her heart and let me in.

Gregory wanted to wipe the smirk off Nick's face. The man was a weasel and made him sick. He reached out unexpectedly and grabbed Nick by the lapel, lifting him halfway out of his seat and onto the table. Some of the other patrons turned and looked in their direction, but Gregory ignored them. "If you're lying to me about Ambrose, you will live to regret it. Do you understand?"

Nick nodded his head mutely.

"Good man." Gregory abruptly let him go. "Go on. Get out of my sight before I change my mind about calling Burnell."

Nick scrambled to his feet so quickly he knocked over his chair. He backed away from the table, making sure that Gregory wasn't coming after him. A couple of "Here, watch it," were heard before he finally fumbled his way out the door.

Gregory pushed away his plate with the half-eaten sandwich. He had lost his appetite. He slammed his fist down on the table, spilling beer everywhere.

"Never mind. I'll get that, sir." The pretty blonde waitress was back. In a second, she had mopped up the beer with a cloth. "Will there be anything else?"

She gave him a wink, but he was no longer in the mood to flirt. "No, thanks. Just tell me what I owe."

She told him and he dug the money out of his pocket. Then she sliced her way back to the bar, disappointed.

As Gregory stood to go, he caught a glimpse of Nick having a very animated conversation in the call box across the road. A smile crossed his lips. "Well, well. I wonder who you could be ringing, Nick old man. Who, indeed?"

そうそう

"Listen, Ambrose. I just ran into Greg in The George and I don't think it was a coincidence. He knows you're still alive and he's coming after you. He won't stop until he finds you, mark my words. And if Greg knows, it's only a matter of time before the others find out. Don't forget his girlfriend is that *Times* reporter. I didn't like it when you first came to me and I like it even less now. This is getting too dangerous for me. I'm out. I don't want to be found in some alley with my brains blown to bits."

Nick severed the connection. He pushed the door open and walked out of the call box.

He saw Gregory coming out of the pub and began running.

Afterward, some witnesses would say that the man stepped off the curb just as the light changed and there was no way the white van could have seen him in time. Others would say that the van was driving erratically and the poor fellow never stood a chance. In the end, Nick lay dead in the middle of Fleet Street. And the only one who was certain that it was murder and not an accident was Gregory.

CHAPTER 9

Emmeline got out of the Tower Hill Underground station and walked the few blocks to No. 1 Virginia Street, the brick-and-glass building which was home to *The Times'* offices. She took the lift up to the newsroom and, at once, was seized by the electric energy reverberating all around her. People were shouting. Some of her fellow colleagues were on the phone conducting interviews. Still others were hurrying out the door on a story.

She remembered the first time her parents had taken her to see "where Mummy and Daddy work." Emmeline was all of four, but she felt very grown up. To this day, she still felt the same awe and giddy thrill of excitement coursing through her veins. How she longed for her parents to be here—to see she had followed in their footsteps. She hoped they would be proud of her. A tear pricked her eyelid. But they had been gone a long time. Twenty-five years. They died covering a story in Lebanon. They were a team. Her father was the well-respected investigative reporter Aaron Kirby and her mother was the prize-winning photojournalist Jacqueline Davis Kirby.

Emmeline was five when it happened. Her whole world shattered the day that Gran broke the news. But Gran, her mother's mother, became her rock. She scooped Emmeline up and took her down to live with her in the lovely, rambling Tudor house in Swaley in Kent. Gran saw to everything. At first, Emmeline couldn't bear the thought of leaving the Holland

Park townhouse she had shared with her parents. However, Gran saw to that, too. She found someone to take care of the house until Emmeline was old enough to live in it on her own, which she did now.

"Emmeline, are you here to do some work or are you merely taking in the sights?" James's voice pulled her out of the past. "Five minutes, in my office. I want to know what you've discovered about the Trent murder."

"Right. I'm coming."

She dropped her handbag on her desk and dug out her notebook and pen. She waved to a couple of the lads as she hurried across the floor. James never put the blinds down in his office and she could see he was already seated at his desk, banging away at his computer keyboard. He wasn't a dashing and handsome man like Gregory, but then not many men were—*was she being completely objective on this point? Could she be?* She pushed this disturbing thought from her mind and focused once more on her editor—it was safer that way. James's features were melded together in such a way that he exuded earnestness, honesty, humor, and a zest for life, all of which were highly appealing to the opposite sex. They also made people feel comfortable in his presence, so much so that they told him things that they had never intended. This rare quality had helped James coax some of his best stories onto the page.

Now, at forty-eight, he used his instincts and innate talents to help guide his reporters to the key that unlocked a compelling story.

Emmeline walked into the office and closed the door behind her. She took the seat opposite James and, without preamble, said, "This is going to be a more intriguing story than we first thought."

"Oh? I'm listening. Impress me." He took off his glasses and leaned his elbows on the desk. His long, oval face was immediately alert and his hazel eyes glinted with a hungry eagerness.

"The man who was murdered in Hyde Park last night, the man who was Claire's fiancé—"

"Yes?" James prompted.

"—is not Ambrose Trent."

"Isn't he? Who is he then?"

"Chief Inspector Burnell doesn't know yet."

"Then how do the police know that the dead man is not Ambrose Trent?"

"Scotland Yard didn't know, actually. Neither did Claire for that matter. Gregory was one who told all of us."

"Gregory? As in Gregory Longdon, your former fiancé and a known jewel thief?"

"Alleged jewel thief. The police have never been able to prove anything against him." These were the same words Gregory had used when they argued about this same subject only yesterday. Why was she defending him?

James tilted his head and gave her a pointed look. "Never mind all that for the moment. Why was Longdon there?"

"Well..." Emmeline looked down the desk and hedged. "...he sort of came with me this morning."

"Uh, huh. I see. Why, may one ask?"

Emmeline hurried on. "He dropped by this morning just before I left the house and I told him I was going to see Claire."

"Why would he want to tag along?"

"I was getting to that point, if you'd stop interrupting me and listen. It came out in a conversation we had yesterday at tea. It seems that Gregory is an old friend of Ambrose Trent's."

James leaned back in his chair and rested his hands behind his head. "Curiouser and curiouser."

"I knew that would pique your interest."

"Interest? Yes, it piques my interest. So where's the real Ambrose Trent and why did someone want him dead?"

"Nobody seems to know."

"What about your chum Longdon? Doesn't he have any ideas?"

"He's not my 'chum.' We are not together anymore," Emmeline said impatiently.

"It doesn't look that way from where I'm sitting."

"Then you should probably get a stronger prescription for your glasses."

James chuckled softly.

Emmeline squirmed in her seat.

"My eyes are perfectly fine. I think it's you who need to get checked."

"Well, you're wrong." She crossed her arms over her chest defensively and glared at him.

"That remains to be seen. In any event, Longdon is suddenly omnipresent. First, he appeared out of the blue last month when you were in the middle of the Charles Latimer murder story. Now, here he is again. *And* we have another murder. Only this time the plot thickens. Longdon is a friend of the dead man, who turns out not to be dead after all. But we still have a body on our hands. You know what I think?"

"No, but I'm sure you'll enlighten me with your pearls of wisdom."

"I will ignore that remark, young lady. I think it smells fishy. I don't like it one bit. I especially don't like the fact that Longdon is mixed up in this affair."

"You can't possibly think Gregory has anything to do with the murder."

"How should I know? From my vantage point, he makes a bloody good suspect."

Emmeline stood up. "You're mad. Utterly mad. As journalists, we are taught to be objective. You've tried and convicted Gregory simply because he's a jewel—" Her mouth snapped shut.

"You weren't going to say *thief* by any chance, were you?"

"No, I was not. Listen, James. Here are the facts that we have thus far." She enumerated them on her fingers. "One, Claire Sedgwick got engaged to a man called Ambrose Trent after a whirlwind romance on a Mediterranean cruise. Two, this man is murdered and it turns out that he is not Ambrose Trent after all. You agree with me on these points?"

James nodded.

"Now, why was this man killed? Was it because someone

falsely believed he was Ambrose Trent? Or was he the intended victim and he had to be silenced because of something he
knew?"

"What's your angle going to be?"

"So you're allowing me to go ahead with the story, despite your prejudices against Gregory?"

"I never said I was going to take you off the story. I just
hope you'll be objective about Longdon."

"I'm always objective."

"Emmeline, I don't want to argue with you on this subject. What's the angle you're going to take?"

"I thought, 'Who is Ambrose Trent?' My instincts tell me
that if we discover who this mystery man is, all the other pieces will fall into place. Where is he? Why was another man posing as him? And, ultimately, who was the real target? As soon
as we're done here, I'm going to get on to Chief Inspector
Burnell to see if the police have been able to identify the victim."

"Go with it, but—"

"But?"

"I needn't have to remind you to tread carefully. This is
an extremely sensitive story because of the victim's connection
to Lord Douglas Sedgwick. One word his lordship doesn't like
and he could crush you. Don't forget that he is a close friend of
the publisher. If push comes to shove, he'll wind up on top."

"I'm not worried about Lord Sedgwick."

"Don't be naive, Emmeline. You're smarter than that.
Men like him revel in their own self-importance for power's
sake. If he doesn't like the story you're writing, the fact that
you're his daughter's friend won't matter one jot."

"I sincerely hope you're not suggesting that if I find out
something that might be disagreeable to Lord Sedgwick, I
shouldn't write about it. Because there is something called
freedom of the press, in case you hadn't heard about it. There
is also the matter of finding out the truth. And justice for a
dead man, of course."

"Justice is one thing and then there's the type of reckless
antics you pulled when you went to the Russian embassy on

your last story and nearly caused an international incident."
Emmeline blushed and had the good grace to look chastened. "I'm sorry. You're right about that. I wasn't thinking rationally. I was desperate to clear Gregory's name and to find out—"
"The truth? Emmeline, we're talking about a murder. The truth will be cold comfort if you're dead."

જાજી

Two constables had been summoned from the Royal Courts of Justice across the road to keep the growing crowd of curious onlookers at bay. Another constable was diverting traffic from the Strand onto Fleet Street. Someone had taken pity on Nick's lifeless body and covered it with a coat. Gregory huddled near the doorway of The George pub. When he saw Chief Inspector Burnell and Sergeant Finch pull up in the unmarked police car, he elbowed his way toward the street. "Oliver, over here."
"I'm sorry, sir. I'm going to have to ask you to keep back. This is a crime scene."
Gregory smiled ingratiatingly. "Oh, it's all right. You needn't worry, Constable—"
"Higgins, sir."
"Constable Higgins. I realize you're simply doing your job, but I rang Chief Inspector Burnell about this sad business. He and I go back a long way. I'm certain he wants to speak to me. Don't you, Oliver?"
Burnell appeared at the constable's side. "It's all right, Higgins. Get back to your post."
"Yes, sir." Higgins turned back to Gregory. "I didn't realize, sir. I'm sorry I detained you." He inclined his head slightly.
"Don't mention it. You couldn't have known."
"Go on, Higgins," Burnell said through clenched teeth.
They watched the constable go. "You know, Oliver, that young man has the makings of a great police officer. Perhaps, with a little guidance, he'll even rise to the rank of chief inspector one day. What do you think?"

"First of all, it is Chief Inspector Burnell."

"Oh, Oliver." Gregory flicked an imaginary piece of lint from the chief inspector's lapel. "I quite understand. We must maintain the formalities in front of the troops. You can count on me." He touched the side of his nose with his forefinger and smiled knowingly.

Burnell threw his hands up in exasperation. "I don't have the energy for your games today, Longdon. What happened here? When you rang, you said it had something to do with the Trent murder."

Sergeant Finch joined them before Gregory could answer the question. "Sir, the forensics team has just arrived." He nodded grudgingly at Gregory. "Longdon."

"Nice to see you again too, Sergeant Finch. You're looking well."

Finch ignored this remark and opened his notebook. He directed his comments to Burnell. "Sir, I spoke to some of the witnesses. It appears that the victim suddenly ran into oncoming traffic. There was no possible way the driver of a white van could have seen him in time."

"Then why didn't the driver stop and wait for the police to arrive, if he had nothing to hide?"

"You know how it is, sir." Finch shrugged his shoulders. "Perhaps he was afraid of getting arrested."

"Mmm." The chief inspector stroked his beard meditatively. "I don't like it. Has the victim been identified?"

"If I may interject, I might be able to elucidate on one or two points," Gregory said with exaggerated politeness.

Both policemen turned their attention toward him. "I was getting around to *your* involvement in all this," Burnell said. "Another body and by coincidence you happen to be on the scene. *Again.*"

Gregory clucked his tongue and wagged a finger at Burnell. "Now, now, Oliver. I'm disappointed to detect an undercurrent of suspicion in your tone. If this continues, it will drive a wedge in our friendship. And that would hurt me deeply."

"Longdon," the chief inspector growled, "stop wasting time and tell us what you know."

"Well, if you want to be that way." The smile vanished from Gregory's lips. "The man's name was Nick Martin. He owned an innocuous rare bookshop in Chelsea. But that was simply a cover for his real occupation. He was...how I shall I put this politely?...what is known in the business as a trader in ill-gotten goods."

"You mean he was a fence."

"If you must be so blunt, yes. And this was no accident. I saw the whole thing. Nick caught a glimpse of me from across the road and started running. The van came directly for him and then sped away before anyone realized what had happened."

"Are you saying this nondescript little fence—" Burnell waved a hand in the direction of the body. "—was murdered in broad daylight in front of dozens of witnesses and no one was the wiser?"

"Yes, Oliver. That's exactly what I'm saying."

The chief inspector fixed his blue stare on Gregory as he digested this information. "Why? Why would anyone want to kill him, Longdon? He doesn't strike me as a chap who would have enemies."

"Obviously, he had at least one since he's dead before his time."

"How do we know he didn't have a congenital heart condition and the exertion of running away from you caused a heart attack?"

Gregory cocked his head to one side. "Oliver, you don't believe that. Now, why are you being argumentative?"

A low grunt emanated from Burnell. "Because—as much as I hate to admit it—I think you're right."

A triumphant smile broke out across Gregory's face. "There that wasn't so hard, was it, Oliver? You should practice being humble. It rather suits you."

"Sir," Sergeant Finch exclaimed.

"Oh, come on, Finch. Don't tell me that you believe this accident business."

"No, but—"

"Then let's stop playing games." Burnell turned back to

Gregory. "Longdon, what else can you tell me about this Nick Martin? Why would someone want him dead?"

"I was with him in the pub for about a quarter of an hour before all this happened." He jerked his head toward The George. "It was one of Nick's favorite haunts."

"Why did you go looking for him?"

"Because I thought he could tell me where Ambrose Trent is."

"What was Martin's connection to your long lost friend—which reminds me. I have a few questions that I'd like to ask you about him?"

Gregory gave Burnell a pointed look. "Let's just say that Nick and Ambrose used to do business together and it wasn't of a literary nature, if you take my meaning."

"Ah. That explains a good deal. It seems that your friend wasn't the squeaky clean businessman you claimed. Did you know he didn't exist until 1995?"

One of Gregory's eyebrows quirked upward. "What are you talking about?"

"Just that. He seems to have been conceived out of thin air. Finch checked. There is no birth certificate in the United Kingdom—or anywhere in Europe, for that matter—in the name of Ambrose Trent. No one had ever heard of him until one fine June day in Paris in 1995, when he purchased an apartment on the Ile de la Cité. And he seems to have dropped out of sight completely about a year ago."

Gregory frowned. "I don't understand."

"Neither do we, but I'm damn well going to find out. Now, what about the chap who was going around calling himself Ambrose Trent? What do you know about him?"

"I can't help you there, Oliver."

"Stop calling me by my Christian name. It's *Chief Inspector Burnell.*"

Gregory sighed wearily and, as if indulging a wayward child, said, "Anyway, *Chief Inspector Burnell,* I'd never seen the bloke until Claire Sedgwick showed us her fiancé's photo this morning."

"Are you quite positive about that, Longdon? You wouldn't lie to me, would you?"

Gregory put his hand over his heart in a theatrical gesture. "Ol—Chief Inspector Burnell, I'm shocked that you think I would even contemplate lying to Scotland Yard."

"Hmm. I wonder."

"Then let me put your mind at rest. I am not lying to you. I have absolutely no idea who the fellow is—was."

Burnell looked at him skeptically for a moment and then shrugged his shoulders. "Well, we do. He has a long string of aliases, but his name is Kenneth Armitage. It seems he worked the Continent, mostly the French Riviera. His specialty was charming women—wealthy women—into giving him their money and then he would suddenly disappear."

Gregory wrinkled his nose in disgust. "Ah, one of those types."

"Longdon, I don't see what you have to feel superior about. You're a bloody jewel thief, for God's sake."

"Oh, Oliver, there you go again. If I didn't know you were under a constant strain at work and couldn't possibly re-alize what you were saying, I'd have you up on slander charg-es."

"Ha. I'd like to see you try."

"I wouldn't tempt Providence, if I were you. You never know what Fate has in store for you."

"All right. That's enough blather from you. I have an in-vestigation to conduct. Make sure you're in my office this af-ternoon to make a statement."

"Aye, aye, sir," Gregory said as he clicked his heels to-gether and gave Burnell a crisp salute.

"Go on. Get out of my sight."

Gregory started to walk away, but Burnell caught his arm. "Longdon, if you discover anything, needless to say that it is your duty to tell the police."

Gregory clapped him on the shoulder. "You'll be the first to know, Oliver. I promise." He gave the chief inspector a wink and then melted into the crowd.

CHAPTER 10

The shouting and the murmur of voices in the newsroom became a dull droning buzz in the background. Emmeline's eyes felt dry and they stung from staring at her computer screen for so long. She had been at it for two hours and still couldn't come up with anything on Ambrose Trent. She had started by checking the National Archives database of all birth, death, and marriage records in the UK between 1975 and 1980. The impostor couldn't have been more than thirty-five, so Emmeline guessed the real Ambrose Trent had to be in the same age range. Nothing. Then it occurred to her that he might be the son of British military personnel who had been stationed abroad. Emmeline made calls to the Royal Navy and the RAF and any other military branches she could think of, but Ambrose Trent remained an enigma. It was very odd. She could find nothing about the man. Not a photo. *Nothing.*

She leaned back in her chair and pressed the heels of her hands to her tired eyes. There had to be something somewhere. "Think, Emmeline, think. What am I missing?" she asked herself in frustration.

It's as if the man does not exist. But that's not possible. Emmeline did not believe in ghosts. Besides, Gregory knew him. Ambrose Trent lived, breathed, and walked the streets of this world. So where was he now and why couldn't she find out anything about him? His past seemed to have been meticulously expunged. Someone had gone to great lengths to ensure that he could not be traced. Why? *Why is this man so important?*

Emmeline sat up suddenly. A kernel of an idea had popped into her head. Perhaps she was going about this wrong way. She was not asking the right questions. That was why she was having so much trouble. *What if Ambrose Trent* never *existed? What if Ambrose Trent wasn't his real name?* The adrenaline started coursing through her veins. She knew she was right. She could feel it. Who would have the power and the means to *establish* a false identity? *The government.* Who would *need* a false identity*? A witness to a crime or a spy.* So which are you, Mr. Ambrose Trent?

Emmeline reached for the phone and punched in a number she had come to know by heart over the last month.

ᴇ/ɔᴇ/ɔ

It was two-thirty when the phone on Philip Acheson's desk at the Foreign Office rang. His secretary still wasn't back from the dentist, so he had to screen his own calls. He felt a sharp twinge in his left arm as he reached for the receiver. Although the wound was healing, he still had stiffness and pain. The doctor told him it would go away in time, but he would have a scar. Philip wasn't worried about a scar. It could have been worse. Much worse. He was philosophical about that awful, tension-filled night about a month ago, when Emmeline had nearly been killed by two Russian spies in St. James's Park. Sergeant Finch had been shot as well, but thank goodness it wasn't as serious as the doctors thought at first.

They were all there that night, Emmeline, Longdon, Chief Inspector Burnell, and Sergeant Finch. Once it was all over, Philip had made sure that they each signed the Official Secrets Act.

Now, the details about what happened and the true nature of Philip's job were locked securely somewhere within the walls of Thames House, MI5's headquarters, located a few hundred yards south of the Houses of Parliament overlooking Lambeth Bridge on the north bank of the Thames.

Ostensibly, Philip worked for the Foreign Office's Directorate of Defense and Intelligence. His area of expertise was Russia. However, his true master was MI5, Britain's counter-intelligence service. Only a handful of people knew this. Maggie, his wife and Emmeline's closest friend, was completely ignorant of this fact and he was determined to keep it that way. There was no reason to worry Maggie needlessly. Besides, they had the twins to think about. And when all was said and done, it was just his job. A job that he was damn good at and in which he took great pride. But he knew his Maggie. She wouldn't see it that way. She had been terrified when he had been shot. It was only a superficial wound. He told her someone had tried to mug him on his way home. She had fussed over him for days. Now, sometimes, when he happened to glance up, he caught her watching him and the look of sheer terror reflected in those beautiful green eyes sent a shiver down his spine. He could only imagine how that fear would be magnified, if she knew the truth. So, for the sake of everyone's peace of mind, Maggie would forever remain in the dark about his work for MI5.

Philip picked up the receiver on the second ring. "Acheson."

"Philip, it's Emmeline."

"Emmeline, to what do I owe this pleasure?" he asked, smiling with delight. "Everything is all right, I hope."

"Everything's fine. I should be asking you that question. Maggie told you that we had our monthly tea yesterday?"

"Yes, she did."

"She told me you're healing very well after..." Her voice trailed off. "After the incident in the park."

"I'll be as good as new soon. Not to worry."

"That's wonderful news." He heard the genuine relief in her voice. Then she cleared her throat. "I felt beastly lying to Maggie. She's my best friend."

"Emmeline, we've discussed this. You know this is the only way. For Maggie's sake, she cannot know."

"Yes, yes. I know and I agree. But I still feel beastly. We've never kept things from one another before."

They both lapsed into silence for a moment. Philip was

the first to speak. "I'm sure this was not the reason you rang me."

"No, it's not. I need some help with a story I'm working on."

"Emmeline, I cannot go on the record. You must understand that."

"I'm not asking you to. Maggie's probably told you about Claire's fiancé."

"Yes, she did. Sad business. But I don't see how I can help. It's clearly a police matter. Who's in charge of the case?"

"Chief Inspector Burnell."

"Well then, you have nothing worry about. He'll get his man or woman in the end."

"Philip, I've been doing some digging and there's something very odd about all this."

"Odd how?"

"The man who was murdered, Claire's fiancé, was not the real Ambrose Trent. He was only posing as Ambrose Trent."

Philip sat up straighter in his chair. "How do you know that?"

Emmeline sighed. "Gregory and the real Ambrose Trent have been chums for years apparently."

"Longdon? Is he still in the picture?"

"There is no picture," she said, irritation creeping into her voice. "He just happened to come with me this morning when I went to see Claire. She showed us a photo of her fiancé. That's when Gregory informed us that the man was not Ambrose Trent."

"Although it's not a common name, did it ever cross your mind that there could be two Ambrose Trents walking this earth?"

"I suppose so, but after last night there's only one."

"I still don't see how I can help. Strange though this matter is, it is not the sort of thing that falls within my jurisdiction."

"There's more."

"Go on," Philip said wearily. "I'm listening."

"I've spent the past couple of hours trying to find out anything I can about the mysterious Ambrose Trent. I think he was the real target and Claire's fiancé was killed by mistake. Though why he was posing as another man, I haven't been able to find out—*yet*. But, I'm digressing. Here's the intriguing part. There's absolutely no record—no birth certificate, no photo—anywhere in the United Kingdom or in Europe on Ambrose Trent, alive or otherwise. Nothing, Philip. *It's as if he never existed.* Don't you find that odd?"

"Where are you heading with this?" Philip didn't like what he was hearing. An icy tendril curled around his chest. Trouble was brewing. There was no doubt about it.

"I'm not sure. That's what I am trying to find out."

"What conclusions have you drawn from all this detective work?"

"It's called investigative journalism, but that's neither here nor there. I think Ambrose Trent is either one of you—" She lowered her voice. "—a spy, I mean, or..."

"Or what?"

"Or someone in a witness protection program. I can't decide which until I find out more about him. That's where you come in, Philip."

"Do I? I don't recall ever having promised to help you. I only said that I would listen."

"But you will help me, won't you? You know I'm right. I can hear it in your voice," Emmeline cajoled, ever so sweetly. "Don't worry. I plan to badger Chief Inspector Burnell as well. That way you won't feel you're being singled out."

"I can't tell you how much better that makes me feel."

"How about if I pop over in, say, an hour? Would that be all right? We can discuss this further then. What do you say?"

"I say...I say that I must be out of my mind." He sighed. "Come by in an hour. I'll be here waiting."

"I knew you would see it my way."

"Emmeline, we poor, defenseless creatures are powerless against you. Once you get an idea into your head, you're like a dog with a bone."

"I just want to find out the truth."

"Take it from me, sometimes it's better to let sleeping

dogs lie. Otherwise, they might rear their heads suddenly and bite you."

☙❧

Emmeline headed out of No. 1 Virginia Street and turned west toward the Tower Hill Underground Station. She would catch the District Line to the Westminster station and then walk the couple of blocks to the Foreign Office on King Charles Street.

The platform was crowded with a group of German tourists. They were all talking loudly. They must have come from visiting the Tower of London. Emmeline glanced up at the electronic display board, which told her the next train would be arriving in five minutes. Thank goodness for that. She walked a short way down the platform, trying to distance herself from the Germans.

It was not long before she felt a warm breath stir the air. She took a step closer to the edge of the platform. People were starting to crowd around her. At precisely the moment when the lights of the train—like two glowing eyes—emerged from the mouth of the tunnel, Emmeline felt a hand between her shoulder blades. Before she realized what was happening, she felt herself falling forward. Her hands flailed, desperately clawing at the empty air. She heard someone scream. Was it one of the tourists or her own voice? She couldn't be sure. All she knew was that she was about to die.

CHAPTER 11

A strong arm yanked her back onto the platform, just as the train whooshed into the station. Emmeline was taking deep, grateful gulps of air as the doors slid open and people started getting off. They gave her odd looks and then shoved past. They had no idea how close she had been to dancing a *hora* in the other world. She was trembling from head to toe. Her legs felt like water.

"Calm down, Emmeline. You're all right now," the voice of her rescuer whispered in her ear. She wanted to thank him. *But how did he know my name?*

She tried to twist her head around to get a look at his face, but it was as if her head was wedged in a vice. He held her close to his chest. "No, Emmeline, don't turn around. It's better this way. Count your blessings that you escaped serious harm. You might not be so lucky next time, if you continue to pursue your search for Ambrose Trent. Take some sage advice and drop it. You *and* Longdon. No good will come of it. I assure you. None whatsoever."

Gregory? He knew Gregory, too. "Who are you?" she asked hoarsely, but her question was lost as the next train pulled in.

The iron hand suddenly slipped away. People were jostling her aside again. But which one was her rescuer with the warning? *Or was it a threat?*

లుృల

When Burnell and Sergeant Finch returned to Scotland Yard, they were surprised to find Emmeline waiting for them in the chief inspector's office. "Miss Kirby? Are you quite all right?"

Her normally olive complexion had faded to a chalky pallor and her dark eyes glistened with an unnatural brightness. "I'm sorry, Chief Inspector Burnell. I always seem to be bringing trouble to your doorstep." Burnell noticed the teacup rattled as she tried to place it back on the saucer. She smiled back weakly. "I hope you don't mind. That very nice Miss Harper said that I could wait for you in your office. She also gave me a cup of tea."

Sally nice? The chief inspector supposed it *was* possible. But then again, even a cold-hearted, sour puss like Sally stood no chance when confronted by the force of Miss Kirby's guileless charm.

Burnell came over and sat on the corner of his desk. He signaled with his head that Finch should take the seat next to Emmeline. "What can we do for you?" he asked softly. "It's obvious something's amiss. Now, how can we help?"

Before she answered his question, she turned to Finch. "You must think me terribly callous, Sergeant Finch. But there wasn't really an opportune moment to ask this morning at Claire's flat. How are you recovering from your wound? From what I can see, you seem to be all right." Finch had been shot in the shoulder the same fateful night as Philip.

The sergeant's face broke out into a broad smile that touched his brown eyes. He was clearly moved by her thoughtfulness. "I still have a bit of stiffness and I don't have full range of motion back yet, but overall the doctor says that I'm doing fine, Miss Kirby. Thank you for your concern."

Emmeline smiled in response. Her color was starting to come back. She turned her attention back to Burnell. "I'm sorry, Chief Inspector."

"Nonsense, we're all glad to see that the lad is on the mend."

Emmeline looked from one to the other and then, in a single breath, said, "When I couldn't reach Gregory on his mobile, I came here straightaway. Someone just tried to kill me at the Tower Hill tube station." Her voice trembled on this last word.

"What?" the two men said in unison.

"I didn't know what else to do. I was so frightened." She had to grip the arms of the chair to prevent her hands from shaking.

Burnell put a hand on her shoulder. "It's all right, Miss Kirby. You did the right thing. You're safe here. No one will hurt you. Just start at the beginning. Take your time. There's no rush. Would you like another cup of tea?"

Emmeline shook her head. The words began spilling from her lips. She told them what she had discovered about Ambrose Trent and her speculation about who he may really be. She gave an objective account about what happened at the station. The only time her voice cracked was when she recalled being shoved from behind and the sight of the train bearing down upon her.

"And that's how I came to be here in your office," she concluded.

Burnell smiled down at her. "You did the right thing, Miss Kirby." He walked around the desk and reached for his phone. "I'll have a car watch your house for a few days. Sergeant Finch will see you home. Don't worry. We'll soon have this mess sorted out."

They were silent until he had finished his brief call. "But, Chief Inspector, what about Ambrose Trent?"

"In light of what just happened, don't you think it would be wiser to step back from this story?"

"That's precisely why I must plunge ahead. Clearly, I'm on to something if they—whoever they are—risked coming after me in broad daylight like that. So what do you think about my theory?"

Burnell folded one arm across his chest and stroked his beard with the other. "This is off the record."

Emmeline nodded solemnly. "Of course."

"A spy or someone in a witness protection program. I'd say that it isn't farfetched at all."

She smiled in triumph. "Philip was not enamored of the idea when I broached it, but he couldn't deny that it was plausible."

"Acheson? You went to Mr. Acheson?"

"Well, I rang him and was on my way to see him. Good Lord." She stood up abruptly.

"What is it, Miss Kirby?"

"Philip. I completely forgot about Philip." She glanced at her watch. "I must ring him."

"By all means, use my phone," Burnell offered.

"Thank you." She quickly apologized to Philip, simply saying she had been unavoidably detained and she would explain everything once she got to his office. "Right. We'll be there in half an hour." She returned the receiver to the cradle. "Philip would like all of us to pop over to his office. I just wish I knew where Gregory was."

Burnell and Finch exchanged glances.

"What? Has something happened to Gregory?" Her nerves betrayed her and her voice rose an octave.

"No, Miss Kirby. Longdon is perfectly all right. The man's like a cat. He has nine lives. Nothing can destroy him."

The tension in her body eased and she resumed her seat. There had been too much excitement for one afternoon. "But something else *has* occurred? And it's connected with Ambrose Trent, isn't it?"

"Why don't we wait to see if Mr. Acheson can provide any insight into the matter?" the chief inspector said as he waved his hand toward the door. "Shall we?"

ფოფ

Gregory made a right off George Street onto Bryanston Mews East in the heart Marylebone. As luck would have it, he slipped his Jaguar into a spot on the corner and turned off the ignition. His eyes flicked to the rearview mirror. No one had followed him. He quickly scanned the street ahead of him. It was deserted, as it should be on a weekday afternoon. He got out and locked the car, glancing up and down once more. The street was wide open and provided no convenient cover for anyone to conceal himself. However, Gregory had taken the precaution of parking a couple of doors down from the lovely mews cottage that belonged to the man he knew as Ambrose Trent.

His footfalls echoed hollowly as he walked the few short steps to Ambrose's door, to the right of which stood a tiny flowerbed. Gregory peered through the three square windows at the top of the door, but could see nothing out of the ordinary in the corridor. He took a small file out of his inside breast pocket and, in a matter of seconds, a soft click was heard. He smiled as the knob easily gave way to his touch. Mere child's play. Ambrose should really have that seen to, he thought. After all, anyone could get in here. He had only taken half a step into the corridor, when he realized that someone had indeed been there. Could still be lurking about.

The door to the spacious living room was slightly ajar. Gregory pushed it completely open with the toe of his shoe. Everything in the room had been overturned. The sofa cushions had been slashed with a knife. A lamp had been knocked off the end table and lay in two halves on the Persian carpet. The drawers of a small desk in the corner of the room had been wrenched open and were dumped upside down on the floor. Papers were strewn all over.

"My, my, how very untidy," Gregory murmured to himself as he righted a painting that hung askew on the butter yellow wall.

He sensed, rather than heard the movement behind him. But it was too late. There was a sharp crack. Searing pain exploding in the back of his skull. Then blackness enveloped everything.

എന്റെ

Emmeline, Chief Inspector Burnell, and Sergeant Finch passed between the Corinthian columns of the Foreign Office's main entrance. They gave their names to the guards and showed their identification. One guard checked a list and said they could go straight up. "Mr. Acheson is expecting you." He gave them badges and waved them on their way.

Their footsteps echoed loudly as they crossed the elegant hall with its high vaulted ceiling, gilded walls, and red-veined marble columns. They walked slowly up the grand staircase. At the top of the landing, they turned left. They passed two men, deep in conversation, as the trio followed the gallery until they reached the office at the far end. Burnell rapped once on the heavy oak door and then turned the knob without waiting for a response.

Pamela Marsh, Philip's secretary, was on the phone, when they entered the outer office. She smiled when she saw Emmeline and nodded at the two police officers. She waved a hand toward the leather sofa against the opposite wall and covered the mouthpiece. "Do sit down. This won't take a minute," she whispered and turned her attention back to the call. When she hung up, she made a note in Philip's diary and then turned to her visitors. "I'm sorry about that. Mr. Acheson has been trying to get a hold of the ambassador for a week."

"Quite all right, Miss Marsh," Burnell said. "We rang Mr. Acheson earlier. He's expecting us."

"Oh, yes, I know. He had me clear his calendar for the remainder of the afternoon. I'll just let him know that you're here." She picked up the receiver again and spoke for several seconds. "Please go in."

Sergeant Finch held the door open for Emmeline and Burnell and then quietly closed it as he fell in behind them. Philip came around the elegant mahogany desk, which dominated the center of the office. He took both Emmeline's hands in his larger ones. "Emmeline, a pleasure, as always, to see you." He gave her a peck on the cheek. Then, he extended a hand to the two detectives. "Burnell. Finch. Now, why don't we all sit down."

Philip shepherded them to the corner, where a Chesterfield sofa and two wing chairs in the same claret leather were clustered around a highly polished oval cherry wood coffee table. This little area sat next to a large window that overlooked King Charles Street. On the opposite side of the room near the desk were two mahogany bookcases with glass doors, through which one espied leather-bound tomes.

Philip took one of the chairs as the others settled themselves on the sofa. In the next instant, the door opened and Pamela came in with a tray laden with a teapot, cups, saucers, and a plate of biscuits. She placed it in the center of the coffee table and wordlessly began pouring steaming Darjeeling tea into the delicate Royal Doulton cups decorated with the tiny pink rosebuds. After she handed the cups around, she asked, "Will that be all for the moment, Mr. Acheson?"

"Yes, that's fine, Pamela. Thanks. Hold my calls until I'm finished here."

"Of course." And with that she was gone.

The room briefly fell silent as they all sipped their tea. Finch reached for a biscuit and munched thoughtfully. Philip smiled. "Now, then, I've made a few calls since we spoke earlier, Emmeline."

"Oh, yes?" She put her cup and saucer down on the table and sat on the edge of the sofa. "I'm sure we're all eager to hear what you have discovered. Then I'll tell you about something that happened after our conversation."

Philip's brow furrowed and a shadow darkened his blue eyes. "From your tone, I take it that this 'something' was not of the pleasant variety."

Emmeline hesitated for a second before answering. "Well, no, I can't say that it was a very pleasant experience and I certainly wouldn't want it repeated. But I'm all right and that's what counts."

A blond eyebrow shot upward as Philip cast a questioning glance at Burnell and Finch.

"Come on, Philip. Don't keep us in suspense. What have you learned about the mysterious Ambrose Trent?" Emmeline pressed, as she took out her notebook from her handbag.

"First, of all, you can put your notebook away. This is not for public consumption."

"I see. Not even an informed source?" she asked hopefully.

"No source at all. Is that understood?"

"All right." She sighed and dutifully dropped her notebook back into her handbag and reached for her tea again.

"Good girl." Philip sat back in his chair and crossed one long, elegant leg over the other. "Emmeline, you're not going to like this."

"Oh? What is *it*?" Her mind danced with excitement. That fire was extinguished with his next words.

"I'm afraid you cannot write a single word about Ambrose Trent. The story ends here in this room this afternoon."

"What do you mean?" Emmeline put her cup down so hard she sloshed tea onto the saucer.

"Just that. Forget you ever heard the name Ambrose Trent."

Emmeline stood up suddenly. "Forget it? *Forget it*? I can't simply file it away and forget it. Just like that." She snapped her fingers in the air. "Besides, the whole London press corps knows that Ambrose Trent—well, a man calling himself by that name—was murdered in the middle of Hyde Park last night. They've been camped outside poor Claire's flat. So don't tell me to forget it."

"Emmeline, calm down. Please sit."

Ooh, how she hated it when someone told her to calm down. She was calm until that moment. Now, she wanted to scream.

Burnell and Finch exchanged worried glances. Although they both admired Emmeline, they knew she had a short temper. Burnell intervened in an attempt to diffuse the tension. "Is there anything you *can* tell us, Mr. Acheson?"

"I'm afraid not."

"I see." The chief inspector leaned back and stroked his beard. "And what am I supposed to do with my murder inquiry? Bury it?"

"That would be best. But I'm afraid that's not possible, since the press is already on the scent, as Emmeline has pointed out. I think another couple of days of investigating and then conclude that it was a simple robbery that went tragically wrong."

"You seem to be afraid of a lot of things, Philip. The only thing I can surmise is that you've been got at. The question is by whom. Could it perhaps be Lord Douglas Sedgwick? Did a little bird whisper something in his ear?"

His jaw tightened and his blond brows knit together. "I will not grace that remark with an answer. You should know me better than that, Emmeline."

The fire fueling her anger had finally gone out. She felt ashamed for what she had just said. She plopped back down onto the sofa. "Sorry, Philip. I didn't mean that. The words slipped out before I knew what I was saying."

"You're forgiven. I realize that it was said in the heat of the moment. We'll say no more about it."

"I'm just trying to understand all this. Can't you tell me something? *Anything?*"

"I'm not at liberty to say anything—officially or unofficially—to any of you." His blue gaze swept over the three of them. "I can easily make a few calls and quash this story in a quarter of an hour. And I can have you reassigned, Emmeline. He held up a hand to forestall the torrent of protest rising to her lips. "But I won't. However, I will give you a piece of friendly advice. Consider this story dead."

"Like Ambrose Trent."

"I'm afraid so."

"My dear Philip, *I'm afraid* that's not possible. Someone just tried to kill me at the Tower Hill Underground station."

His brows shot up and he scalded his tongue as he took a sip of tea. "W—what?" he spluttered as he sat bolt upright. "Why didn't you tell me this earlier?"

Emmeline ignored his question. "I don't know about you, but I take great exception to being murdered. So you see, this has become *very* personal. Nothing will induce me to drop the story."

℘℘℘

Gregory wished whoever was jumping on his head with heavy boots would stop. He shifted his body and moaned. Pain exploded in the back of his skull, which felt as if it had swelled to the size of a watermelon. When the throbbing had subsided somewhat, he cautiously opened one eye.

"Sorry, old chap," the man sitting in the chair across from him said.

Gregory closed his eye and grunted. "Ambrose."

"Got it in one. It's good to know the old gray matter is still working. No permanent damage, then."

With a supreme effort, Gregory pushed himself into a sitting position on the sofa. It was not one of his more brilliant ideas. The pain radiated in a thousand different directions. "Why did you hit me?"

"I didn't realize it was you until it was too late. I thought you were one of them. Does it hurt awfully?"

Gregory gave his friend a pointed look. "What do you think?"

"Silly question," Ambrose replied with a sheepish grin. "How about if I get some ice for your head?"

"Later. First, you have a lot of explaining to do."

Ambrose arched one fair eyebrow. "Do I?"

"Yes, you do. We'll start with who you really are."

"I must have hit you on the head rather harder than I thought, old man," Ambrose said with a forced laugh. "You seem to be a trifle confused. I'm Ambrose. Why don't you lie back down again and I'll nip into the kitchen for that ice?"

"I don't know what game you're playing at, but it's a dangerous one, judging by the friends who created this lovely interior design for you." Gregory waved a hand at the mess that had been made in the living room as he unsteadily rose to his feet. "By the way, in case you haven't heard, they—whoever they are—killed Nick this afternoon. Ran him down on the Strand in broad daylight." Ambrose blanched at this. "Therefore, a little explaining is the least you can do. *For the moment*," Gregory continued. "Who are you?" he asked again as they climbed the stairs to sit on the roof terrace.

The mews house was arranged on three floors and the terrace was at the back. The March afternoon was mild and the sunshine warmed their faces as they sat drinking coffee. Gregory nursed the growing lump on his head.

Ambrose shook his head, as if he were carrying on an argument with himself. Finally, he let out a long, low sigh. "It doesn't really matter, Greg. Ambrose Trent is as good a name as any. The rest...well..." His voice trailed off and his brown eyes fixed on a spot somewhere over Gregory's shoulder, lost in the past.

"You're wrong. It does matter. First of all, I don't like being lied to by my friends. Second, people seem to be dying right and left and that does not give me a great sense of comfort and well-being."

"I'm sorry you got involved in all this."

"No, you're not. You deliberately dragged me into it. You sent me that wedding invitation to 'your' and Claire Sedgwick's wedding. Didn't you?"

The corners of Ambrose's lips curved into a half smile. "How did you guess?"

"It was not hard. And it was you on the Vespa this morning, wasn't it?"

"Guilty as charged."

"You've gone to great lengths to get my attention. I'm here now, so start talking. It's the least you can do after coshing me on the head."

"Diamonds, Greg. It all has to do with a fortune in diamonds." Then his voice fell to barely a whisper. "And *murder*."

CHAPTER 12

Gregory remained silent. He waited for Ambrose to collect his thoughts. "Where to begin?" Ambrose rested his elbows on the table and pursed his lips. "Antwerp. That's where this tale has its roots. Antwerp, the on-again, off-again center of the diamond trade for over 500 years. Amsterdam temporarily took on this mantle in the seventeenth and eighteenth centuries. However, Antwerp's long history of diamond cutting dates back to the early 1500s. But when the Spanish took control of the city in 1585, most of its Jewish diamond cutters fled to Amsterdam, halting diamond production.

"Greg, I know you're a...shall we say?...connoisseur of jewels, diamonds in particular. Do you know the city's history or shall I go on?"

"Go on because I don't think that what is happening today has anything to do with the 1500s."

"Maybe not the 1500s, but you're wrong about the past not having anything to do with the present. It has everything to do with it. I—we have reached this point today because of what happened so many generations ago. The sins of the father," Ambrose murmured. "You can never escape the sins of the father."

"Then tell me, so I can help you," Gregory implored as he touched Ambrose's arm.

Ambrose's brown eyes searched his face for a long moment without uttering a word. "It's too late. Nothing can help me now. But I'll tell you the story so that you understand.

"By the end of the Napoleonic wars in 1815, Antwerp was incorporated into the Netherlands and all religious groups were granted equality. As a result, the city's Jewish community was officially established in 1816. Its Hasidim *diamantairs*, or diamond cutters, opened their first formal diamond trading exchange, *Bourses*, in 1863.

"By the mid-nineteenth century, the diamond trade was growing rapidly. The discovery of the Kimberley diamond fields in South Africa in 1871 allowed Antwerp to once again become a leader in the world diamond market after 300 years.

"Although its diamond industry was hit hard by the German occupation during World War I, the city was able to rebound after the liberation in 1918 and to flourish until the Depression in America began to affect Europe in the early 1930s. Not surprisingly, as the Depression took hold, the demand for diamonds and other luxury goods plummeted. By 1934, De-Beers, the renowned mining company, began to hoard diamonds, restricting supply to stabilize prices. As the situation worsened, the Antwerp and Amsterdam diamond exchanges slashed production in half to limit overcapacity. This prompted factories and trading centers to severely curtail their operations, either by reducing work-hours or eliminating 25,000 jobs. By the end of the 1930s, the diamond industry recovered briefly because speculators were seeking safe investments in commodities that were highly portable and which had a fairly stable value. This would not last long because war clouds were looming once again.

"As World War II erupted in 1939, many of Antwerp's *diamantairs* fled to Cuba, England, Palestine, Portugal, and America. They took as many stones as they could with them to prevent them from falling into German hands. By 1940, up to eighty percent of Antwerp's Jews were involved in the diamond trade. Those who didn't flee—" The words caught in Ambrose's throat, and his hand curled into a fist so tight that his knuckles turned white.

"Well, we all know what happened to those poor souls.

Now, where was I? Oh, yes. Two *diamantairs*, Romi Gold-muntz and Herman Schamisso, with the help of Antwerp's mayor and the British government, established the Correspondence Office for the Diamond Industry—COFDI. This office registered and stored the smuggled diamonds until the end of the war.

"My grandfather, David, a boy of fifteen, and his parents and brother managed to flee Antwerp in April 1940, just one month before the Nazis occupied the city." Gregory raised his eyebrows, but said nothing. "The family had been *diamantairs* for generations," Ambrose continued. "In fact, David's brother, Paul, who was four years his senior, had entered the business a year earlier. David had planned to follow when the time came, making their parents, Nathan and Sarah, very proud. However, the Germans changed these plans. Nothing would ever be the same again for anyone.

"The family's escape was harrowing to say the least. I'm a little fuzzy on some of the details, but they made their way to the North Sea and bribed a fisherman to take them across to England. The country welcomed the refugees with open arms and helped them to adjust to their new lives.

"Nathan, like his fellow *diamantairs*, had smuggled out all the diamonds he could and immediately went to register them at the COFDI. Paul, grateful to his adopted country for taking them in, went to join up so that he could fight the German bastards. Within two months of the family's arrival in London, he received his papers from the RAF and was preparing to be sent out for training to become a pilot. This left a hole in the tight-knit family, but Nathan, Sarah, and David pulled together and tried to go on as best they could. While they worried about Paul, they understood why he joined up.

"Through word of mouth, their new life slowly started to take shape. No longer able to cut diamonds, Nathan had to find work. He had always had an ear for languages, so he offered his services to the government as a translator. After being thoroughly vetted by the War Office, Nathan soon was doing his bit for the war effort just like his son. Meanwhile, Sarah found work as a bookkeeper. Only David felt at loose ends. He longed to be doing something to fight the Germans, but he was too young so he was placed in school. Like Nathan, he had always been good at languages and soon was able to keep up with his lessons. He even made a few friends.

"And so, life took on a certain rhythm. Every time the air raid siren wailed and they had to run to the nearest Underground station for shelter, their thoughts immediately turned to Paul and whether he was safe. He always called them after a mission and sent a letter whenever he could. Then one day, there was another voice at the end of the line. A Lieutenant Prescott. He was sorry to have to tell them that Paul was involved in a firefight over France and both engines were hit. There was no time to eject.

"They were devastated. Suddenly, they were three. How could they go on? They managed, though. With the help of the new friends they had made and the support of the city's Jewish community. Nathan even discovered he had a distant cousin living in London. That was in November 1941. But that wasn't the end of the tragedy that touched this family—my family.

"In April 1943, Sarah was on her way home from doing the shopping and was caught in an air raid. She didn't have time to reach the shelter. Nathan and David were there when they pulled her body from the rubble. Only steps from the family's home, which was unscathed. *Only steps*. Sarah's death shattered Nathan. Overnight, he changed. He no longer cared about anything. This thrust David into the role of father and son. And this is how, at the end of the war, he came to find himself at the COFDI to seek the return of the diamonds Nathan had registered there back in 1940.

"By this time, David was twenty, young in years but an old man already. Like all of the children who were born during or just before the war, he was forced to grow up fast. They had no adolescence. Life's responsibilities were thrust upon their young shoulders before they should have been. In David's case, it came sooner because he had to take care of his father and their household. But he didn't complain. This is what families did. It was only the two of them in this world and if they didn't watch out for one another, who else would?"

Ambrose reached out for his cup, took a sip of coffee, and shuddered at its bitterness.

Gregory saw that his hand was trembling and the muscle in his jaw twitched. He placed a hand on Ambrose's arm. "Are you all right, old chap?"

Ambrose stared at the hand as if trying to figure out how it got there. Then he gave it a squeeze. "Yes, I'm fine. Fine. It's important that I finish the story." He cleared his throat. "What David was unprepared for—and what shook his faith in his fellow man—was the fact that someone would deliberately set out to cheat his family.

"When he went to the COFDI, he was told that there was no record of Nathan ever having registered any diamonds. In fact, the official said that they had never heard of Nathan Steinfeld. David couldn't believe his ears. This was sheer madness. *A horrible mistake.* He waved the papers in the official's face that proved what he was saying was true. But the official would have none of it. He took a cursory glance at the papers and had the temerity to say that they were forged. He 'advised' David to leave the premises immediately, otherwise he would be forced to call in the police.

"David stumbled out of the building somehow, tears stinging his eyes. What was he going to tell his father? This would certainly kill him. He wandered about the streets for a couple of hours, wracking his brains. When he had calmed down sufficiently and started to think clearly again, there was only one conclusion that he could come to. Someone in the COFDI had stolen his father's diamonds and wiped the record clean. Who was the bastard? And how could he prove what he knew was truth? Who would listen to a refugee? He didn't know what his legal rights were. He needed help. But who could he turn to? And then he remembered that Nathan's cousin had a son, Simon, who was studying to become a lawyer. He had met him a few times at the synagogue. Simon was a nice, friendly chap. David decided to go and talk to him. At this point, he had nothing left to lose.

"Simon listened to everything David had to say and was incensed. He agreed that it was an inside job. He pledged to do anything he could to right this wrong and restore the diamonds to Nathan. And thus, the two cousins banded together. It took weeks of painstaking work—and don't ask me how they managed it—but they were able to trace the crime to one man who worked in the COFDI. The older son of a privileged aristocratic family, whose history stretched back to the Normans. He was a wastrel, who drank and gambled and never had time for his new wife. He was only a few years older than David and Simon, but a world apart. He was given the job in the COFDI to keep him out of trouble and to learn some responsibility.

"The two cousins took the evidence they had pieced together to the head of the COFDI. David would always remember him. A soft-spoken, little man in his early sixties with a head of thick steel-gray hair and icy green eyes. He thanked David and Simon for their diligence in bringing the matter to his attention. He promised to review the information most carefully.

"A month later, the two cousins still had no word about Nathan's diamonds. Simon called the COFDI man's office several times, but was told by his secretary that he was not available. Frustrated, David and Simon decided to waylay the man and demand an answer. After two hours of waiting outside the building one afternoon, they were finally rewarded when the small figure appeared through the double doors. They allowed him to walk on a bit, before confronting him near Green Park.

"He pretended that he had never seen them before in his life. He said that if they didn't stop harassing him, he would summon a constable. This shook the confidence of the two young cousins. They had been manipulated from the start. Without the files that they had turned over to the little man, it was their word against the COFDI. To add insult to injury, he informed them that the young lord who they had 'so viciously maligned' with their lies had been transferred. They had no chance. Their case was lost.

"Simon blamed himself. He had walked right into the trap they had set. As a student of the law, he should have known better. David did not see it this way and was grateful to his cousin for the help that he had offered. But what could he tell Nathan? He had failed his father.

"Sadly, two months later Nathan died. He had sunk into a deep depression and without his dear Sarah anymore, he had simply given up. On the day of his father's funeral, with Simon at his side, David vowed that if it took the rest of his life he would get the lord that had done this to his family. No matter what he had to do, he would make sure that Lord Gerald Sedgwick paid."

Gregory blinked. "*Lord Gerald Sedgwick?* You mean—"

"Yes, the father of Lord Douglas Sedgwick, QC, MP."

Gregory let out a low whistle. "Now, I'm beginning to understand."

"Do you, Greg? I don't think so," Ambrose snapped. His brown eyes were ablaze with decades of hatred. "I don't think you realize what that family is capable of—what cold, black hearts hide within their aristocratic breasts. You see, it wasn't enough that Lord Gerald broke Nathan's spirit. He destroyed David's life as well. Although he married and had a son, David became consumed with the idea of revenge. He wanted to hurt Lord Gerald for essentially stealing his family from him. This notion gnawed at David. Anthony, my father and his son, watched as this obsession ate away at David's soul bit by bit every day until there was nothing left and he died of a heart attack at the age of forty.

"And so, Anthony assumed the mantle of avenging angel. Although only ten, he had inherited David's tenacious spirit and promised that his father's death would not have been in vain. But the bloody Sedgwick family—" Ambrose pounded his fist against the table so hard it rattled. "—would triumph over the Steinfelds once again.

"Years later, when I was just a lad of seven, Dad was arrested for embezzlement. It was a trumped up charge orchestrated by the now extremely powerful Sedgwicks. The family had their fingers in every pie imaginable. Lord Gerald had built up a huge international conglomerate that had holdings in oil, shipping, mining, newspapers, magazines, and real estate. In addition, he was a member of the House of Lords.

"Dad was an accountant and he was determined to prove that his lordship had gotten the money to start his company with the diamonds that he had stolen from Nathan. It took Dad several years to untangle all of the company's business ventures. Along the way, he discovered that some of them were not very kosher. However, Dad built up a solid case against Lord Gerald. But once again the Sedgwicks, and not justice, prevailed. They had somehow found out that he was about to take the evidence to the authorities. So, they paid someone off to make it look like Dad had been stealing from his company for years. The Sedgwicks were very thorough. They even set up a Swiss bank account in Dad's name and made it appear he had been making regular monthly deposits.

"Dad was given twenty years. The prosecutor in the case was a young, up-and-coming barrister by the name of Douglas Sedgwick. The judge was a snob and Douglas's aristocratic background had won his sympathy from the first day of the trial. With the judge on his side, it was not hard to persuade the jury to find Dad guilty. Unfortunately, Dad's lawyer was not as sharp and calculating. But then, Simon Kirby was ill at the time and couldn't take on his case. If he had, I'm sure Dad would have won. Instead, he died in prison."

Gregory's head throbbed. Perhaps, he hadn't heard him correctly. "Simon *Kirby*?"

"Yes, the QC. His cousin. The same one who had tried to help my grandfather recover Nathan's diamonds all those years earlier."

"But, Ambrose, Simon Kirby was Emmeline's grandfather."

"Yes, I know."

"That makes you—"

"A distant cousin."

CHAPTER 13

"Does she know about you?" Gregory asked. "About any of this?"

"I very much doubt it. She was only two when it all happened. As for me, I remember there was a family gathering at Simon's home a few months after Emmeline was born. I was five at the time and felt grown up compared to the tiny squirming bundle. She was such a good-natured baby." Ambrose smiled at the memory of that happier time. "I remember her parents, too—vaguely. A handsome couple. They died five years later and Emmeline's grandmother took her under her care. I never saw her after that."

"It must be the knock on the head because I'm still confused. I need something stronger than this cold coffee." Gregory pushed his cup and saucer away and closed his eyes for a moment, in the hopes of clearing his jumbled thoughts. "Why are you living under an assumed name? Are you afraid that Lord Douglas Sedgwick will come after you? And if so, what on earth was the whole charade with that chap who was posing as you and on the verge of marrying Claire Sedgwick?"

The smile of a few moments ago vanished from Ambrose's lips. "His name was Kenneth Armitage and he worked the Riviera. You know the type. Seduced rich women and took everything he could before moving on to his next victim. He was quite successful at it. He was also a heavy gambler and owed a lot of money to a lot of nasty chaps. The night I ran

into him at the casino in Monte Carlo, he was losing quite badly. I simply made him an offer that he was only too grateful to
accept."

"And that was?"

"Pretend to be me and romance Claire Sedgwick."

"The plan being to dump her after what…a few weeks, a
few months?"

Ambrose stiffened and sat up straighter in his chair.
"Don't look at me like that, Greg. She's a Sedgwick."

"Claire's not like her father and grandfather. I know her.
She went to university with Emmeline."

Ambrose snorted. "Don't be fooled. That family is all the
same under the skin, male and female. Black poison runs
through their veins, not blood. They deserve to rot in Hell for
what they did to my family, Greg."

"I understand that, but I repeat, not Claire."

"Have it your own way. She's of no consequence to me.
In any case, things started to unravel." He leaned forward and
rested his elbows on the table. He dropped his head between
his hands. "That idiot Armitage fell in love with her and was
planning to unburden himself in an effort to soothe his conscience."

Gregory raised his eyebrows and asked quietly, "Did you
kill him?"

Ambrose's fair head jerked up and he nearly toppled the
chair over as he hastily got to his feet. "How dare you? I
thought you would have known me better than that."

"What am I supposed to think? You've been lying to me
from the first day we met."

"I—am—not—a—murderer," Ambrose enunciated slow-
ly through clenched teeth. "I want the bloody Sedgwicks *alive*
so they can know what it is to suffer. It's no good sitting there
primly and coming over all holier-than-thou. You have no
right to judge me or my actions. No right whatsoever. After all,
you're a common thief."

At this, Gregory stood up and snatched both of Ambrose's lapels. They stared at each other for an uncomfortable
moment. Their faces were only inches apart. They fell into a

tense silence. Gregory was the first to speak. "So who killed Armitage?" he asked as he released Ambrose and resumed his seat. Calmness and sanity had prevailed.

Ambrose wavered for a fraction of a second and then wearily dropped back into his own chair. He reached out and gave Gregory's arm a quick squeeze. "Sorry, old chap. I didn't mean it. It's the strain of it all."

Gregory clapped him on the shoulder in response. Their friendship, although bruised and shaken, had been restored. "Who killed him?"

Ambrose hesitated. "I don't know."

"But you have a suspicion, don't you?"

"I wouldn't put it past Sedgwick."

"Why? What would be his motive? Unless—"

"Unless what?"

"Were you blackmailing Lord Sedgwick through Armitage?"

Ambrose put a hand to his chest. "Me? I don't know what you mean, Greg."

"Don't play the innocent with me. You heard what I said. That's the only thing that makes sense in this whole convoluted mess. Out with it. What did you have on him?"

A grin as wide as the Cheshire cat in *Alice in Wonderland* curled around his lips. "I found my father's files on the stolen diamonds. He was very meticulous. I also discovered a bit of dirt on Lord Douglas himself. It seems that our fine, upstanding lord is more like his father than anyone realizes. He drinks—and he likes to play cards. He's not good at it, but he likes to play. And he owes money, quite a lot of money to some unsavory types."

A low whistle escaped from Gregory. "I would never have guessed that Lord Douglas Sedgwick had any vices. I wonder if Lady Vanessa knows."

"Never mind her. There's more. About ten months ago, Sedgwick was driving back to London from some conference in Cambridge, when he struck and killed a woman. He was drunk at the time. The party sent in its minions to clean up the mess and it was all hushed up. They paid off the family and made the nasty situation disappear just like that." Ambrose brushed his hands together. "Naturally, it wouldn't do to have the country's star politician, possible future prime minister, tarnished."

"So you're saying that the same thing is happening now. Sedgwick realized that Armitage was after Claire's money—at least he was at the beginning, anyway—and he whispered a few words to the party bigwigs about the blackmail. And poof, Armitage is shot dead in Hyde Park."

"That's the most likely scenario."

Gregory caught something in Ambrose's tone and his eyes narrowed. "But?"

"But what?"

"What *aren't* you telling me?"

"I've told you everything now, Greg. You know my life story."

"No, I don't. First of all, what's your real name?"

Ambrose's brown eyes searched Gregory's face. He sighed and ran a hand through his sandy hair. "Jonathan. Jonathan Steinfeld."

"Well, that's a start at least. Now, *Jonathan*, if you're running around London under an assumed name, it must mean that Lord Sedgwick realizes who you are or at least of your existence."

"I would say that was a fair assumption."

"I'm glad that you concur. The only problem is, if he had Armitage vetted—which I'm certain he did—then he would have known immediately that he was a minor crook and not the Ambrose Trent he was looking for. The Ambrose Trent who threatened to ruin not only his career, but more importantly his family's name. So that means you're not telling me the truth or at least not all of it." Gregory leaned forward. "Let's start with why you've assumed a false name."

Jonathan said nothing.

"No answer," Gregory asked with an arched brow. "Shall I tell you? I think that there's something else going on here. Look at you. The fear's written all over your face. The first thing you said to me when I came round after you hit me was,

'Sorry, old chap, I thought you were one of them.' One of
who? Who else is after you?"

Jonathan blanched under that intense cinnamon gaze. "In
for a penny, in for a pound," he replied at last. "I'm afraid it
was diamonds and Antwerp again, Greg. It seems that it's in
our blood. We Steinfelds can't seem to get away from them.
You remember the big diamond robbery at the Antwerp Diamond Centre in February 2003?"

"Remember? How could anyone forget the 'heist of the
century'? I marveled at the sheer nerve of the thieves. They
emptied 123 of 160 vaults, making off with at least $100 mil-
lion in loose diamonds, gold, and jewelry."

"That's right. The vaults were thought to be impenetrable.
After all, they were protected by ten layers of security, includ-
ing infrared heat detectors, Doppler radar, a magnetic field, a
seismic sensor, and a lock with 100 million possible combina-
tions."

"What does this have to do with you, Jonathan?" It was
funny how the name came so easily to his tongue, Gregory
thought. Jonathan suited his friend much better than Ambrose
ever did.

"The jewels were never found, but based on circumstantial evidence Leonardo Notarbartolo, a diamond merchant who
rented an office in the Antwerp Diamond Centre and had been
to the vaults on several occasions, was arrested. He was sentenced to ten years. He denied having anything to do with the
crime. However, the Italian anti-Mafia police contend that he
has ties to the Sicilian mob and that his cousin was tapped to
be the next *capo dei capi*, the head of the entire organization.

"Notarbartolo was the only one who was caught. The rest
of his gang vanished into the ether and it is thought that the
spoils are hidden somewhere until Notarbartolo gets out of
prison. Everyone's wrong, of course. He doesn't have the loot.
I do."

"What?" Gregory was incredulous. "*You* have a $100 mil-
lion worth of diamonds."

"It's not just diamonds, but let's not quibble. Yes, I have
the stuff."

"But how? Were you in on the heist?"

"Certainly not," Jonathan said indignantly. "If I'd planned it, to this day the police would be wondering who pulled it off. No, I found the loot."

"*Found*? What do you mean found? Where?" Jonathan pursed his lips and shook his head. "Best not to ask, old chap. What you don't know can't hurt you."

"So the gang or the Mafia are after you because they want the diamonds back?"

"That and the fact that I testified against Notarbartolo at the trial." Gregory sat back stunned and confused. He couldn't believe his ears. Jonathan nodded. "I was placed in a witness protection program. Only it seems they've managed to track me down."

"Armitage was a pawn, wasn't he?"

"I needed time to get Sedgwick and then I was going to disappear with the stash." Jonathan rubbed the back of his neck. "Only things got a little complicated."

"Only a little? Frankly, I don't see how the situation can be any worse."

"Well, it's just possible that they believe Emmeline has the diamonds now."

"What?" Gregory exploded as he jumped to his feet.

Jonathan hurried on. "It was yesterday—when she nearly collided with Armitage outside the tea shop. They were watching. I know because I saw them watching. They know we were working together. They probably reckoned that it would only be a matter of time before he led them straight to me. I'm fairly certain that they think Armitage passed the jewels on to Emmeline."

"Bloody hell."

"Yes, I think that would be an accurate assessment of the situation."

CHAPTER 14

As Gregory rang the doorbell to Emmeline's townhouse in Holland Park, he wondered what he was going to say to her. His head still ached from Ambrose's—Jonathan's, he corrected himself—blow, as well as everything he had learned that afternoon. Jonathan had sworn him to secrecy. He didn't want Emmeline to find out about the family connection because of her friendship with Claire Sedgwick, nor did he want her to know anything about the loot from the diamond heist.

"Listen, Greg," Jonathan had implored, "telling her won't solve anything. In fact, it could only make things worse. She's in enough danger as it is."

"And whose bloody fault is that?" Gregory fired back.

He shook his head as he rang the doorbell again. Something caught his eye on the other side of the square, as he heard a muffled "I'm coming" from inside. There was a slight movement in the shadows. He was sure of it. He took a step backward and peered hard across the dark expanse of the park. He was about to go and investigate further, when Emmeline flung open the door. She was wearing a burgundy velvet dress with a V-neckline that accentuated the string of creamy pearls around her throat. The light was streaming out from behind her and her face was half in shadow.

"What are you doing?" she asked suspiciously, her dark eyes narrowing.

"I—" He was half-turned away from the door with one foot on the top step and the other on the one just below. He shot a look over his shoulder and then focused his attention on Emmeline, joining her on the top step. "I must say that is not a very friendly greeting, love. No kiss. No welcoming embrace. Shall we start all over?" he said with a roguish wink as he leaned down and attempted to give her a kiss.

Emmeline pushed him away. "I am in no mood for your games, Gregory. Not after the afternoon I've had. You can either come inside and we can go to dinner, or you can turn around and take yourself off somewhere else. The choice is entirely yours."

He shot a quick glance up and down the street and then quietly shut the door behind him, making sure that the bolt was fastened. Emmeline had disappeared into the living room. Like everything else in this house, the room had an understated elegance and charm. The pastel peach walls gave off a soft, warm glow in the lamplight and served as a perfect backdrop for the various landscape oil paintings decorating the room.

She was sitting on the sofa, arms crossed defensively over her chest. He shrugged out of his coat, which he dumped haphazardly on an armchair. He sat down next to her and squeezed her knee. "Shall I ask or are you going to tell me what happened?"

Emmeline was quiet for a long moment as her eyes roamed over all the familiar nooks and crannies of his face. "Someone tried to kill me this afternoon at the Tower Hill Underground station."

He gripped her knee harder and the muscle in his jaw twitched. "Are you hurt?" There didn't appear to be any outward sign of injury.

A sheen of unshed tears glistened on her eyelashes as she shook her head. Gregory could see that it was taking all her powers of self-control not to cry. "Come here." He pulled her toward him and instinctively she settled in the crook of his shoulder, her head against his chest. "Tell me," he whispered in her ear as he placed a kiss against her dark curls.

Emmeline explained everything that had taken place since

they had parted that morning. She told him about her research into Ambrose Trent's background and her theory that he was either a spy or in some sort of witness protection program. Gregory raised an eyebrow at this, but said nothing. He had always admired her intelligence and perspicacity.

She tilted her head back so that she could look up into his face. "What do you think?"

He cleared his throat. "I think—I think it's a logical deduction. But go on. I want to hear what else you discovered."

Emmeline nestled back against his shoulder. "Ha. Philip tried to fob me off, but I know I'm right. The fact that someone tried to kill me proves it. Chief Inspector Burnell and Sergeant Finch are on my side, though."

"You mentioned your theory to Acheson *and* Oliver?"

"Yes. Sorry, I'm getting a bit ahead of myself. When I hit a brick wall in my research on Ambrose Trent, I rang Philip to ask if I could come round to see him. With his MI5 links, I thought he might be able to help. Although he agreed to hear me out, I could tell he was quite skeptical. Anyway, I was on my way to the Foreign Office when someone tried to shove me in front of a District Line train at the Tower Hill station."

Gregory could feel her body start to tremble against his rib cage. He held her tighter.

Her voice lowered a pitch. "I really thought I was going to die. I saw the train coming straight toward me and I couldn't grab on to anything." She took a deep gulp of air, as if the whole scene replayed itself before her eyes. "Then all of a sudden, I felt a strong arm pull me back onto the platform. I was a bit disoriented. People were shoving past me as they got off the train and he was whispering in my ear. I couldn't see his face because held me fast against him. But he told me that everything was all right. That I was safe. Gregory, he knew my name. And yours. He warned me to drop my investigation into Ambrose Trent. He said I had been lucky once, but I might not be a second time. How did he know us? How?"

Gregory cursed Jonathan. For he was certain, it had been Jonathan who had saved Emmeline. He cursed Jonathan for not telling him about the attempt on Emmeline's life and for swearing him to secrecy. She had a right to know that he was her cousin, as well as the fact that the Mafia or some equally unpleasant types thought that she had $100 million in stolen diamonds.

"I'll kill him," Gregory muttered under his breath. "I'll throttle him with my bare hands."

"What did you say?"

"Nothing, darling." He gave her forehead a distracted kiss and patted her knee. "You're safe now. I'll see that no one tries to harm you again. But I think it was time we were off. I made the reservations for eight."

Emmeline pushed herself up, confused by his change in manner. She fixed Gregory with her dark stare. "What's wrong? You've found something out about Ambrose Trent, haven't you?"

Gregory stood up wearily. "I found out more than I ever cared to know."

"I'm not leaving this house until you tell me what you've discovered."

He recognized the stubborn look that flitted across her face and sighed inwardly. "Darling, I promise to tell you everything. But at this moment, my head is swimming and I need a stiffener. Now, come on." He tugged at her arm.

"What's wrong with your head? It looks perfectly sound to me." Emmeline reached out and playfully tapped his crown.

Gregory winced at her touch, gentle though it had been, and recoiled. The color drained from her cheeks and he saw the concern flooding her eyes.

"You're hurt. Who did this to you?"

"It's funny you should ask that. It was none other than our elusive friend Ambrose Trent." Emmeline's jaw dropped. "Now, are you coming?" he asked. "Or would you rather sit here dying of curiosity?"

ⱸⱺⱸⱺ

Lord Sedgwick had been closeted in the study of his Lowndes Square mansion for the past hour, but he had gotten very little done on his final speech for the trial the following day. He ran a hand through his hair and crumpled another sheet of paper. It was no good. He couldn't concentrate. He stood up and paced the length of the room. It had been a waking nightmare since Ambrose Trent walked into his life. Sedgwick cursed Trent and he cursed his father for bringing this shame down upon the family. It was a good thing his father was no longer alive. But that meant that now *he* had to clean up his father's mess.

Sedgwick thought that, once Trent was dead, the whole thing would simply go away. He had been wrong. A mirthless laugh escaped his lips. So very wrong. He went over to the sideboard and poured himself a large whiskey. He downed half the glass in one gulp. The amber liquid burned his throat, but he didn't mind. He topped up the tumbler and walked back to his desk.

He felt as if things were slowly slipping out of his control and he didn't like it. Not only was Claire's fiancé *not* Trent, now he had to contend with Emmeline Kirby. He took another swig of the whiskey and reread the advance copy of the article she had written for tomorrow's edition. Long ago, he had thought it prudent to have his own spy in the *Times'* newsroom. Someone he could rely on to keep him abreast of any exposés the paper might be planning on him, or more importantly, on his enemies. After all, knowledge is power. And the more power one had in Whitehall, the better.

He dropped the article on the desk in disgust. "Bloody Jews. Father was right," he murmured to himself. "You can't trust any of them. They all stick together." The thought had crossed his mind that perhaps she was somehow involved with this Ambrose Trent, but he quickly dismissed it. However, he had always been a little wary of the fact that two of his daughter's closest friends were Jews. He held his tongue, naturally. And of course, if all Jews were like Emmeline and Maggie and knew their place, well then, there wouldn't be any problems in the world. Still, the friendships bothered him.

Claire's friend or not, he had to do something about Emmeline. She was trouble. Sedgwick reached across for the phone and dialed a number from memory. It was answered on the second ring. The conversation only lasted a few minutes, but as he replaced the receiver a broad smile creased his face. "One problem solved," he said with satisfaction.

"Now, where is Trent—or whatever his name is? And where is that blasted file on Father's diamonds?" He had to find it and destroy it. If it fell into the wrong hands, it would mean instant ruin. He would lose everything. He couldn't allow that to happen. "I *won't* allow it to happen." Sedgwick pounded his fist on the desk.

"What was that, Doug?"

Sedgwick was startled by the sound of his wife's voice. He hadn't heard her come in. "What? Sorry, Vanessa."

"Doug, is everything all right? You look a little peaked. Are you coming down with something?" She came over and felt his forehead. "Shall I call the doctor?"

He caught her hand and turned it over to kiss her palm. "I'm fine, dear. Just a minor problem. Nothing for you to worry about."

Vanessa cocked her head to one side and studied her husband. "Are you certain? We always said that we would tell each other everything. You know you can trust me, darling. With anything."

"Yes, I do know that, my love. But nothing is the matter. I assure you." He gave her hand a reassuring squeeze. "Now, what was it you wanted?"

Vanessa hesitated a moment and then gave a slight shrug as she seemed to change her mind about something. "I came to tell you that it was time to get dressed, otherwise we'll be late for the dinner at the French embassy."

"It completely slipped my mind, darling. What would I do without you?" Sedgwick stood and put an arm around his wife's shoulders as they walked to the door.

"Luckily, you'll never have to find out. But, Doug, are you sure nothing's wrong?" Her brown eyes searched his face for some clue as to what was bothering him.

"Nothing I can't handle. So stop worrying." Sedgwick kissed her cheek and changed the subject. "How's Claire doing?"

Vanessa sighed. He could see the little lines around her eyes deepen. "Oh, Doug, she's completely shattered. I've never seen her this way."

He gave her shoulders a reassuring squeeze. "She'll get over it and find a nice chap. Not a gold digger like Trent."

Her brow furrowed and she shook her head. "I'm not so sure about that. We both know Ambrose was a scoundrel of the worst sort, but she won't listen to a word against him. I'm very worried about her. I feel so helpless because I don't know what to do. I feel as if she's slipping away from me."

"Nonsense, darling. Claire knows you love her, that *we* both love her. She just needs time. Perhaps, if she had taken a little more time to get know him in the first place, she would not have brought down all this trouble on the family."

Vanessa turned sharply at this remark. "Trouble? What do you mean, Doug? What trouble has Ambrose Trent brought to our family?"

Sedgwick was quiet for a moment. "Nothing. Just a silly figure of speech. I'm tired, that's all. I don't know what I'm saying anymore. Come on, let's go and dress for that dinner."

Silently he concluded, *You can't outrun the past. So you just have to destroy it, before it has a chance to work its evil. Yes, that seems only fair. Eminently fair, in fact.*

CHAPTER 15

B ut *where* are the diamonds?" Emmeline whispered as they sipped their coffee. Gregory had told her an abridged version of Jonathan's story over dinner.

"He didn't trust me with that information."

Emmeline snorted. "I'm not surprised. He probably thought you'd go straight out and pinch the stuff. It takes a thief to know a thief."

"Darling, how can you say such a thing?" Gregory clucked his tongue at her. "I didn't realize you had such a cynical streak in you. I'll have you know I'm a model citizen of the world."

"Ha."

"Naturally you're entitled to your opinion, wrong though it may be."

"I'm not wrong. Neither are Interpol and Scotland Yard. Everyone knows you're—" She dropped her voice. "—a thief."

"I'll have you know that is a slanderous statement and I would be well within my rights to file a lawsuit against you." He raised an elegant hand to forestall the argument he could see kindling in her eyes. "But at this moment, love, your safety is uppermost in my mind because that bloody fool has made you a target."

"Piffle. Ambrose Trent simply made up that story. I'm mean really, *the Mafia*? It sounds like something out of a movie. I think there is more to this and you're just not telling me."

"Emmeline, I don't think you should dismiss this so lightly. Someone thinks you have $100 million in stolen jewels and they're willing to kill to get them back." Gregory grabbed her wrist roughly. "For God's sake, they saw you talking to that chap outside the tea shop. Now, he's dead because they think he passed the jewels to you."

"But I don't have them." The reality of the situation was obviously starting to sink in.

"I know that, but they don't. And when they realize that…well, you see my point, darling. I think they may have been behind that car that nearly ran us down outside the tea shop."

"So what am I supposed to do? Turn tail and run. As I told Philip this afternoon, I'm not dropping this story. I can't help feeling there's more behind it than just a seven-year-old diamond heist. I'm sure Ambrose Trent's real identity is the key. And another thing—" She wagged a finger at him. "—I'm certain *you're* hiding something. As usual."

Gregory's eyes widened. "*Me*? What could *I* possibly be hiding?"

Emmeline leaned over the table and tugged on his cherry-red silk tie so that her head was nearly touching his. "I don't know, but I'm going to find out."

e∽∾∾

Something simply did not make sense. Emmeline frowned as she punched the button in the lift and rode up to the newsroom. "Well, let's face it," she murmured aloud. "A lot of things about this story don't make sense." But if the Mafia truly believed that she had the jewels, *why* would they try to kill her? How could they recover the jewels if she were dead? And if the Mafia hadn't tried to run her and Gregory down, who did? An icy tendril of fear curled around her heart. *Who did?*

The question echoed in her ears as the lift doors slid open. She stepped into the corridor and felt the hairs on the back of her neck prickle. Emmeline straightened her shoulders and tried to shake off the sense of foreboding. But it only increased when she pushed open the door to the newsroom, which instantly fell silent.

Emmeline shivered involuntarily as a dozen faces stared blankly back at her. "What's all this, chaps? I'm certain it can't possibly be such a slow news day." No one laughed at her weak attempt at a joke. "What's the matter has the cat got your tongues?" She turned from one of her fellow reporters to another, but the silence continued. It looked like Bob Ellis, the features columnist, wanted to say something. She took a step toward him. "Yes, Bob?"

"Emmeline, I'd like a word," James called from his office.

"I'll be there in a tick."

She turned back to Bob. His clear gray eyes were filled with pity. All he said was "It's wrong," and looked away, ashamed.

What's wrong? She slowly walked toward her editor's office and felt a dozen pair of eyes boring into her back.

"Close the door, Emmeline."

She did as she was bid and sat down in the chair opposite him. For a moment, neither of them spoke. There were purple smudges under his bloodshot eyes. It looked as if he hadn't slept the night before.

She reached out and touched his hand, concerned for her boss and friend. "Are you all right?"

He sighed and pulled his hand away. "There's never an easy way to say these things. So I'll just come right out and say it. But you must understand, I'm doing this with great regret. You must believe that. I have no choice in the matter."

"James, you're scaring me. What's all this about?"

He sighed again. "I'm afraid you're sacked."

She felt the blood drain from her cheeks and sat back stunned. She couldn't have heard him correctly. "Would you mind repeating that?"

There was a slight tremor in his voice. "I said you're sacked."

"I see." She nodded once, frowning as her mind tried to

digest this information. Rage smoldered in her mind. "And what, may I ask, is the reason for my dismissal?" Her tone was clipped.

"It was felt that your work...that, well..."

She could almost feel sorry for him as he struggled for words. Almost, but not quite. "That what, James?"

"That your work was...well...not up to *The Times*' professional standards."

"I see," she said again. Her voice was dangerously low. She knew if he had been a bit more perspicacious, he would have recognized this warning sign. "Since when has my work not been up to...how did you put it?...oh, yes, 'professional standards'? I seem to remember that several of my stories won a string of awards for investigative journalism."

He swallowed hard. Good. She wanted to make him squirm.

"Emmeline, look—"

"I don't have to look. It is as clear as the end of my nose that I've upset the apple cart and someone doesn't want me poking into the Ambrose Trent murder. Isn't that right?"

"I assure you. It's not me. It came from the top."

The last remnants of her self-control abandoned her and she gave full vent to her anger. She slammed her fist on the desk and exploded, "But you're allowing it to happen, aren't you?"

She stood up and yanked the door open. With her hand on the knob, she turned back. "I respected you. I never thought you would cave in in such a cowardly manner. Friends usually stick up for one another. I guess that was another delusion under which I was laboring."

The door rattled on its hinges as she slammed it behind her. "I'm sorry, Emmeline," he murmured as he watched her walk across the newsroom to her desk. "You don't know how sorry I am."

She began wrenching open drawers, cursing at the entire world under breath. Her vision blurred as salty tears stung her eyelids. But she would not give any of them the satisfaction of seeing her cry. Oh, no. She was going to walk out of this place with her head held high.

"Looks like the Jew has finally fallen out of favor with management and about time, too."

Her head snapped up. "Which coward said that?" Her voice dripped venom. There was a sudden low murmur, but no one answered. No matter. She knew exactly who it was. The only person who had always resented her talent and success. Ian Newland. An arrogant, anti-Semitic misogynist who thought women were only good for one thing. He was a mediocre reporter who was only kept on the paper because of his family connection to the publisher.

She marched across the floor to his desk, her fists balled tightly at her side. "I dare you to repeat that again."

He tilted his chair back and threaded his fingers together to create a pillow for his head of wavy red hair, his blue eyes twinkling with amusement. "I beg your pardon. I have no idea what you're chuntering on about."

She wanted to slap that smug smile from his lips. "You don't have the courage to repeat it, do you, you bastard?"

He clucked his tongue. "Language, language. It seems they don't teach your kind manners."

She heard a sharp intake of breath somewhere behind her. "What is that supposed to mean?" she demanded.

"I would have thought it was fairly obvious. However, that's neither here nor there. It is refreshing to see that Shylock no longer holds sway in this newsroom and the right people are finally getting the attention they deserve."

"By 'right people,' I take it you are referring to yourself, Ian."

Again that reptilian smile slid across his lips. "I see that you're not as dim as I thought. That's right. The cream has finally risen to the top. But just between us—" He lowered his voice conspiratorially. "—I am now working on the Ambrose Trent murder. It seems Lord Sedgwick thought the story required a reporter with a bit of tact and sensitivity."

That was it. Emmeline's tenuous hold on her temper snapped with an almost audible crack that reverberated around the newsroom. She leaned down, braced her hands on the arm-rests of Ian's chair, and brought her head very close to his face. "You can go burn in Hell," she said through clenched teeth. "You are nothing but a spineless opportunist without talent or morals. However, in the end—to borrow your own very charming phrase—'your kind' always overreaches because you are too arrogant and too stupid to know any better. I'll be waiting for that day and will take immense pleasure in watching you plunge into ignominy. In the meantime, here's a little push to start you down that road." She leaned harder on the chair until it tipped backward and a stunned Ian landed heavily on the floor. "Don't forget your morning coffee. I know you can't live without it." Before he had a chance to recover his wits, she dumped the contents of his cup on his head.

"You bitch," he screamed as the hot liquid splashed onto his crisp, white shirt.

She raised her forefinger. "Ah. Ah. Language. Well, Ian dear, if there's nothing else, I must dash. After all, I have a story to write. You see, I may no longer work for *The Times*, but the Ambrose Trent murder is still *my story* and I'm not giving up on it. I hope I make myself quite clear on that point. So I suggest you stay out of my way."

With that, she turned on her heel and walked over to her desk to gather her things. Emmeline was surprised when the newsroom broke out into thunderous applause. They all stood—except for Ian, of course—as she made her way across the floor.

There were a few "Good lucks" and "Keep your chin up."

Tears were rolling down her cheeks. She couldn't control them anymore. She thought she was alone, but she was wrong. She didn't look back, though. No, that would have been a mis-take. She had to look forward. She pushed the door open and stepped out into the corridor with determination. She pressed the button and waited for the lift. Yes, she had to look forward so she could unravel the mystery swirling around Ambrose Trent and the stolen diamonds.

She couldn't quite put her finger on it yet, but there was something else at work here. Something distinctly unsettling.

And if she did not tread carefully, she might wind up dead.

First things first, she had to find out why Lord Sedgwick had turned on her. What was it she knew or he *thought* she knew that made him feel threatened? More importantly, was he willing to kill to keep it a secret?

Emmeline didn't know the answer and this disturbed her even more.

CHAPTER 16

Emmeline passed under two intricately carved porches fitted with iron gates as she entered the Royal Courts of Justice through the Gothic doorway in the Strand. The carving over the outer porch featured the heads of eminent judges and lawyers. Over the highest point of the upper arch there was a figure of Jesus, while to the left and right at a lower level Solomon and Alfred the Great could be seen. Moses appeared too on the building's northern façade.

Her heels clicked loudly along the elegant marble foyer as she headed toward the public gallery in Court 2. She quietly slipped into an empty seat at the front, which gave her a perfect view of the courtroom below. The proceedings hadn't started yet. This afforded Emmeline a chance to cast a glance at the handful of spectators seated around her.

A woman with silvery hair tucked into a loose bun at the back of her head was knitting as she waited. She briefly looked up and smiled at Emmeline, who returned the smile. "Should be an interesting case," the woman said.

Emmeline merely nodded her agreement.

A couple, probably married—heads bent close together—was whispering earnestly two rows behind her. At the back by the door, there was a sour-looking old gentleman with rheumy green eyes, who was muttering to himself. Down below, the court reporter and another functionary took their places. A sign that the trial would resume soon.

Emmeline turned around and rummaged in her handbag for her pad and a pen. When she looked up, she saw a young man with sandy blond hair at the other end of the gallery staring fixedly at her. He quickly averted his gaze, but not before she saw a flash of warm brown eyes. She tilted her head to the right and contemplated the stranger. She judged that he was only a few years older than she was. There was something vaguely familiar about him, but she couldn't place her finger on exactly what it was. She bit her lip. Had she met him before?

These thoughts were interrupted by the bustle of activity down below. In the space of only a few minutes, the prosecutor and jury had come into the courtroom. Emmeline's eyes became narrow slits when she saw the defense sweep through the doors. There in the flesh was the man responsible for having her sacked. Lord Douglas Sedgwick, QC, MP, all decked out in his black silk gown and gray, curled wig, looking the epitome of pompous arrogance. He must have sensed her intense scrutiny because he suddenly looked up at the gallery, which had filled up by now. Sedgwick frowned briefly when his green gaze fell upon Emmeline. Her eyes shot daggers at him in return, leaving no room for doubt about her frame of mind. However, this silent battle was short-lived for the judge arrived and the court clerk ordered everyone to rise.

For two hours, Emmeline sat transfixed as Lord Sedgwick made mincemeat of the prosecution. He was going to win this new trial by sheer force of his personality and his silver tongue. She could see that he had already swayed many members of the jury to his side. By the time closing arguments rolled around, the entire jury would be absolutely convinced that the appeal overturning the Crown Court's original conviction ... new trial for his client—a former-Russian-

CHAPTER 15

"B ut *where* are the diamonds?" Emmeline whispered as they sipped their coffee. Gregory had told her an abridged version of Jonathan's story over dinner.

"He didn't trust me with that information."

Emmeline snorted. "I'm not surprised. He probably thought you'd go straight out and pinch the stuff. It takes a thief to know a thief."

"Darling, how can you say such a thing?" Gregory clucked his tongue at her. "I didn't realize you had such a cynical streak in you. I'll have you know I'm a model citizen of the world."

"Ha."

"Naturally you're entitled to your opinion, wrong though it may be."

"I'm not wrong. Neither are Interpol and Scotland Yard. Everyone knows you're—" She dropped her voice. "—a thief."

"I'll have you know that is a slanderous statement and I would be well within my rights to file a lawsuit against you." He raised an elegant hand to forestall the argument he could see kindling in her eyes. "But at this moment, love, your safety is uppermost in my mind because that bloody fool has made you a target."

"Piffle. Ambrose Trent simply made up that story. I'm mean really, *the Mafia*? It sounds like something out of a mov-

She came from privilege and never worked a day in her life. Whatever she wanted, she got. And one day, Aleksei Propov crossed her path at a dinner party and she wanted him. Good-looking, charming, and cunning, Propov easily bewitched the spoiled woman. After a torrid affair that shocked even the most blasé of the upper classes, Propov and Anthea were married. There had been whispers from the start about his former employer and the source of his wealth, but no one was willing to examine the matter too closely. It was easier to turn a blind eye. After all, if Anthea had no interest in her husband's business dealings, why should they?

For the first year, Propov and Anthea were seen everywhere together. They summered on the French Riviera in St. Jean Cap Ferrat and wintered in Gstaad. They bought a penthouse in New York, an apartment on Boulevard Haussmann in Paris, and a villa on Lake Como in Italy. Then, as usually happens with two such tempestuous personalities, the initial attraction began to pall. Husband and wife began drifting apart. Rumors began to fly about Propov's string of indiscreet affairs and not-so-ethical business deals. Eventually, Anthea sought to nurse her wounded pride. She did so by seeking solace in someone else's arms. At last, she had found "true love" and started proceedings against Propov. Two weeks later, she was found dead in her bed of an overdose and Propov was soon arrested for her murder.

"And I put it to you, members of the jury," Sedgwick was saying in his summation, "that after listening to the woefully circumstantial evidence presented by the prosecution, there can be but one verdict—" He paused theatrically for emphasis. "—that of not guilty. For it is clear, that my client was convicted solely because he was a foreigner and did not have the same pedigree as those in the circles that he and his late wife were often seen."

He plunked down on the bench and mopped his patrician brow, seemingly exhausted from his strenuous efforts. The message he intended to convey was that he had given his all to defend his innocent client. Emmeline looked down at the faces of the jury. It was clear Sedgwick had swayed several mem-

he passed the j...

"But I don't have them." The reality of the situation was obviously starting to sink in.

"I know that, but they don't. And when they realize that…well, you see my point, darling. I think they may have been behind that car that nearly ran us down outside the tea shop."

"So what am I supposed to do? Turn tail and run. As I told Philip this afternoon, I'm not dropping this story. I can't help feeling there's more behind it than just a seven-year-old diamond heist. I'm sure Ambrose Trent's real identity is the key. And another thing—" She wagged a finger at him. "—I'm certain *you're* hiding something. As usual."

Gregory's eyes widened. "*Me?* What could *I* possibly be hiding?"

Emmeline leaned over the table and tugged on his cherry-red silk tie so that her head was nearly touching his. "I don't know, but I'm going to find out."

ഌരുഌ

Something simply did not make sense. Emmeline frowned as she punched the button in the lift and rode up to the newsroom. "Well, let's face it," she murmured aloud. "A lot of things about this story don't make sense." But if the Mafia truly believed that she had the jewels, *why* would they try to kill her? How could they recover the jewels if she were dead? And if the Mafia hadn't tried to run her and Gregory down, who did? An icy tendril of fear curled around her heart. *Who did?*

The question echoed in her ears as the lift doors slid open. She stepped into the corridor and felt the hairs on the back of her neck prickle. Emmeline straightened her shoulders and bers to his cause and he knew it. He obviously tried to smother the ghost of a smile that flitted across his lips for the briefest instant. Probably no one saw it, except Emmeline.

It took the jury just under an hour to find Propov not guilty. Emmeline bustled out of the public gallery as quickly as possible. She wanted to corner Sedgwick before he left the court. By the time she made it downstairs, a small group of reporters was already huddled around him in the corridor, firing questions about the case and Propov. This was her milieu.

She pushed her way to the front and waited for him to finish answering a question. Then, she pounced. "Lord Sedgwick?"

"Yes? Ah." Annoyance was reflected in his green eyes as he turned to find himself face to face with her.

"Emmeline Kirby, *The Times*. I have a question for you, sir."

"That's not quite true anymore. Is it, Emmeline?" There was a hard edge to his voice.

"What isn't true, Lord Sedgwick?"

"I hear you are no longer with *The Times*."

"Where exactly would you have heard that, Lord Sedgwick?" she asked innocently.

"Oh, you know how these things get about."

"No, I don't actually. Perhaps you could enlighten me."

"I don't have time for this game." He took a step closer to her. "I suggest you leave before I call a constable and have you removed from the building."

"Why would you do that, Lord Sedgwick? A guilty conscience, perhaps? I know you're the one who had me sacked. Why would you do that? What are you hiding?" She had no intention of being intimidated.

Sedgwick's voice was a dangerous hiss. "I've had enough of this innuendo. I suggest you leave. *Now*. Don't come near me or my family ever again. Do you understand?"

"My, that sounds very much like a threat, Lord Sedgwick."

He straightened his tie and attempted to regain his composure. "Not a threat. Just a little sage advice which you would

be wise to follow." With that, he turned back to the rest of reporters and said aloud, "I'm afraid that's all, ladies and gentlemen. Good afternoon."

Emmeline called to his retreating figure. "And if I don't
heed your advice, Lord Sedgwick, what will happen? Will I
become a liability like Ambrose Trent? Is that what you're
worried about?"

Sedgwick kept walking down the corridor, but she knew
her arrow hit its mark because she saw his back stiffen.

"You haven't answered the question, Lord Sedgwick?
Are you afraid your secret will come out?"

Someone bumped into her and hissed in her ear. "A public confrontation was a mistake, Emmeline." Then the voice
came over her other shoulder. "The Sedgwicks are a dangerous
enemy. Don't let your guard down. You're being watched."

"What?" The unexpected warning jarred her. She had
heard that voice before. Where? The Tower Hill Underground
station. *My Good Samaritan.*

She swept around and scanned the people milling outside
the various courtrooms. She saw the blond man that had been
in the public gallery slicing his way through the crowd.

"Wait. Come back," she yelled after him. "Come back."

A few people turned to stare as she tried to elbow her way
through the crowd, but the man didn't stop and soon she lost
sight of him. It was no use going after him.

"Damn and blast," she muttered under breath. "Who the
bloody hell *are* you?"

"Emmeline?"

She felt a soft tap on her shoulder and turned to find herself staring into Claire's very green, very bewildered eyes.
"Claire, what are you doing here?"

"I came to find Dad. I needed to discuss something with
him. I didn't expect to find you here. A bit out of sorts today,
are we?"

"Sorry." Emmeline reached up and gave her friend a distracted peck on the cheek. "A lot's been happening. Look,
there's a free bench in the corner. Let's go sit down." She took
Claire by the elbow and led her across the corridor. "That's

much better," Emmeline said as they settled themselves on the bench. "Now, we can talk. How are you coping?"

Claire's golden tresses were swept high atop her head today, drawing attention to the pallor of her translucent skin and the purplish half-moon smudges beneath her lovely eyes. The unrelieved inkiness of her somber suit only served to heighten this ghostly impression.

"You don't look like you're getting any sleep," Emmeline remarked.

Claire sighed and shook her head. "I haven't slept a wink since—" Her voice cracked as she fumbled in her handbag for a tissue. "Well, since the night Ambrose was—was murdered. Mum said I should continue taking the sleeping tablets the doctor prescribed, but they made me so horribly muddled that I decided I'd rather live with the insomnia."

"Oh, you poor dear." Emmeline gave Claire a hug and asked gently, "Is there anything I can do to help?"

"No." This was a mere whisper. A number of emotions drifted across Claire's tear-stained face. "Just find the person who killed my Ambrose and make sure that he's brought to justice."

"That's easier said than done. I was sacked this morning."

"What?" Claire's eyes became like two enormous emerald saucers. "You're pulling my leg."

"I wish I were. James—you know, my former friend and editor—he called me into his office this morning and very succinctly told me that my work was not...what was the phrase?...oh, yes, 'not up to *The Times'* professional standards.'"

"That's bloody insane. He must have been in his cups when he said it."

"I can attest to the fact that he was stone-cold sober."

"I can't believe it. It doesn't make any sense. Look, let me have a quiet word with Dad. He knows the publisher. I'm certain that this is simply some horrid mistake."

Emmeline cleared her throat. "I'm afraid that would be rather pointless."

"But why? It's worth a try at the very least."

"Because your father is the one who had me sacked," Emmeline replied as calmly as her raw nerves would allow.

Claire stared at her open-mouthed for several seconds. "I don't understand."

"It's not that complicated a concept to grasp." Emmeline leaned closer, her gaze pinning her friend to her seat. Her voice was low and full of pent-up emotion. "Your father had me sacked because he was afraid I was getting too close."

"*Too close*? Too close to what?" Claire looked around in confusion. "What are you saying?"

"Your father is hiding something, and I believe it has to do with Ambrose Trent's murder. Or rather, the man calling himself Ambrose Trent."

Claire jumped to her feet. "You're mad. Do you hear yourself? My father is a member of the House of Lords and a well-respected barrister. He couldn't have had anything to do with Ambrose's murder."

Emmeline stood slowly and hitched her handbag strap over her shoulder. "Not more than five minutes ago, your father threatened me because he believes I know his secret."

"Threats? Secrets? Now, we really are entering the realm of fantasy. I'm sorry you were sacked. I can see you're terribly upset about it, but making my father the villain in all this is simply not on." Claire started to walk away, but then turned on her elegant heels. "In the circumstances, I think it might be best if you didn't come around for a while. At least until you come to your senses."

Emmeline swallowed down the anger bubbling in her throat. "Funny, you sounded just like your father when he *ordered* me to stay away from your family. Permanently. Like father, like daughter. I guess it runs in the genes. Goodbye, Claire. You needn't worry. I shan't be troubling you anymore."

She brushed past Claire without a backward glance. There was nothing left to say. Emmeline never would have dreamed it was possible that their close friendship could be irrevocably broken in the space of a few short minutes. *Ah, well. You live and learn.* The problem was, could she stay alive long enough to discover who killed the phony Ambrose Trent? She hoped so because she wasn't giving up on this story. Not now.

❧

Emmeline's brain was awhirl as she stepped out of the Royal Courts of Justice and into the brilliant sunshine streaming down upon the Strand. She suddenly stopped in her tracks. Where was she going? She didn't know. There was no newsroom to go to, not anymore. Maybe she'd walk for a bit to collect her disjointed thoughts. Yes, that was a good idea. A little exercise always helped to chase the cobwebs away. Then she'd track Gregory down to see what he was up to and pop over to Scotland Yard to have a word with Chief Inspector Burnell. Maybe she'd even tackle Philip again. That would require a little delicacy, though.

With this plan of action in mind, Emmeline headed west. She turned down Southampton Street, slowly wending her way to Victoria Embankment. The Thames was a shimmering ribbon of silvery-green. She leaned her elbows on the parapet and watched the river traffic. A sigh escaped her lips. The argument with Claire upset her more than she had realized. It had hurt to see the look of disbelief in her friend's eyes. Emmeline shrugged her shoulders. She'd ring Maggie this evening to discuss what had happened. Perhaps, between the two of them, they could come up with a way to heal the rift with Claire. Emmeline felt better about the situation. Maggie was always full of good advice.

Now, if only Emmeline could make sense of the rest it. What was Lord Sedgwick hiding? She heard the Good Samaritan's voice in her head. '*The Sedgwicks are dangerous. Don't let your guard down. You're being watched.*'

That's all very well and good, but *who* was doing the watching?

The attack, when it came, was so swift and unexpected Emmeline didn't even have time to scream or run. There was a sharp pain in her right side. Then a sticky wetness. When she looked down, to her horror, she saw her own blood seeping through her coat. She had been stabbed.

CHAPTER 17

L ord Sedgwick's hand trembled as he hastily took a swig of whiskey. Some of it dribbled out of the corner of his mouth. He wiped at it absently and downed the rest of the tumbler. His eyes darted around the staid confines of the reading room at his club. He drew comfort from the low murmur of voices; the dark, wood-paneled walls; and the claret leather Chesterfield sofas and armchairs of this male bastion. He always sought refuge within these walls when his mind was troubled. Much as he loved and adored Vanessa, sometimes he just needed a little distance to gain the proper perspective.

Sedgwick signaled to the waiter for another whiskey. As a defense against any unwanted conversation, he snatched up the copy of *The Times* that had been left on the table at his elbow. He opened it with a crack. The words blurred before his eyes. What his brain needed was time to think. And, oh, did he have a lot to think about. Perhaps, though, the first thing he should do was to get rid of the gun.

೧೦೧೦

Ignoring the *CLOSED* sign in the window, Gregory easily gained entry into Nick Martin's spotless rare bookshop on Kensington Church Street in Chelsea, where some of London's finest antique dealers could be found.

The shop, a narrow white-washed Georgian building, had

a large picture window. It had been shuttered by the police since Nick's untimely demise. Ah, well, Gregory was so certain Chief Inspector Burnell wouldn't begrudge him a quick look around the premises that he hadn't bothered to ask for the detective's permission to visit the shop. Out of courtesy, naturally. Since Burnell was *so* busy, it was one less thing for the poor chap to worry about.

"Isn't that right, Oliver?" Gregory asked the empty shop.

The shop was laid out like a doughnut on two floors. A hush immediately enveloped him as the thick apple-green, wall-to-wall carpeting muted his footfalls. The upper gallery overlooked the main floor and was accessed by a spiral wrought iron staircase on either side. Highly-polished oak bookcases lined the walls all around. The main floor boasted first editions of Dickens, Austen, the Brontes, and other novelists of their stature on one wall, while rare antiquarian and children's books peered out at customers along the opposite wall.

Gregory pulled out a few of the pristine books and admired their elegant leather covers and bindings. He carefully flipped through one or two of the novels and then slipped them back into place.

He stood in the middle of the shop—one arm crossed over his chest and his head cocked to the right as his chin rested on his other hand. "Now, Nick old man," he murmured aloud as his gaze raked the shelves, "where would you hide $100 million in diamonds?"

He was certain the jewels had to be somewhere in the shop. He had searched Nick's flat and the jewels were not there. Well, he hadn't really expected to find them in the flat. That would have been too easy. But it had been worth a look, just in case there had been some clue as to where Ambrose and Nick had hidden them. One thing Gregory was confident about was that Burnell remained completely in the dark about the stolen jewels. If Burnell had found them, Gregory would have known about it. If the Mafia had them, they would not have ransacked Ambrose's mews cottage.

Gregory took another turn about the floor, but his search

elicited nothing. Instinct told him that the jewels had to be in the shop. There was nowhere else. But where? He started to climb one of the spiral staircases to the second floor, the home to modern first editions. An entire bookcase was dedicated to Agatha Christie, while Dorothy L. Sayers and Ngaio Marsh nestled together in the space adjacent. A little farther down the line, the shelves sported first editions of spy thrillers by such authors as John LeCarré and Ian Fleming. Gregory stopped in his tracks. John Le Carré and Ian Fleming. It couldn't be that simple, could it? He trailed a finger along the spines and a smile suddenly broke out across his face.

"Nick, old man, I tip my hat to you. You were always smarter than anyone gave you credit for. May you rest in peace."

At that moment, Gregory heard the tinkle of the bell as the shop door opened and closed. Male voices floated up to him. He leaned over the railing and felt a twinkle of amusement. "Oliver, Sergeant Finch, what a delightful surprise. Were you looking for something to read? I can make a few recommendations, if you like."

The detectives' heads snapped up in the same instant. "Longdon, what the devil are you doing here?" Chief Inspector Burnell barked. "*How* did you get in here?"

Gregory started wending his way down the staircase. "Really, Oliver. What a question. Can't you see the lock on that door is rather flimsy? A mere child could get in here. I must say Nick was very lax about security, considering all these rare books lying about." He waved a hand airily around the shop. "Perhaps someone should report it to the police. Oh wait, you *are* the police." He clapped the chief inspector on the back. "What a jolly good thing you turned up, Oliver."

"Hmph," Burnell grunted.

Finch rolled his eyes, but said nothing.

"I'm not amused, Longdon. How did you get in here? This is a crime scene, you know."

"Is it really? How fascinating."

"We've just come from Martin's flat. To the casual observer it wouldn't be obvious, but I'm certain that someone had a look round. You wouldn't happen to be that someone, would you, Longdon?"

"Who me?" Gregory's eyes widened in mock innocence. "I wouldn't presume to do such a thing. Breaking and entering is against the law, I believe."

A weary sigh escaped the inspector's lips. "I give up, Longdon. I'm too tired for this today. Have you discovered anything that could help us find Martin's murderer?"

"So you're convinced it *was* murder and not an accident?"

"Everything points to it. Finch spoke to a number of the witnesses at the scene and they all said the van clearly seemed to target Martin. But there's a piece missing from this puzzle, and I'm damned if I know what it is." Burnell paced a few steps and scratched his head, his thoughts clearly all a jumble. His piercing blue gaze slowly came to rest on Gregory's face. "However, I have a feeling that *you* know a lot more than you're letting on."

"*Me*? What could I possibly know that the great Scotland Yard does not?"

"For starters, you know our elusive friend with the checkered past, Ambrose Trent. Everything seems to come back to him. Where is he by the way?"

"Ambrose does not keep me apprised of his comings and goings. He's what is known as a free spirit."

"So you'd have us believe he hasn't tried to contact you since all this business unfolded."

"That's right."

"Longdon, you're a bloody liar. I can arrest you for perverting the course of justice."

Gregory simply smiled and put his arm around Burnell's shoulders. "Oliver, Oliver." He shook his head as if he were indulging a wayward child. "That would not be a very sporting way for friends to deal with one another, now would it?"

The chief inspector's face flushed slightly, as if with annoyance. "We have never been friends nor will we ever be. Now, what are you hiding?"

Gregory turned to the sergeant. "Don't look so worried, Finch. All families have their little tiffs now and again."

"Mr. Longdon, I'd have a care, if I were you. If you know something, I'd advise you to tell us at once. Two men are already dead," Finch said.

The tense silence that ensued was broken when Gregory's mobile screamed to life. He quickly flipped it open. "Hello."

"Greg? You must come quickly."

Gregory stared incredulously at his phone. "*Ambrose?* Where are you? Half of London's looking for you."

"This is not the time for explanations or recriminations. Just come. Emmeline's hurt."

All other thoughts flew out of Gregory's head at the sound of her name. "Where are you?"

"Her house in Holland Park." The line went dead.

"So you don't know *where* your friend is?" Burnell asked pointedly.

"Listen, Oliver, we can get back to our squabble later. I'm afraid I'm going to have to leave you gentlemen. Apparently, Emmeline's been hurt. I don't know by whose hand or how badly."

"Miss Kirby hurt? Well, that's a different matter altogether. Where is she?"

Gregory hesitated for only a fraction of a second. Ambrose—no, Jonathan, or whatever he chose to call himself—would simply have to fend for himself. "At her house."

"Right. Come on. We'll take you in the car. It'll be faster that way."

Gregory shot him a grateful look. "Thanks, Oliver. You're a good chap."

Burnell dismissed this with a wave of his hand and gave Gregory a small shove toward the door. "Stop dawdling. I'm not doing this for you. My concern is for Miss Kirby."

Gregory smiled and said over his shoulder, "Under that gruff exterior, you're just a woolly lamb, aren't you, Oliver?"

"Oh, go on with you. Come along, Finch," Burnell mumbled.

e/s e/s

"Lie still, Emmeline," Ambrose said as he smoothed the

damp curls from her forehead and eased the pillow under her head. "It's all right. The blood's stopped. It could have been much worse."

"Gregory?" Her voice was a hoarse rasp.

"Shh. Don't worry." He patted her shoulders gently. "I rang him. He's on his way. He'll be here soon."

"Who—who are you?"

The corners of his mouth twitched into a grin. "Don't you know? I thought a sharp woman like yourself would have had it all worked out by now."

Emmeline shook her head slowly from side to side.

He felt the pull of her dark eyes pleading with him. "I'm Ambrose. Ambrose Trent."

"Not your real name. Who—"

"Hush. Names are not important. Ambrose will do just as well as any other."

Emmeline squeezed her eyes shut for a moment. "Thank you."

"For what?"

She opened her eyes again. "That's twice you saved my life. It *was* you in the Tower Hill station, wasn't it?"

"Yes," he said gently. "But you didn't listen to me. And now look what's happened. I was a bit late this time."

"They think I have the jewels, don't they?"

Ambrose's soft brown eyes widened in surprise. "So you know about that?"

She nodded. "But there's more—to the story. I—"

Emmeline passed out before she could finish her sentence. It was just as well. The conversation was getting dangerously close to home. Ambrose eased himself off the edge of her bed and tucked the blanket around her.

"Yes, there's more, Cousin Emmeline," he whispered from the doorway as he tiptoed out of the room. "I'm sorry that this ugliness had to touch you. But I swear I won't allow the Sedgwicks to harm our family anymore. You have my word on it."

Ten minutes later, the car pulled up to the curb opposite Emmeline's townhouse near Stafford Terrace in Holland Park.

Gregory didn't wait for Sergeant Finch to turn off the engine. In two strides, he was across the street and bounding up the steps. The door opened before he had a chance to ring the bell. "Ah, Longdon. There you are."

Gregory took a step backward. He wasn't expecting to see Philip—all golden, immaculate and unruffled as ever— standing on the threshold. "Acheson? What are *you* doing here?"

CHAPTER 18

Gregory stepped into the hall and cast a glance around. "Where's—"

Philip cut him off. "I expect you want to see Emmeline."

"Of course, I want to see Emmeline," Gregory retorted irritably. "What's happened?"

"She was stabbed this afternoon along the Thames, near Victoria Embankment Gardens," Philip said succinctly. "But she's fine. The doctor's been and gone. It's nothing life-threatening. Emmeline was very lucky. She's asleep at the moment. I wouldn't wake her, if I were you."

"Naturally, I won't. But I'll just poke my head round the door to satisfy myself that she's all right." Gregory was halfway up the stairs when he turned back. "Acheson?"

"Yes, Longdon?" Philip's blue eyes were an impenetrable mask.

"I was wondering whether you'd care to explain why a Foreign Office official-cum-MI5 agent is here investigating what clearly is a police matter."

"I'd rather not, old chap. Suffice it to say that I'm here in the capacity of an old friend."

"I see," Gregory murmured as he took a step back down. "Then perhaps you can tell me where's Ambrose?"

"Ambrose? Ambrose who?"

"Ambrose bloody Trent. That's who." The last thread of Gregory's patience snapped. "The man Emmeline came to speak to you about the other day. The man *you* said you didn't know."

Burnell and Finch entered the house. "Mr. Acheson?"

Philip extended a hand to the two detectives. "Nice to see you again, Chief Inspector Burnell, and you, too, Sergeant Finch."

Burnell inclined his head. "I must say that I'm rather curious to find out why you're here?"

"As I was telling Longdon, it is merely the concern of an old friend. Nothing more." The words sounded unconvincing.

"I see. Therefore, you wouldn't know why someone would want to attack Miss Kirby?"

"No idea whatsoever, Chief Inspector."

"Uh huh. And you don't know anyone called Ambrose Trent?"

"Why does everyone keep asking me that? I've never heard of the bloke."

"That's funny, Mr. Acheson, because Finch and I were in your office only yesterday with Miss Kirby to discuss the very same Ambrose Trent."

"Really? I can't seem to recall the conversation."

Philip and Burnell stared at one another for a long, uncomfortable moment.

Burnell was the first to break the silence. "We had the impression that Ambrose Trent was here."

"As you can see—" Philip made a show of looking around. "—I'm the only one here."

The chief inspector rubbed the back of his neck. The smile crossing his lips failed to reach his eyes, which were as hard as steely blue daggers. "Mr. Acheson—" His voice was dangerously low. "—while I have tremendous respect for you and the delicacy with which you must carry out your work, my job is just as important. If there's one thing that I cannot tolerate from *anyone*, it's being lied to." He paused to let these last words sink in. "Especially with two murders on my hands and this new attack on Miss Kirby."

"And what, may I ask, makes you think I'm lying, Burnell?" Philip's tone was clipped.

Gregory came back down the stairs to join the little trio standing in the middle of the hall. "Your very presence and Ambrose's glaring absence strike a dissonant chord, *old chap*." He poked Philip in the chest with his forefinger. "Why is MI5 interested in this case at all? And why was Emmeline brought home? Surely she should be in hospital, at least overnight for observation. Unless *you* wanted the attack and Ambrose's involvement hushed up for some reason. Could that be it?"

Philip felt three pairs of eyes upon him. He ran a hand through his blond hair as he wrestled with his conscience. "Come in here." He motioned with his head toward the living room. "We don't want to disturb Emmeline."

Gregory and the two policemen silently followed him into the cheery room with its peach-colored walls. They ranged themselves awkwardly on the sofa with Burnell's bulk wedged between Gregory and Finch.

Philip remained standing, three expectant faces watching him. "This is all highly irregular."

"Never mind all that. It wouldn't be the first time. Just get on with it," Gregory snapped.

"I needn't have to remind you that nothing goes beyond these walls."

"Emmeline will have to be told."

"I'm afraid that's impossible, Longdon. It's a very sensitive situation."

"You're a bloody fool if you think you can stop her from pursuing this to the bitter end. We are talking about Emmeline, after all. This afternoon's attack—the second in two days, I might add—will only serve to make her more determined to ferret out the truth, heedless of any danger that may follow."

A wan smile creased Philip's handsome features. "You're right, of course. Our Emmeline tends to be a bit headstrong."

This seemed to ease the tension that had hung thickly upon the air.

"Where to begin." Philip started to pace the length of the room, his hands folded behind his back. "About six months ago, your friend Ambrose came to us with evidence that top-secret British weapons were getting into the hands of terrorist groups—Basque separatists in Spain, African dictators, Colombian rebels—you get the idea. Anyone, and everyone, who was willing to pay was received with open arms. It does not fall within my purview, so it was not my case. I only became involved yesterday when I made a few discreet inquiries for Emmeline about Ambrose Trent. I was quickly told, in no uncertain terms, to cease and desist *at once* and to persuade *anyone* else to forget that Ambrose Trent ever existed."

"But he doesn't exist," Finch pointed out in his usual calm and quiet manner. "We've already established that it's a false identity. Who is he?"

"I'm afraid there are a number of questions that remain to be answered. As I said, I just happened to stumble into this case. According to our chaps, he has evidence Renato Gamborelli brokered these arms sales and received a very generous cut for his troubles. Do you chaps know who Gamborelli is?"

Burnell spoke up before the others could answer. "Mafia, isn't he? An exceedingly enterprising bloke, if my memory serves me correctly. I came across his Interpol file a few years back. Drugs, prostitution, assassinations."

"Very good, Burnell. Gamborelli also has a lucrative sideline in arms trafficking."

"But how are the British weapons getting into Gamborelli's hands?" Finch asked.

"After months of painstaking investigation, MI5 has been able to narrow it down to someone in army intelligence. Most likely a disgruntled officer lured by cash or women, or both, who is actually procuring the weapons. However, the interesting bit of the case is that Gamborelli's girlfriend is the one who put him in contact with the officer. She happens to be English."

"Who is she? Surely MI5 doesn't think it's Emmeline?"

"No, Longdon," Philip replied, his voice tinged with irritation. "Do give us some credit. Trent was going to give us the girlfriend. Apparently, she's a stunner *and* well-connected. That's what likely caught Gamborelli's eye. For her part, she's

the type that only has to crook her little finger and she gets
everything she wants in life. She was probably bored. Gamborelli offered a bit of excitement and danger."

"They sound like a charming pair," Burnell said with dis-
gust. "So who is she and what does all this have to do with
Kenneth Armitage, alias Ambrose Trent and my body in Hyde
Park?"

"Ah, here's where it all gets a bit sticky." Philip dropped
into the wing chair and crossed one long leg over the other.
"Trent hasn't given us her name. He promised to deliver the
evidence to my colleague yesterday. When he didn't turn up at
the rendezvous, MI5 dispatched a couple of agents to his mews
cottage only to find that someone had been there before them
and left the place in a right old mess. Coming on the heels of
his namesake's murder in Hyde Park, I think Trent went into
hiding. It's an odd coincidence, though, that he would choose
the moment when Emmeline's been attacked to resurface."

"Distinctly odd," Gregory murmured.

He wanted to throttle Ambrose with his bare hands for
telling him that yarn about the stolen jewels. Unless...Could
the two be tied together somehow? Gregory frowned and
shook his head. Gamborelli was an unpleasant and dangerous
twist in the tale. What if Gamborelli or his cohorts tracked
Ambrose down through Nick? Nick was obviously terrified
when he had seen him in the pub yesterday. Gregory remembered that Nick nearly went into apoplexy when Ambrose's
name came up in the conversation. The jewels were right up
Nick's alley. He always loved a challenge. Nick was a master
at making illicit goods disappear into the ether, while turning a
hefty profit on the transaction. Only, this time, he made the
mistake of tangling with Gamborelli. A mistake that he paid
for with his life. Gregory had to get back into Nick's shop as
soon as possible.

"What was that, Longdon?"

Gregory hadn't realized that he had spoken aloud. "Nothing. Nothing. Don't forget there's Nick Martin's murder as
well. He knew Ambrose, too."

"We haven't forgotten him. Another one of your illustrious contemporaries. I must say you have very poor taste in friends, Longdon," Burnell noted cynically.

Gregory smiled and put his arm around the chief inspector's shoulders. "No need to feel jealous, Oliver. I still like you."

"Oh, get off. You'll be the death of me yet," Burnell grumbled.

"Well, gentlemen *and* Longdon, now you know as much as I do. The question is how do we proceed from here? And how do we keep Emmeline out of it?"

"I must say I find it extremely disheartening to discover you are conspiring against me behind my back the moment I've been incapacitated." Four pairs of eyes looked up at this unexpected interruption to find Emmeline standing in the doorway of the living room wrapped in a rose flannel robe with her dark curls slightly tousled. Her slippered feet had muffled her approach.

Gregory jumped up, put an arm gently around her waist, and led her to the sofa. "Emmy, *what* are you doing up? You should be in bed, love. Come sit down."

Burnell and Finch made room for her. Emmeline winced as she eased herself against the pillows Gregory tucked behind her back.

"How's that, love? Are you comfortable? Shall I get you a cup of tea?"

Emmeline's face softened for a moment as she saw the look of concern reflected in his cinnamon eyes. "I'm fine. Thanks." She squeezed his hand briefly. "Really."

Gregory remained unconvinced, but took the armchair opposite, and watched her closely.

"Miss Kirby, I must say that in this instance I agree with Longdon," Burnell said. "You should really be in bed."

Finch nodded. "That makes three of us."

"Four," Philip corrected. "Now, *why* must you be so headstrong, Emmeline? You have nothing to prove to us. We all know that you are a brave and intrepid soul and a crusading journalist, but this is unwise. You were stabbed this afternoon and need some rest."

"I have rested." She thrust her chin forward with determination. "Besides, the doctor said that it's not as bad as it first appeared."

"Be that as it may—"

Emmeline cut Gregory off in mid-sentence. "I want to make it perfectly clear to all of you." Her eyes raked over their faces. "I am *not* going back to bed. I will not have all of you sitting in *my* house and devising a plan of attack without me. Now, the first thing that we absolutely must do is to find Ambrose Trent. Aside from the fact that he saved my life— *twice*—he is at the heart of this convoluted mystery. I must say that Gamborelli's involvement changes the entire dynamic. We must try to trace the girlfriend. After all the trouble that she's gone to thus far, she has to know where Gamborelli is hiding. The tricky part is to get her to give him up."

The four men were stunned into silence and then Gregory started laughing. "*How* long have you been listening at the keyhole?"

Emmeline lowered her gaze and plucked an imaginary piece of lint off her lap. Her cheeks flushed the same shade of pink as her robe. "Not long." When she looked up again, she pinned him with her dark eyes. "But it was a good thing I did listen because you weren't going to tell me anything. Were you? You were going to leave me in the dark."

Gregory held up an elegant hand and flashed a triumphant grin at her. "Ah, you're wrong there. I did explain to Acheson that it would be tantamount to high treason to keep such revelations from you. Knowing you so well, darling, I predicted that this would be precisely your reaction."

"You don't know me." She crossed her arms over chest and immediately grimaced. Her wound did not appreciate such rough treatment. "Not anymore," she said through gritted teeth.

"Let's leave that old argument for another day, shall we, Emmy? It's obvious that you heard everything."

"Not quite everything," she admitted grudgingly. "But enough to draw some conclusions."

Philip sighed. He felt as if he was fast losing control of

the situation. "Right. Let's hear them. God's knows the rest of us are stumped."

Emmeline hesitated for a second and then met Philip's steady blue gaze. "I think Gamborelli is after Ambrose Trent because of the jewels."

The blood drained from Gregory's cheeks.

"Jewels? What jewels?" Philip and Burnell asked in unison.

Emmeline frowned in confusion. "Surely Gregory told you. The jewels from the 2003 Antwerp Diamond Centre robbery."

Philip sat on the edge of his chair. Burnell cast a sidelong glance at Gregory and probed gently, "No, Miss Kirby, Longdon hasn't told us about the jewels, *yet*. Perhaps you would be so kind as to enlighten us."

Emmeline suddenly felt very warm. She loosened her robe a bit. She had the distinct impression that she had put her foot in it. "Gregory—I—I'm sorry. I thought you told them."

Gregory had regained his composure and shot a cheeky grin at Burnell. "It's all right, darling. There's nothing for it. The cat's out of the bag now. You might as well plunge ahead."

The chief inspector's blue eyes narrowed in response. "Yes, Miss Kirby. Please tell us the story. We're terribly interested."

"Well, all of you must remember the robbery. It was in all the papers at the time. One hundred million dollars in diamonds and other jewels were stolen from the Antwerp Diamond Centre, which was thought to be impenetrable. The jewels were never found. The Belgian police thought a ring of Italian thieves was responsible. The only one to be arrested was Leonardo Notarbartolo, who had posed as a diamond merchant. He was sentenced to ten years. The Italian anti-Mafia police claimed that Notarbartolo was connected to the Sicilian mob and that his cousin was poised to become the next *capo dei capi*."

"Fascinating, Miss Kirby. Do go on." Although Burnell spoke to Emmeline, he was looking directly at Gregory.

"I think Gamborelli is the cousin and Notarbartolo passed the loot on to him. But somehow the jewels fell into Ambrose Trent's hands. I'm not sure how. I haven't worked that bit out yet. That's why Trent went through the whole charade of finding a double. He knew Gamborelli was on his trail."

"So your theory is that Gamborelli tracked down the impostor, believing him to be Trent, and then killed him when he realized the truth?" Philip asked.

"Yes. Don't you see? Gamborelli had never seen Trent before."

Philip sat back and propped his elbows on the armrest. "It makes sense, Burnell."

"Yes, Mr. Acheson. It most certainly does."

"That explains why Trent's house was ransacked," Finch piped in. "Although he knows his prey now, Gamborelli obviously hasn't found the jewels."

"And he's getting desperate," Emmeline said. "I think Gamborelli is behind that incident at the Tower Hill station and this afternoon's attack."

"But why come after you, Emmeline? You're not connected to Trent in any way. It simply doesn't make sense," Philip asked, trying to work out the pieces of this complex puzzle.

"It all boils down to being in the wrong place at the wrong time."

"What do you mean?"

"When I went to meet Maggie the other day for our monthly tea, I nearly collided with the phony Ambrose Trent—not that I knew who he was at the time. He was leaving the tea shop as I was walking in. We exchanged a few words and that was the end of the episode. But I think that Gamborelli's minions must have been watching him and now they believe that I have the jewels. Which I don't."

"Naturally. No one in this room suspects that for one minute," Philip asserted.

"However, there *is* one person here this afternoon who is quite capable of it," Finch suggested. All eyes turned toward Gregory.

"Yes," Burnell said with a glint in his deep blue eyes. "Someone with a long and checkered past, and *present*. Someone who loves nothing better than a flamboyant jewel theft."

"It's no good looking at me like that, Oliver," Gregory replied calmly. "I have no idea what you are referring to."

"Don't you, Longdon? Everyone else knows exactly what I'm talking about."

"Chief Inspector Burnell, you can't possibly think Gregory has anything to do with this. It's absolutely ridiculous."

"Respectfully, Miss Kirby, I don't think that you can be objective about Longdon."

Emmeline sucked in her breath. She could feel the blush searing her cheeks. "I am not naïve, Chief Inspector. I, better than the rest of you, know Gregory has his faults—*many of them*." She gave Gregory a pointed look. "But he was just as surprised by this story when Trent told him about the jewels." As soon as the words came out of her mouth, she wanted to take them back. She had dropped Gregory into the soup for a second time. She looked over at him and mouthed *Sorry*.

"Never mind, love. Oliver is determined to think the worst of me."

"So, Longdon, you've been in touch with Trent. Did you have any intention of mentioning it to us? Or did it slip your mind?"

"You know how it is, Oliver. A chap has so many claims on his time," Gregory said with a casual shrug of his shoulders.

"I'm conducting a murder inquiry, not hosting a parlor game." Burnell slapped his fist against his knee. "It is your duty to tell me if you have any information pertaining to this case. I can arrest you right now for perverting the course of justice."

"Really, Oliver?" Gregory arched his right eyebrow. "Wouldn't that be a waste of your time? After all, you don't seriously believe I'm involved. You simply feel a bit put out that's all."

"Longdon, I'd watch my step if I were you," Philip warned.

"Thank you for your concern, Acheson, but it's not really warranted."

"Oh, please, all of you. Stop this childish bickering," Emmeline cut in. "This is not getting us anywhere."

Burnell recovered his equanimity. "You're right, of course, Miss Kirby. I apologize." He turned once again to Gregory. "When did you see Trent?"

"Yesterday at his house. He coshed me over the head."

The chief inspector's face broke out into a broad smile. "Did he? I think I'm beginning to warm to this chap after all. He seems to have good sense."

"Ha, ha, Oliver. I must have arrived soon after the visit from Gamborelli's men. The place was as Acheson described, 'a right old mess.' Everything was tossed. Drawers were pulled out, papers scattered about, china smashed, cushions slashed. You get the idea. I didn't hear Ambrose come in. He clearly thought that I must have been one of his new interior decorators. Before I realized what was happening, he had hit me. I woke up a little while later with a bump the size of a goose egg on the back on my head." Gregory unconsciously rubbed the still tender spot. "That's it. End of story. He apologized, offered me a cup of tea, and we parted friends once more."

"That's it? Oh, come on, Longdon. You can't expect us to believe that you and your chum didn't talk about anything. The jewels seemed to have come up in the conversation at some point. Miss Kirby just told us that."

Emmeline winced, but not from the pain of her wound.

"Ah, the jewels from the 2003 heist, is that what you mean, Oliver?"

"Yes, Longdon, that's what I mean," Burnell said, as if he were speaking to a demented child.

"Why didn't you say so?" Gregory always enjoyed teasing Burnell whenever the opportunity arose.

The chief inspector and Finch looked at one another and rolled their eyes in frustration. "Well, Longdon? We're waiting."

"Let's see." Gregory's brows knit together in concentration, as he stroked his chin thoughtfully. "Yes, I believe he did mention something about the jewels."

"Good. Now, what did he say exactly?"

"I can't remember word for word. It must be the bump on the head."

"We'll accept the general gist of the conversation."

"He didn't tell me how the jewels fell into his possession, but he did say he has them and the Mafia wants them back. Gamborelli's name did not come up."

"Did he say anything about his double?"

"It's as you surmised, Oliver. He was hoping to divert the Mafia's attention long enough to disappear. It's clear from all this that his plan failed miserably." Gregory had no intention of revealing to Burnell that Ambrose, née Jonathan Steinfeld, had hired the impostor as an instrument of revenge to ruin the Sedgwicks. That was something Burnell did not need to know. It was a personal matter and not relevant to this case.

Emmeline saw Burnell, Finch, and Philip exchange skeptical looks. They were certain that Gregory was keeping something back, but they couldn't figure out what it could be.

"All right, Longdon. Keep yourself available. We may have more questions for you."

Gregory fluttered his eyelashes at Burnell. "Oliver, I'm always at your beck and call. Night or day. I can't bear to be away from you for very long."

The chief inspector opened his mouth to reply, but shut it without saying anything.

"It's not worth it, Burnell," Philip pointed out. "He'll never change. We have more important matters to concern ourselves with at the moment. It is imperative that we find Gamborelli and Trent. I suggest that we pool our resources. Since MI5 is already searching for Gamborelli in connection with the British weapons, I could tackle that end of things while you focus on Trent."

"That sounds fine to me, Mr. Acheson. I'll have a word with Superintendent Fenton as soon as we finish here to apprise him of the latest developments."

"Good man." Philip stood and glanced at his watch.

"Gentlemen, it's getting late. I'm afraid I must be getting home or else my wife will murder me. We have guests for dinner."

"Bully for you, Acheson," Gregory said facetiously as he crossed one leg over the other.

Philip ignored him and continued speaking to the two police officers. "I think we've accomplished everything that we can at this stage. We'll compare notes tomorrow afternoon." He crossed the short distance and bent down to give Emmeline a peck on the cheek. "Emmeline, no more heroics, please. My heart can't stand the shock and Maggie would never forgive me if I allowed something to happen to you."

She patted his hand. "Thanks, Philip. My love to Maggie and the twins."

"Of course. Make sure you get some rest." He was shrugging into his coat. "Don't go in to the office tomorrow. Work from home. Better yet, don't work at all. *The Times* can do without its star reporter for one day."

A shadow fell across Emmeline's features. "You don't have to worry about that, Philip. The paper will be doing without me for many days to come."

"I don't understand."

"It's very simple. I was sacked this afternoon."

CHAPTER 19

Emmeline could feel four pairs of eyes on her, but Gregory was the first to speak. "That's ludicrous. Why were you sacked?"

They all knew how much she loved her job.

Tears stung her eyelids. The events of the day had suddenly caught up with her and a dam broke inside. The men squirmed uncomfortably as Emmeline wept for a few minutes.

Gregory knelt down beside her and put an arm around her. "It's all right, love. Tell us what happened."

She put her head on his shoulder. "James called me into his office this morning and said my work was not up to *The Times'* professional standards." She sniffled and took a deep breath. "So he had no choice but to let me go."

"What? I've never heard anything so daft in my life," Gregory said.

"The chap must have been drunk," Burnell added.

"Emmeline, I know a few people. I could have a quiet word, if you like," Philip offered.

She shook her head against Gregory's neck and mumbled, "Thanks, but it won't help."

"Of course, it will, darling," Gregory said encouragingly. "Acheson may not look like much, but I'm certain that he can be a very persuasive fellow when he wants to be."

Emmeline lifted her head and sighed. "It won't help because Lord Sedgwick is the one who instigated the whole thing."

"Did he now?" Burnell's eyes narrowed. "That's *very* interesting."

She turned to him. "I think Lord Sedgwick was worried about the negative publicity engendered by my article on Ambrose Trent. Because Trent, or rather the man calling himself Ambrose Trent, was Claire's fiancé."

"It seems rather excessive to me, especially in view of your friendship with Miss Sedgwick."

A mirthless laugh escaped Emmeline's lips, which she instantly regretted because it sent a pain shooting through her side. "Well, gentlemen, that's one more thing you can cross off the list. Today was not a very good day at all. I wish I had not gotten out of bed this morning. I really do." She sighed when she saw their perplexed faces staring back at her. "My 'friendship' with Claire is at end as well. She took umbrage because I had the nerve to criticize her father for having me sacked and for suggesting that he had something to hide. Heated words were exchanged. We both said things that we didn't mean and we parted on acrimonious terms. You have to understand that I was still seething from my confrontation with Lord Sedgwick, when Claire suddenly materialized. He made me so angry." Her fists were balled tightly in her lap.

Finch let out a low whistle. Burnell cleared his throat.

"Your *what* with Lord Sedgwick? I couldn't have heard you properly," Philip said as he exchanged looks with Gregory.

Emmeline thrust her chin out defiantly. "You heard me perfectly well and I don't need a lecture."

"Emmy, darling, that was—"

She turned on Gregory. "I especially don't need a lecture from *you*. I know it was a mistake to tackle him at the Royal Courts of Justice."

Philip groaned and slumped down into the chair that Gregory had vacated. He dropped his face into his hands and shook his blond head in disbelief. "This gets worse. Not only did you confront Lord Sedgwick. You did it in one of the most public places that you could find. Oh, Emmeline, what possessed you?"

Her eyes glistened with unshed tears. "I told you. I was angry. I wasn't thinking clearly."

"That's an understatement." He lifted his head and wearily fixed his blue gaze on her. "This is as reckless as your foray to the Russian embassy last month. Sedgwick is a very powerful man. He can make your life miserable. Even I won't be able to help you, if he chooses to do so."

"That's what Ambrose Trent said."

"What? Trent was there at the courthouse?" Burnell's ears perked up at this last remark.

Emmeline nodded. "I saw him in the public gallery during the trial, although I didn't know who he was at the time. Then he brushed past me in the corridor just after my quarrel with Lord Sedgwick. He said a public confrontation was a mistake. He also said the Sedgwicks are dangerous and that I was being watched."

"Our Mr. Trent seems to be a veritable fount of knowledge. I wonder why he was at the courthouse?" the chief inspector murmured.

Gregory held his tongue, but he privately cursed Ambrose. Although he couldn't fault the chap for seeking to right the wrong done against his family, Gregory was worried that things were now spiraling out of control and Emmeline was being put in harm's way. On top of that, she still remained in the dark about the family connection. Gregory was sorely tempted to make a clean breast of everything, but he had given his word to Ambrose. Besides, he wasn't sure if the knowledge would help her or hurt her. The only thing that he could do was to find those jewels and dispose of them as quickly as possible. Before Emmeline unwittingly stepped into the killer's sights, *again*. After all, nobody's luck lasted forever.

⊘⊘⊘

Lord Sedgwick quietly let himself into his graceful white-stucco mansion. He dropped his briefcase by the hall table and shrugged himself out of his Burberry coat. He picked up the post and gave it a cursory glance. He would deal with it later.

It was awfully quiet. "Vanessa?" he called. But there was no answer.

Where was she? Then, he remembered that they had tickets for the ballet tonight. He had promised her. She must be upstairs getting dressed. Bloody hell. The last thing he was in the mood for was the ballet.

Sedgwick sighed and shook his head, which throbbed from the whiskey he had consumed at the club. He climbed the stairs with a slow and heavy tread. When he reached the top of the stairs, he heard the sound of running water and Vanessa singing. A crooked smile touched his lips. She always sang in the shower, off key. He tapped and opened the door a crack. He raised his voice over the escaping steam and torrent of water. "I'm home, darling."

The singing stopped and his wife's sodden head popped out from behind the curtain. "Oh, good, Doug. I was getting worried that you wouldn't get back in time. How was the trial?"

"I won."

"Naturally," she said as she ducked back into the shower. "That goes without saying."

He smiled. Vanessa was the only person in the world who had complete confidence that he could do absolutely anything. She was a woman in a million.

"I'll be out in five minutes and then you can have your shower."

"Right," he replied wearily.

Sedgwick closed the door and crossed the hall to their bedroom. The singing started again as he loosened his tie. Vanessa had already laid out his tuxedo on the bed. He took off his gold cuff links and dropped them on the vanity table. For a moment, he was caught off guard by the face staring back at him mirror. He almost didn't recognize himself. His skin looked sallow and there were dusky purple smudges under his green eyes. This Ambrose Trent business was taking a terrible toll on him and his family. As this thought entered his mind, his gaze fell on the dresser across the room. Sedgwick's jaw tightened.

He straightened his back and squared his shoulders. Right, he had to make this mess disappear before it could damage the family any further. He had to protect the Sedgwick name. *At any cost.* He turned away from the mirror and slowly walked over to the dresser. Calmly, he pulled open the second drawer, his hand fumbling blindly on the outside at the back until his long fingers came into contact with something hard and metallic. Sedgwick drew the gun from its hiding place and held it in his hand. He felt its cold weight in his palm.

"Doug, what are you doing?" His wife's voice suddenly filled the room like a thunderclap. He hadn't heard her come in.

Sedgwick dropped the gun into the drawer and pushed it closed. He quickly recovered his wits and turned around to face her. "I didn't hear you come in, darling. All finished? Then I'll just have a quick shower. I wouldn't want us to be late. I know how much you're looking forward to the performance." He quickly kissed her temple and began unbuttoning his shirt.

Vanessa stood stock still in the middle of the room. Her brown eyes flitted to the dresser for the briefest instant before returning to watch her husband divest himself of the remainder of his clothing. "Doug?"

"Yes, darling?" he asked distractedly as he shrugged into his robe.

"Is anything wrong?"

He widened his eyes innocently. "Wrong? What could possibly be wrong?"

She bit her lip. "I don't know."

Sedgwick saw her eyes drift over to the dresser. "Of course nothing's wrong, dear." He took her by the shoulders and tilted her chin up to look into his eyes. "There's absolutely nothing to worry about. Nothing. Trust me."

She searched his beloved face, desperately seeking reassurance. "You would tell me if there were, wouldn't you? On our wedding day, we promised we would always tell each other everything. We said we would never keep secrets from one another."

Sedgwick smiled and pressed a soft kiss on her lips. "From that day, my love, I have shared my every thought and fear with you. I'm an open book. Now, if I don't get in that shower in the next sixty seconds we'll be late." He gave her bottom a playful pat and hurried out of the room.

Vanessa stared at the closed door and shivered slightly. A lump formed in her throat as a single tear escaped from beneath her lashes. She didn't know which hurt more—that Doug had lied to her for the first time in their entire married life. Or was it because *she* hadn't told *him* the truth?

CHAPTER 20

Gregory had spent the morning with Emmeline. Considering she had been stabbed the day before, she was fairing remarkably well. He waited until the doctor had called round again. Before he took his leave, Gregory made her swear that she would remain in bed and rest. She had earnestly promised to do so. But knowing Emmeline, she had probably thrown the *bedclothes* off before he was barely out the door and was now happily ensconced in her front of her computer or on the telephone.

Overnight, she had decided to offer the story as a freelance investigative piece to *The Telegraph*. Gregory sighed and shook his head wearily as he turned his Jaguar into Bryanston Mews. There was nothing he could do about it. She wouldn't be Emmeline if she didn't pursue the story. His only consolation was that she was safely tucked up at home and not roaming about London placing herself in danger.

Ah, well, he would go back this evening to see that she hadn't gotten into too much mischief during his absence. He also made a mental note to drop by Burnell's office this afternoon to find out if there were any developments in the case.

Gregory had taken a circuitous route across the city in an attempt to shake off any unwelcome shadow he may have attracted. He was satisfied he hadn't been followed. Again there was no one about as he got out of his car and walked the few steps to Ambrose's door.

He had made inquiries all over London and had drawn a blank. If someone had seen Ambrose in the last twenty-four hours, he or she was too frightened to say anything in the wake of Nick's murder. Gregory concluded that the only logical place Ambrose could have gone was his own house. The police had been there already and so had MI5 and the Mafia, therefore it was a fairly safe bet they wouldn't be coming back anytime soon.

He let himself inside the mews cottage with the assistance of his file. Everything had been returned to its proper place. The living room was once again spotless. "Ambrose?" he called out. No response. "Jonathan?" Still nothing. "I know you're here so stop playing this little game of hide-and-seek. I'm alone and I wasn't followed."

At this, he heard a shuffling noise from the upper floor and then footsteps on the stairs. A moment later, Ambrose materialized. He waved Gregory over to the sofa. "You might as well sit down. How's Emmeline doing?" he asked as he dropped into the chair opposite.

"She'll be all right. She's a fighter."

Some of the tension eased in Ambrose's face. He looked as if he hadn't slept all night. "That's a relief. I was worried about her, but I didn't dare hang about after Acheson arrived."

"Speaking of Acheson. You lied to me. *Again.*"

"Ah. That's not strictly true, old chap."

"No? Then, it simply slipped your mind to mention the fact that you had stolen the diamonds from none other than Renato Gamborelli, one of the biggest and deadliest *capos* operating in Italy today?"

"It's not a case of *stealing*, rather it's a matter of justice. Like the Bible says, 'An eye for eye.'" A muscle in Ambrose's jaw twitched and his knuckles turned white as he clasped his hands together in his lap.

Exasperated, Gregory threw his hands up in the air. "That doesn't make any sense, Ambrose. Or would you prefer if I called you Jonathan?"

"We've been through this already. Ambrose is fine. You haven't told Emmeline?" he asked anxiously.

"That you're her distant cousin? No, I have not. I gave you my word that I wouldn't, but it's only a matter of time before she finds out. She knows about the diamonds and Gamborelli, though. She also knows about your little arrangement with MI5 to provide the evidence on the arms trafficking and the name of Gamborelli's girlfriend. What were you thinking when you dragged Emmeline into your sordid little affair? Thanks to you, she's nearly been killed *twice*. No, I lie. Make that three times, if you count the car that tried to run us down outside the tea shop."

"Greg, you must believe me. I never had any intention of involving Emmeline in this. On the contrary, I was trying to stay as far away as I possibly could. Unfortunately, she stumbled into Armitage and then things started to get complicated."

Gregory snorted. "That's an understatement." He leaned forward and shook his head. "I ought to throttle you."

"You are well within your rights to feel that way. But when I realized Emmeline was in danger, I did what I could to protect her. But I could kick myself for not following her closely enough yesterday afternoon after she left the courthouse. Perhaps if I had, she wouldn't have been stabbed. It's just that I was afraid Sedgwick would see me. After I warned Emmeline to be on her guard, I felt very exposed hanging about in that corridor. I tried to make my way out of the building as quickly as possible. In the process, I lost track of Emmeline for a bit. I caught up to her by the river, just after she had been stabbed."

"Did you see anybody?"

"I'm afraid I was too focused on Emmeline to pay much attention to my surroundings. She had passed out. I managed to get her into a taxi and I rang MI5 on the way to her house. Then, I rang you. Acheson was waiting with the doctor when we arrived at the house. He was not my contact. It was the first time I had ever laid eyes on him and I was a bit wary. Rather a cold chap, if you ask me. Over the last few years, I've learned to give my trust sparingly. However, Acheson assured me he was an old friend of Emmeline's. I saw that was the case when she came round. She was happy to see him. But I have to tell you, she kept calling for you. I don't know if she realizes it or not."

A faint smile touched Gregory's lips at this last remark. He leaned back and rested his head against the sofa. "There's something wrong here and I can't put my finger on it. Why would Gamborelli—because who else could it be?—go after Emmeline like that in broad daylight?"

"It's clear enough. He wanted the diamonds and was willing to throw all caution to the wind to get them back."

Gregory sat up and stared directly into his friend's brown eyes. "But don't you see? That's just it. If he thought she had the jewels, why would he try to kill her? He would never be that foolish. Otherwise, he would never get them back."

Ambrose blanched. But he said nothing.

"What am I missing? Perhaps it's not the diamonds that are important. Maybe it's some other secret Emmeline discovered about Gamborelli and she doesn't even realize it. Something that *you* on the other hand know, Ambrose old chum. What else haven't you told me?"

"I've told you everything."

Gregory gave him a pointed look. "Hmph. Judging by your track record, I very much doubt it."

"What do you think I'm keeping from you? I told you about how the Sedgwicks cheated my family out of what was rightfully ours. I told you that Emmeline is a distant cousin. I told you about the diamonds—"

"Ah, but you neglected to mention the bit about Gamborelli, the arms dealing, and MI5."

Ambrose waved a dismissive hand in the air. "Mere details. The less involved you are the better it is for you, Greg. Safer."

"But I *am* involved. You saw to that the minute you sent me that invitation to 'your' and Claire's wedding. More importantly, Emmeline is involved in this mess. And that's the part I don't like." He poked Ambrose in the chest with his forefinger. "Especially with people dying left and right."

"I'm sorry, Greg. More than you'll ever know. It's just that the diamonds—"

"Yes, about those troublesome diamonds. I know you don't have them. Nick did and *I* know exactly where he hid them."

An uncomfortable silence hovered in the space between them. Ambrose's face froze and his back stiffened. They stared at one another for a long moment. Ambrose was the first one to speak. "You can't possibly know. You're simply fishing."

Gregory smoothed the corners of his mustache and crossed one leg over the other. "Nick wasn't a complicated chap. If you knew him well—as we both did—he was very easy to read."

Ambrose swallowed hard as his brain furiously tried to work out his next move.

Gregory finally left a quarter of an hour later. Ambrose was glad to see the back of him. All his carefully laid plans were up in smoke. Damn and blast. Did Greg take the diamonds or were they still in their hiding place? He didn't know. Greg was always a good poker player and could bluff his way out of anything. Ambrose ran a hand through his hair and began pacing the length of the living room. The shrill peal of the telephone on the end table halted his nervous perambulations.

He hesitated before picking it up. No one except Greg knew he was here. At least he *thought* no one else knew. He didn't recognize the number. "Hello?" he said tentatively.

Ambrose listened for a few seconds. "So you've found me." His heart hammered in his chest and his breathing became a shallow rasp. The blood drained from his cheeks as he tried to brazen it out. His voice sounded strange to his own ears. "What do you want?"

The caller's last words reverberated in his ears long after the connection had been severed. "The diamonds, of course, Mr. Trent. I want the diamonds. What else?"

"I don't have them."

"Please, Mr. Trent, this little game of yours is becoming rather tiresome. The late Nick Martin didn't have the diamonds, so that leaves only you. I want my property returned."

"It's not your property. You're nothing but a liar and a cheat. You're also a *murderer*. I *know* you killed Nick and

Armitage and I'm going to make sure the bloody world knows it too."

"That would be a grave mistake. And I do mean grave in the literal sense. You do value your life and that of Emmeline Kirby, don't you, Mr. Trent?"

౮ඁඁ

As Gregory had surmised, the minute he was out the door this morning Emmeline leaped—well, not quite leaped—out of bed and shrugged into a comfortable pair of old trousers and a sweater as fast as her wound would allow. Then she gingerly made her way downstairs to the living room. Emmeline had every intention of keeping her promise to rest. She slipped a disc into the CD player and waited until the sparkling sounds of Albinoni filled the room. A smile curled around her lips. How she adored Baroque music.

Emmeline pulled a history of the Roman Empire from the glass-enclosed bookcase and settled herself on the sofa. Ever since she could remember she had been a voracious reader. Her reverence for the written word was first instilled in her by her parents, and, after they died, by her grandmother. As a testament, Emmeline always had to have a book to read and every room in the house sported shelves or a bookcase bursting to the seams with biographies, novels, and volumes of poetry that fired her imagination or opened the door to other worlds. Emmeline's natural inquisitiveness had led to an affinity for history. Her mind always wanted to know what happened in the past so that she could better understand why the world was the way it is today.

This soothing interlude worked for half an hour, but in the end, the siren call of her laptop on the desk by the window overlooking the garden was too strong. After yesterday's revelations, Emmeline threw herself into the story with renewed vigor.

౮ඁඁ

Emmeline had been hard at it all day, following leads and

making phone calls. She yawned and massaged her stiff neck. Her eyes ached from staring at her computer screen for so long. She glanced at the Limoges ormolu clock on the mantelpiece. Four o'clock. She couldn't believe it. Where had the day gone? Her stomach growled in protest. She hadn't eaten all day. So she decided to take a small break for tea. She still had some of that delicious poppy seed cake Gran had made when she had been down to see her the previous weekend. That would do very nicely indeed. She rubbed her hands together in anticipation as she made her way to the kitchen to put the kettle on.

Sated and refreshed, Emmeline was ready to get back to work half an hour later. However, her enthusiasm soon evaporated and, in its wake, was an icy fear that pressed against her chest. For an olive-skinned man in a well-tailored navy suit was waiting for her in the living room.

"Ah, there you are, Miss Kirby," he said calmly.

Her first instinct was to run. She half-turned in the doorway, only to find a swarthy-looking young man blocking her path. Emmeline's eyes widened and she sucked in her breath. Before she could utter a scream, he clamped a large hand over her mouth and pulled out a gun from inside his jacket. He slipped his other hand around her waist and nudged her—none too gently—toward the other man. Pain shot up her side as she was deposited like a sack of potatoes onto the sofa.

"I must apologize for Vincenzo, *signorina*. He comes from the country and is still a little rough around the edges," the older man said as he jerked his head in the direction of the armchair. Vincenzo took the hint and stopped looming menacingly over Emmeline.

"Now then, *signorina*," the older man resumed, "allow me to introduce myself."

The fear was ebbing and was fast being replaced by anger at this brazen intrusion into her home. "There's no need. I know exactly who you are, Signor Gamborelli. Your face is well known in international law enforcement circles. The Italian police have been looking for you for years," Emmeline responded with disdain.

The Mafia boss cocked an eyebrow at her, as if he was amused by her boldness. Most likely no one ever spoke to him in such an insolent manner. They wouldn't dare—if they wanted to continue living.

"I see your reputation is well deserved." His English was flawless. He had only the merest trace of an accent.

"Why did you break into my house? What do you want?" Out of the corner of her eye, she saw Vincenzo perched on the edge of his seat, like a panther ready to pounce. At a look from Gamborelli, he relaxed slightly and leaned back.

"*Signorina*, I have indulged you until now, but I would advise you to curb that tongue of yours. One day, it will get you into serious trouble."

Paolo Talamini had used virtually same words only a month before in Venice, where the hunt to find Charles Latimer's murderer eventually led her and Gregory to a Russian spy in the Foreign Office. Well, Talamini, an international industrialist who was hand-in-glove with the Mafia, was now dead. The victim of his own nefarious business dealings. *What goes around comes around*, she supposed. Talamini had tried to frighten her, too. Although Gamborelli was doing a much better job at it, Emmeline still seethed at his gall in breaching the security and tranquility of her home.

She swallowed hard. "To what do I owe this unexpected visit?"

Gamborelli smiled, revealing a row of perfectly even and very white teeth. She guessed that he must be in his midforties. He was a good-looking man, with straight raven hair brushed to the right across a wide forehead. Tell-tale strands of gray were just beginning to appear at his temples. But what was most disturbing were his eyes. They were jet-black and burned with an intensity that sent a shiver slithering down her spine. A killer's eyes. "That's better, *signorina*." He smiled again, but there was no warmth it.

Emmeline said nothing. She gripped the nearest pillow tightly to her side and simply stared at him as he began to pace back and forth in front of the fireplace. "You know, Miss Kirby, you and your friend Mr. Trent have caused a lot of problems for me." He stopped and casually rested an elbow on the mantelpiece. "And I'm in two minds about what to do about it."

"Ambrose Trent is *not* my friend. Until a few days ago, I had never even heard his name."

A deep-throated chuckle erupted from Gamborelli. "Come now, Miss Kirby. Do you really expect me to believe that?"

"You can believe whatever you like, but it happens to be the truth."

Gamborelli sighed. "I am beginning to lose my patience. We know that you were involved from the start in Trent's elaborate charade and his plot to steal my diamonds." Emmeline opened her mouth to refute this, but he held up hand to stop her. "Please it is no use denying it. My men *saw* you with the ill-fated Mr. Armitage the other day at the tea shop. They also saw our friend Trent come to your rescue after that unfortunate incident yesterday down by the Thames. You have my sincere apologies for that." He put a hand over his heart to emphasize his sincerity. "It was rash and foolish—and I must admit rather messy." His brow furrowed in irritation. "Boys like Vincenzo sometimes get a little too enthusiastic about their work. How are you by the way? I hope that your wound is not giving you too much discomfort."

Emmeline's eyes widened in bewilderment. She could hardly believe that she was sitting here in her own living room and one of the most notorious *capos*, a *pezzo grosso* among *capos*, was calmly admitting that he had been responsible for her stabbing. "I...I..." she stammered, at a loss for how to reply.

Gamborelli's lupine smile curled around his lips once more. "Good. I am glad to hear it. Now, as a businessman, I have very little time to waste. And, as you so charmingly pointed out, I cannot count the police among my intimate friends. So please let's stop this little game. All I want is my diamonds and then I won't trouble you any longer." Emmeline very much doubted this. How could he afford to let her live after she had seen him?

"I told you—" Her voice cracked and she had to clear her throat. "—I have no idea what you're talking about and I certainly don't have any diamonds. You can search the house, if you like."

Gamborelli laughed again. "Miss Kirby, you are very amusing. We have already taken the liberty of searching the house. Don't treat me as if I were some naïve child who can be fobbed off with a tall tale. You are much too intelligent and pretty to engage in such tactics. I would be truly sorry to have to hurt you, but if you left me no choice...well, you understand how it is." He shrugged his shoulders apologetically.

"I don't know how else I can convince you. I don't have your diamonds and I don't know where Ambrose Trent is."

He took a step toward her, his hands thrust in the pockets of his custom-made trousers. "I'm in a generous mood today. I will grant you a reprieve. Mind you, it's only a temporary one. I realize that your wound must be bothering you, so I will give you one more day to see sense. Talk to your friend Trent." He leaned down and braced a hand on either side of her, his face was only inches from hers. She felt his warm breath against her cheek. "Tell him he has until tomorrow to return the diamonds. If I do not have them in my hands by tomorrow evening, then I will kill you both."

Emmeline shuddered. Her heart was pounding so hard that she was certain that he could hear it. "You—you can't come into my home and threaten me like this."

Gamborelli's inky eyes bore straight into her very soul. "It was not a threat, Miss Kirby. It was a *promise*. No one crosses me. *No one*. Besides—" He stood up and shot his cuffs nonchalantly. "—I'm Renato Gamborelli. I can do whatever I like."

CHAPTER 21

Chief Inspector Burnell sat in his office and stared out the window, his fingers tapping unconsciously on the medical examiner's report. It came as no surprise. Dr. Meadows had concluded that Armitage had been shot twice in the chest at very close range. Therefore, he likely knew his killer. Burnell's instincts told him this case would be trouble from the outset. But it had gone from bad to worse. First, it was Lord Sedgwick breathing down his neck and now Gamborelli's involvement added a particularly explosive element to the mix. The chief inspector shook his head. He didn't like it. There were so many loose ends that gnawed at the back of his brain. The biggest of these was Ambrose Trent. His men still hadn't been able to track down the bloke.

It was as if he was some sort of ghost who materialized whenever the mood struck him. The only bright spot in all of this was that Superintendent Fenton was not being his usual supercilious and interfering self. Acheson had kept his promise and had a quiet word with Fenton about the delicacy of the matter and MI5's unofficial interest. Inwardly, Fenton was probably seething because Burnell was in charge of the case and would be the one to get the glory. The chief inspector chuckled aloud at this thought.

"Well, it's nice to see you smiling for once, Oliver. You should do it more often it suits you. It brightens your whole face."

Burnell's good humor of a moment ago evaporated. He looked up to find Gregory leaning in the doorway with his arms crossed over his chest. As usual, his double-breasted suit—Savile Row, naturally—was perfectly pressed and the creases in his trousers were razor-sharp. Not a trace of a wrinkle. How did the man manage it? the chief inspector wondered. He grumbled. "Why are you cluttering up my office, Longdon? Haven't you anything better to do than to harass hard-working policemen?"

"Old friends pop over to see one another all the time, Oliver. They don't need a reason to do so."

Burnell swiveled his chair around and folded his hands together on his desk. "Friends do so, yes. However, we do not fall into that category."

"Oh, Oliver, I don't know why you persist in denying it. I mean, after all, you have so few friends, it doesn't do to alienate them." Gregory flashed him a smile that was calculated to stoke the flames. "May I?" He crossed the room and sat down in the chair opposite Burnell, before the chief inspector had a chance to say a word. "I must admit it feels good to get off my feet for a bit."

"Comfy?" Burnell inquired facetiously.

Gregory wriggled his body from side to side for a second and then smiled. "Since you ask, this chair *is* a bit hard but I suppose it will have to do. Thanks for your concern, though."

"I could care less about the bloody chair," the chief inspector roared as he slammed his palm on the desk. "What do you bloody want, Longdon?"

Gregory clucked his tongue. "Temper, temper, Oliver. You'll do yourself an injury, if you go on like that."

Burnell grunted and ran a hand over his face. Gregory chuckled inwardly. He had had enough fun at the chief inspector's expense. It was time to get down to business. "I came to see if you'd made any progress on the case."

"With what? Gamborelli? The girlfriend? The arms? The diamonds? Your friend Trent? Which *particular* aspect were you interested in? They're all so fascinating." He threw a pen across the room in disgust and frustration. The chair gave a squeak of protest under the strain of his weight as he leaned back.

"Ah, I see. It's going that well, is it?"

"Yes, it's going *that* well. You wouldn't happen to have any idea where we could find your friend?"

"I don't think it will help if you haul him in, Oliver."

"On the contrary, I think he would be a treasure trove of information. It's no good protecting him. If you know where Trent is, it is your duty to tell me. Otherwise, I can have you charged with obstructing a police investigation. And believe me, I will take tremendous pleasure in throwing you in prison."

"Oh, Oliver. You wouldn't do that."

Burnell's deep blue eyes glinted with malicious glee. "Wouldn't I?"

"No, I don't think so for an instant. As it happens, I saw Ambrose this morning."

The chief inspector sat bolt upright. "You what?" he spluttered. "Where? Why didn't you inform the police?"

"I *am* informing you, Oliver. Now, be a good chap and listen carefully. I saw Ambrose at his house this morning. He's in over his head and I'm very much afraid he'll do a runner because he knows Gamborelli is closing in on him."

"Why doesn't he come in? We'll place him in police protection."

"He would never agree to that. He doesn't trust anyone—well, except for me and even so he hasn't told me everything."

"What *has* he told you? Did he give you the diamonds?"

"No. I can honestly say I do not have the diamonds." Gregory didn't see the need to mention that he had a fairly good suspicion of where they could be.

Burnell raised a quizzical eyebrow. "Honest? *You*? That's a contradiction in terms."

"Oliver, you're becoming more and more cynical in your old age. I do not have the diamonds."

"Hmph," was the chief inspector's response.

"There's something else, Oliver—"

"Why am I not surprised?" Burnell interrupted. "With

you, there is always something else. And it's usually something rather unpleasant. I don't understand what an intelligent woman like Miss Kirby sees in you. No matter how much she tries to deny it, anyone with eyes can see she's still in love with you. I pity the poor woman. Perhaps that's the problem. *She* needs to get *her* eyes checked. Then maybe she'll see you for what you really are."

The corners of Gregory's mouth twitched with amusement. "Faint heart never won fair lady. Is that jealousy speaking, Oliver? Emmeline happens to have extremely good taste."

"In this matter, she categorically does not. But that's beside the point at the moment. How is she?" Burnell asked in all seriousness.

"I popped over this morning. She looked a bit pale, but the doctor said that she would be all right."

The chief inspector's face muscles relaxed. "Well, that's one bit of good news, anyway."

"If I know my Emmeline, she's probably been at work—against doctor's orders—on this damned story all day. As soon I leave you, I plan to go over to see her again to make sure that she doesn't get herself into too much trouble."

"If it's trouble she wants to avoid, then she should stay far away from you, Longdon."

"Oliver, we digress. I've been thinking about this case."

Burnell's ears pricked up at a tone in Gregory's voice. "Oh, yes?"

"There's something wrong. I think this Gamborelli business is a distraction."

The chief inspector propped his elbows on the desk and rested his chin on his plump hands. "I wouldn't call one of the biggest Mafia bosses a distraction. But do go on, I'm fascinated."

"There are some things I cannot disclose to you because I gave my word as gentleman—"

"Ha."

Gregory ignored this sarcastic outburst. "But I will endeavor to put you in the picture. Ambrose, as we all now know, is not his real name. He assumed another identity to right an old wrong done against his family."

"What sort of wrong?"

"Well, there it starts to get a bit complicated. The story begins with Ambrose's great-grandfather, a Jew who fled with his family from Belgium to London to escape the Nazis during World War II. His great-grandfather was a *diamantair,* a diamond cutter—"

"Diamonds again? What is this obsession with diamonds all of a sudden?"

"Oliver, listen, I'll try to make this story as brief as possible. Ambrose's great-grandfather, like his fellow *diamantairs,* smuggled out as many diamonds as he could. The British government set up the Correspondence Office for the Diamond Industry—COFDI—to register and store these diamonds until the end of the war. The only problem was that when Ambrose's great-grandfather attempted to retrieve his stones, he was told that COFDI had no record of them."

"Bloody hell. What happened?"

"As you can surmise, they were stolen. And not just by anyone. It was a very high-ranking COFDI official, who came from one England's noble families and of course was completely above suspicion."

"Who?" Burnell demanded.

Gregory paused for effect. "Lord Gerald Sedgwick."

The chief inspector's face froze. "Sedgwick," he whispered incredulously. *"Sedgwick?"*

"There's more."

"I was afraid of that." The chief inspector sighed heavily. When it rained, it poured.

"I won't go into all the details, but the present Lord Sedgwick, as we know first-hand, is not the most amiable chap in the world." Burnell snorted his agreement. "Well, history repeated itself in the next generation. Our illustrious QC, MP, desperate to keep the scandal, as well as his own indiscretion a secret, also exacted a toll against Ambrose's family. Understandably, there is only so much one can take and Ambrose has vowed to destroy the Sedgwicks."

"How?"

"Oliver, I'm telling you this in confidence. I must have your word that you will not arrest Ambrose. I remind you that you have no evidence of anything. We are merely having a friendly chat."

"I make no promises, Longdon." Burnell held up a hand to forestall the protest that was about to spill from Gregory's lips. "But I will keep an open mind."

"I suppose that will have to do for the moment."

"I'm glad to hear it. So *how* does Trent intend to destroy the Sedgwicks?"

"Blackmail figures rather prominently in the scenario."

Burnell let out a low whistle. "*Blackmail Lord Douglas Sedgwick?* One of the most powerful men in England? Your friend has taken leave of his senses."

"There I agree with you, Oliver. As I said earlier, he's in over his head. He's intent on exacting revenge, but as they say there's no smoke without fire."

"What are you implying, Longdon?"

"Let's think back a bit, Oliver. Didn't you find Sedgwick's attitude toward your investigation a trifle odd? One would think that a father would do everything in his power to help the police find out who murdered his daughter's fiancé, wouldn't you? Not Lord Sedgwick, though. He seemed almost relieved that Ambrose Trent, rather the man he *believed* to be Trent, was dead. And then there's the matter of Emmeline being sacked. Why would he go out of his way to do that? Could it be because she has inadvertently stumbled across something that was too close to home?"

"You're not saying that Sedgwick—"

"That Sedgwick killed Armitage and is trying to cover it up? Yes, that's exactly what I'm saying."

"You have no evidence of any of this. It's just your friend's word against Sedgwick. And he clearly has an ax to grind with the Sedgwicks."

Gregory smoothed down the corners of his mustache as a sly smile slid across his lips. "Oliver, you know I'm right," he said quietly.

"I know nothing of the sort." Burnell waved a hand dismissively. "I can't go haring off to arrest a man merely on the basis of a suspicion or innuendo. I need irrefutable proof, especially against a man like Sedgwick. Do you have such proof, Longdon?"

"You know very well that I do not."

"Then we appear to be at an impasse."

Gregory leaned forward. "Can't you at least bring Sedgwick in for questioning?"

"What, and put him on his guard? No, that's the last thing we need. We have to let him think that he's managed to fool us."

Gregory smiled impishly. "So what *are* you going to do, old chap?"

Burnell reached for the phone and covered the mouthpiece. "I'm going to have a surveillance team follow Lord Sedgwick day and night. Everywhere he goes, everyone he sees, I'll know about it. Anything out of the ordinary. Anything that doesn't smell right. And I'll haul in the bastard in a flash for questioning."

Gregory extended one of his elegant hands and Burnell shook it. "Thank you, Oliver. You're a man after my own heart. I'm glad we had this little conversation," he said as he rose to his feet.

"What conversation, Longdon? I have no idea what you're talking about. I don't associate socially with the criminal classes. Now, go on." He jerked his head in the direction of the door. "I have work to do. Give my best to Miss Kirby."

The minute Longdon was gone, Burnell turned his attention back to the phone. "Finch, could you come in here a minute? I have a little matter to discuss with you."

ℰℐℰℐ

Emmeline hugged the pillow tightly to her chest in an attempt to stop the trembling. Gamborelli and Vincenzo had left more than half an ago, but she was rooted to the sofa. She wondered if she would ever feel safe in her own home again. How had they gotten in without her hearing them? Worse yet, were they still out there, watching? She suddenly felt very cold and it had nothing to do with the temperature in the room. More than anything, she wished that Gregory were here with her. She needed his calm strength. Where was he? He promised to come back in the evening to check on her. Just as this thought crossed her mind, she heard a key turning in the front door. Relief swept through her body.

Emmeline called out, "I'm in the living room. I'm so glad that you're back—" The rest of her sentence died on her lips.

Her eyes widened and fear seized her as the door from the hall opened because the man who walked into the room was *not* Gregory.

CHAPTER 22

Emmeline scooted down the sofa until her back made contact with the armrest and there was nowhere else to go. "What do you want? Who are you?"

Ambrose took a step toward the sofa. "Emmeline, I'm not going to hurt you. You must believe me. I never meant you any harm."

She held a hand up in warning. "Stay right there. Don't move."

"Fine." He put his arms at his sides and stood very still. "All right? Feel better now?"

"No, not really. How did you get into my house?"

"May I?" He pointed to his jacket pocket. Emmeline hesitated a moment before nodding her head. "Thank you. I got in with this." He pulled out a key. "I had a copy made yesterday when I brought you home after the stabbing. I wanted to be able to get to you quickly in case...well, in case anything else should happen."

Her cheeks flushed a dusky pink. "Oh. You must think me very ungrateful, but I seem to be very nervy since this whole nightmare began."

The mood in the room had changed, so Ambrose ventured, "May I sit?"

She nodded silently, her eyes never leaving his face. "Gamborelli threatened to kill us both if you didn't return the diamonds to him by tomorrow night."

Ambrose rested his elbows on his knees. With his head

between his hands, he murmured, "I was afraid of something like that. Especially after the phone call I received this afternoon."

She touched his arm. "We must go to the police. We have no choice. Chief Inspector Burnell—"

His head snapped up. "No." Then seeing the fear flicker across her face once more, he said more gently, "No, Emmeline. We can't go to the police. Scotland Yard can't help us now. That's why I came. I'm getting you out of London until all of this blows over. Greg would never forgive me if I let anything happen to you. And *I* would never forgive myself."

"But—"

He held up a hand. "No. I will hear no arguments. I'm taking you down to Swaley tonight. The safest place for you right now is with your grandmother. How quickly can you get ready?"

Her confusion left her tongue-tied. How did this stranger know about Gran? For that matter, he seemed to know an *awful* lot about her life and she knew absolutely nothing about him. Not even his real name. "Get ready?" she repeated dumbly.

"Yes. Get ready. Get packed." He gently pulled her to her feet and gave her a push toward the door. "We don't have much time."

"Yes. Yes, of course." A calm seemed to settle over her. It was as if another part of her brain was taking charge, pushing the fear to one side. "It'll only take me ten minutes to throw a few things into a bag."

Ambrose smiled. "Good girl."

Emmeline stopped in the doorway. She cocked her to one side and stared at him for a second. "I'm indebted to you once again, but *who* are you?"

"All you need to know is that I care very much about what happens to you. The rest doesn't matter."

She was not satisfied, but she shrugged her shoulders in resignation. She knew she wouldn't get an answer from him. Then, a thought struck her. "I must ring Gregory to let him know. He said he would pop over and—"

"There's no time. You can ring him once we're on the road or from your grandmother's house. Please, Emmeline, *hurry*."

જ઼ઝ

The charcoal mantle of dusk had draped itself across the city earlier than usual because of the menacing clouds that had been gathering all afternoon. Sergeant Finch was certain the sky would open up at any moment. It never failed. Whenever he was stuck following a suspect, it always seemed to be the storm of the century. What had he ever done to God to deserve such ill treatment? He leaned over the steering wheel and peered out the windscreen again. The sky looked even more ominous than it had just a minute ago, if that were possible. He sighed and resigned himself to his fate. For the last hour and a half, he had been parked across the street from Lord Sedgwick's chambers. From this vantage point, Finch could see the light still burning in Sedgwick's office window. It was widely known that his lordship was a workaholic. Finch was not looking forward to the prospect of pulling an all-nighter in the middle of a raging monsoon.

However, as the first big, fat raindrops started to plummet out of the darkness, the light flicked off in Sedgwick's office. Finch was suddenly alert. Five minutes later, his lordship was standing in the building's entranceway. Sedgwick glanced up at the sky and pulled up the collar of his Burberry. He glanced to his right and left before fumbling for something in his brief case. It was too dark and Finch was too far away to see what Sedgwick stuffed into his pocket. His lordship hesitated a moment as if he were debating with himself about something. Then, Finch saw him square his shoulders and unfurl his umbrella. The sergeant watched as Sedgwick plunged with grim determination into the foul evening. His lordship's car was in the opposite direction. What the devil was the old boy up to?

જ઼ઝ

Gregory shook the rain from his hair as he pressed the doorbell. He waited a few seconds and rang again. No answer. Perhaps Emmeline was sleeping. He quietly let himself in with his key. The light was on in the living room. He poked his head round the door, which was slightly ajar. "Emmy?"

She wasn't there, but a few of the cushions lay on the floor. He frowned. That was not like Emmeline. Everything always had to be neatly in its place. He went back out into the hall and called up the stairs, "Emmy, love, I'm back. *Emmy?*"

No response.

He walked down the short corridor to the kitchen. It was empty too. The hairs on the back of his neck began to tingle as he returned to the hall. A few rumbles of thunder could be heard outside, but the house remained as quiet as a grave.

⊘⊘⊘

As they exited the M20, the storm intensified. The wipers were going at a furious pace but seemed to be fighting a losing battle against the relentless onslaught of wind and water. When the ever-increasing flashes of lightning burst through the murky gloom of the car's interior, Emmeline caught glimpses of Ambrose's tense profile. The only movement was the rhythmic fluttering of his eyelashes as he blinked. He hadn't said a word since they left London an hour ago. His white knuckles were gripping the wheel so tightly that she thought he would wrench it out of the steering column. For the last five minutes, his eyes flicked nervously between the windscreen and the rearview mirror. *Windscreen. Mirror. Windscreen. Mirror.*

She shivered involuntarily. "What's wrong?"

He didn't say anything at first.

"Ambrose?" Her tone telegraphed her urgency.

"I don't want to alarm you, Emmeline."

"Too late for that. From the minute, I stumbled into your…your little intrigue, for want of a better word, I've been alarmed."

He turned his head slightly toward her. She couldn't be

sure because of the wind, but she thought he said, "Sorry."

"It's no use being sorry so you might as well tell me what the problem is?"

His eyes returned to the road. "We're being followed."

Emmeline craned her neck to look over her shoulder. Two steady beams of light were drawing closer. She turned back to face forward. "Are you sure?"

"Yes."

"Do you think it's Gamborelli?" His silence told her more than if he had answered her question. "What are we going to do?" She swallowed hard and tried to keep her voice calm, even though the blood was throbbing against her temples.

"There's not much we can do. This is the only road until we get to Barfrestone. We're not far now." He reached out blindly and gave her hand a reassuring squeeze. "Perhaps a little music will help to soothe our nerves." He fiddled with the radio dial until he found a station playing classical music. "Ah, Vivaldi. That's better, isn't it?"

Emmeline glanced over her shoulder again. The lights appeared to be within a hair's breadth of their tail. "Ambrose."

"I know." He glanced in the rearview mirror again. "If anything happens—"

The jolt was harder than she had anticipated.

Ambrose swerved a little, but managed to regain control quickly. "Listen, Emmeline, if anything happens to me tonight, tell Greg that he was right about the diamonds and Nick. He'll understand. It's all about justice. An eye for an eye. Tell him."

Another bump. This one was stronger than the first. Emmeline's head banged against the window, briefly stunning her. She couldn't see anything except for the lights from the car behind that was trying to run them off the road. There was no one else about.

Well, let's face it, who else would be crazy enough to be out for a drive in the middle of the country on a night like this? Just as this thought crossed her mind, the car lurched.

There was a terrible screeching sound as Ambrose desperately slammed on the brakes. Sheer momentum kept the car hurtling forward into the black abyss.

Something shattered the window.

Emmeline heard a low moan coming from Ambrose. *Boom.* Metal crunching. Her head cracked against the dashboard. The roar of a car engine. Pain. Oblivion.

CHAPTER 23

Gregory had made a thorough search of Emmeline's house. Nothing seemed to be disturbed, except for those damn pillows on the floor in the living room. He was not a nervous man by nature, quite the contrary, but those pillows seemed to be screaming at him. Emmeline would not have left the house without telling him, especially after yesterday's attempt on her life. He grabbed the phone on her desk and punched in her mobile number. One ring. Two rings. Three rings. Click. "Hello, you've reached Emmeline Kirby. I can't take your call…"

He severed the connection when heard her voicemail message.

"Where are you, Emmy?" he asked aloud of the empty room. Instinct told him that she was in trouble. A gnawing fear whispered that she might be hurt—*or worse*. "No." He tried to crush this last thought before it had time to fully formulate in his brain. "No," he said once more. He would *never* allow anything to happen to Emmeline.

He reached for the phone again. He waited a few seconds. "Burnell."

"Ah, Oliver, thank goodness you're still at the office."

"Longdon? Of course, I'm still here. The Metropolitan Police does not have banker's hours like you. And for the thousandth time, it's *Chief Inspector Burnell*. Now, what do you want? I'm very busy."

"Oliver, I didn't ring to engage in one of our little sparring matches. It's about Emmeline."

Burnell heard the strain in Gregory's voice. "What's happened? Has there been another attempt on her life?"

"That's just it. I don't know what's happened. After I left you, I came round to her place straightaway. Oliver, she's not *here.*"

"Perhaps she went out to the corner shop."

"I've been here for three-quarters of an hour. There is no sign of her. Nothing. It's not like her. She knew I was coming back. She would not have gone out without leaving a note or ringing me."

"I agree, that does not sound like Miss Kirby. Has anything been disturbed? Were there signs of a struggle?"

"Only a few cushions on the floor in the living room. Nothing else."

"Cushions? That's why you rang me. Because of a few cushions on the floor. That's a bit much even for you, Longdon. Maybe she simply wanted to get away from you. Did that thought occur to you?" His tone was even and matter-of-fact, but he knew it was not case.

"Oliver, I *know* Emmeline and something is definitely wrong."

Burnell glanced at his watch. Seven o'clock. He sighed and pushed himself wearily to his feet. "I'm on my way, Longdon. Don't touch anything else."

As he shrugged himself into his raincoat, a deafening clap of thunder rattled his office window. Burnell sighed again. He should have become a banker like his father wanted. Then, he'd be tucked up at home at this very moment with a good book and a glass of port at his elbow. Instead, he was preparing to brave the elements to meet with a jewel thief. Why was it that on nights like these the only ones out were doctors, policemen, and murderers?

℘℘℘

Emmeline struggled to open her eyes. Even the slight fluttering of her eyelashes sent arrows of agonizing pain shooting to every corner of her head. She groaned and passed out again. When she came to a few minutes later, she forced herself to concentrate on her surroundings. She had to stay awake. Fighting a wave of nausea, she slowly turned her head and realized she was in a car.

Her fingers fumbled to free herself from the shackles of her seatbelt. Ah, that was better. It was slowly starting to come back to her. The storm. The car with the bright headlights. The crash. They had hit a tree. Her eyes closed for a second. She was so tired.

No, her brain screamed. *Wake up*. Through sheer willpower, her eyes popped open wide. *Concentrate. Think. Use your brain*, Emmeline told herself.

Ambrose Trent. How was Ambrose?

With a supreme effort, her head made the tortuous arc necessary to face the driver's seat. "Ambrose?" Her voice was a hoarse whisper. He didn't move. She cleared her throat and tried again, a little louder this time. "Ambrose?" Still nothing.

Pain and fear suddenly entwined to send her heart racing. She tried to lift her hand to rouse him, but it fell limply back onto her lap. "Ambrose?"

Only the angry rain lashing at the window answered her. Emmeline felt warm tears streaming from the corners of her eyes.

When the next flash of lightning illuminated the car's interior, her worst fear had been confirmed. Ambrose Trent's unseeing brown eyes stared back at her. He was dead.

☙❧

Burnell had been true to his word. In less than twenty minutes, he was ringing Emmeline's doorbell.

"Thanks for coming so quickly, Oliver."

Burnell gave Gregory a pointed look as he was relieved of his raincoat.

"Sorry. Slip of the tongue, Chief Inspector," Gregory said as he ushered Burnell into the living room.

With a practiced eye, the chief inspector's blue gaze swept over the room.

Gregory held up the whiskey decanter and a tumbler. "Can I offer you something to take off the chill and the damp?"

"What would Miss Kirby say if she knew you were being so free with her liquor?"

"For you, Oliv—Chief Inspector, she wouldn't mind. She wouldn't deny you anything. Strange as it may seem, she likes you."

"Hmph."

Gregory took that as an assent and poured two large whiskies. He crossed the room and handed one to Burnell. They clinked glasses. "Cheers."

They were quiet as they each took a sip of the amber liquid.

"Longdon, I have to be honest with you. I don't know what I can do. No crime seems to have taken place here." The chief inspector heard his knees crack as he lowered himself into an armchair. "There is no sign of forced entry. Nothing appears disturbed. Anything gone missing?"

"Not that I can see, but I can't be sure." Gregory slumped down on the sofa, suddenly bone tired. He leaned back and took another sip of the whiskey. "Oliver, it's just a gut feeling I have. I wouldn't come to you if I wasn't certain that Emmeline is in trouble. Isn't there anything at all that you can do to try to find her? Perhaps Sergeant Finch can make a few calls. Speaking of Finch, where is he?"

Burnell stroked his beard. "I don't know why I should tell you anything, but he's following Sedgwick."

For the first time since he entered Emmeline's house that evening, Gregory smiled. He asked eagerly, "Anything on that end?"

"Not yet."

"Mark my words, Oliver. Sedgwick is our man. He's bound to make a mistake soon. He's already rattled."

"I'm not as confident about that as you are, Longdon." Burnell took another swig of his drink. "Sedgwick is one cold fish and I certainly wouldn't want to have him as *my* enemy."

"Precisely. Unfortunately, that is what Emmeline seems to have done single-handedly in her zeal to get to the heart of this bloody story."

"Yes, well," the chief inspector murmured. "About this story. Where *is* your friend Trent? This entire drama can be traced directly to his doorstep."

"I've no idea." Gregory frowned as he rolled his tumbler between his hands. "And in light of Emmeline's disappearance that is beginning to worry me."

"Only beginning to, Longdon? I'd say your friend has been a walking menace from the outset."

Gregory opened his mouth to reply, but at that exact moment his mobile came to life in his pocket. There was an insistent quality to the ringing. His eyes narrowed when he saw the number. "Emmy, where are you?"

Burnell sat on the edge of his seat as he listened to Gregory's side of the conversation.

"Emmy, can you hear me? Emmy?"

Gregory was quiet for several seconds, his jaw tightening. The chief inspector leaned closer.

"Don't worry, darling. Stay calm. Everything will be all right. I promise you. Help will be there soon. Trust me. Yes, I'm coming." Gregory snapped his mobile shut.

"Well?" Burnell prompted impatiently.

"Emmeline's been in a car accident. She's hurt. I don't know how badly. She said someone tried to run them off the road."

The chief inspector jumped to his feet. "Come on, man, don't just sit there." He was pulling his own mobile out of his pocket "Where is she? Wait a minute. *Them?* Who else was with Miss Kirby?"

"Ambrose Trent," Gregory responded without emotion.

Burnell scowled. "What the devil does your friend think he's playing at, Longdon?"

"Nothing. Nothing at all. He's dead."

CHAPTER 24

The voices grew louder as Emmeline gradually began to stir. "I think she's awake," she heard someone say. The voice was comforting, familiar. "Come on, love, open your eyes."

Gran. It was Gran. Emmeline blinked several times. Bright, golden sunlight reflected off the pristine walls of the private room of the hospital in Swaley. "Gran. It is you. I'm not dreaming."

And there in the chair beside her bed sat her grandmother. Her blonde curls—which had long since been coming out of a bottle—bounced with every turn of her head and her warm brown eyes were full of love, affection, and concern.

Helen smiled and stood to lightly kiss her granddaughter's forehead. "Of course, it's me. In the flesh. Perhaps a little bit too much flesh these days," she said as she cast a downward glance at her plump midsection, hidden by her rainbow-hued silk blouse, and shrugged. "But in the flesh nonetheless. Now, what's this I hear? You've been getting into mischief again."

Emmeline tried to sit up, but pain mingled with dizziness forced her to sink back down.

"There, love." Her grandmother adjusted the pillow beneath her head and smoothed her hair away from her face. "You just lie still. You have a concussion and a few bruises.

The doctor says you need to rest quietly."

Emmeline squeezed her eyes closed. "Gran?"

"Yes, darling?"

"He's dead." She opened her eyes and fixed her grandmother with a stare. "He tried to protect me. He was bringing me to you. I don't know how he knew about you, but now he's dead. It's all my fault."

Helen took one of Emmeline's small hands in her own and rubbed it. "Nonsense. Gregory explained it all to me. That young man had his own demons. You simply stumbled into something you shouldn't have by mistake."

"But, Gran, if hadn't been for me—" Emmeline felt tears stinging her eyelids.

"Hush, now. I don't want to hear such talk. You are not to blame. Do you understand me? Emmy, look at me." With her forefinger, Helen gently forced Emmeline's face to turn toward her. Already petite to begin with, her granddaughter looked even smaller against the crisp, white hospital sheets. "You are not to blame."

"Yes, Gran," Emmeline mumbled obediently.

"That lacked conviction, love. You used to 'Yes, Gran' like that when you were a little girl. I didn't stand for it then and I certainly will not accept it from you now."

Emmeline giggled. The situation was still grave and complicated, but suddenly she felt much better. Gran always had a way of making everything better. She was so glad that she was here. "I love you, Gran."

"Oh, my precious girl, I love you, too." Helen brought her granddaughter's hand to her lips and brushed it with a soft kiss. "Now, if you're feeling up to it, there's someone else here who is anxious to see you. He's been here all night. He slept in this incredibly uncomfortable chair. No mean feat for a man nearly six feet tall."

Emmeline raised an eyebrow. "Gregory?"

"No, the Prince of Wales. Of course, Gregory, you silly girl. I think you should see him."

"Yes, I'd like to see him," Emmeline whispered. She realized that she wanted to see him very much indeed.

Helen was surprised by her granddaughter's placid acquiescence. She had expected an argument. "Well, I think that the accident has knocked some sense into you at last. I'll go get him." She hurried to the door. Under her breath, she crowed and rubbed her hands together with glee. "Wait until Maggie hears about this development. She'll be tickled pink."

"I heard that," Emmeline said. "I knew you and Maggie had gotten your heads together and were plotting against me."

Helen lifted her chin in the air and sniffed. "I don't know *what* you mean. If I may say so, that is not a very flattering remark. I'm sure that Maggie will take great exception to it, too."

"Uh-huh. Have it your way, Gran. I know I'm right."

"How did I ever raise such a cheeky, ungrateful girl?" Helen flounced out of the room in mock anger.

Though it sent pain shooting across her skull, Emmeline chuckled. She kept her eyes glued to the door. In the next second, it swung open and Gregory's trim and elegant frame was filling the space. "Hello, Emmy."

His voice was low and thick with affection. He was carrying a large bouquet of coral roses, her favorite. He hesitated a moment on the threshold. She lifted a hand and motioned for him to come over to the bed.

Gregory smiled. "These are for you."

She blushed. "They're lovely. Thank you."

"I'll ask a nurse to put them in water for you," he said as he laid the bouquet on the table. He bent down and kissed her cheek. Gingerly, he sat on the edge of the bed and took her hand in his larger one.

Emmeline saw the purple half-moon smudges beneath his bloodshot eyes and the rumpled state of his navy suit, a testament to his sleepless night by her bedside. She suddenly felt self-conscious in the presence of this handsome man whom she knew so intimately on several levels and yet, didn't know at all.

"How are you?" he asked.

"My head feels like it's going to explode. Other than that, everything is simply spiffing," Emmeline said in a half-hearted attempt to lighten the situation with humor.

Gregory's fingers entwined with her own. "The doctor says that the headaches will probably continue for a few more days, but overall no real damage was done. Thank God. Is your other wound bothering you?"

Emmeline tentatively probed the side where she had been stabbed—was it only two days ago? "It's a bit tender, but it seems to be all right."

He gave her a lopsided grin. "That's good."

They fell silent. It wasn't an uncomfortable silence. They both had a lot on their minds.

"I'm glad you're here." She gave his hand a squeeze to let him know she meant it.

"There isn't any place I'd rather be."

"Gran told me you were here all night."

Gregory looked away. "Well, you know how it is. Someone had to make sure they were taking proper care of you."

"Thank you."

"No need for thanks. Anyone else would have done the same."

"Aside from Gran, I don't think that's true. Gregory?"

"Yes, love."

"I was very frightened." She tasted the saltiness of her tears as they trickled down her cheeks.

He smoothed them away with his thumb. "It's all right. You're safe now."

Emmeline swallowed the lump in her throat and went on, "I really thought I was going to die. First, when Gamborelli and his henchman came to the house and then in the crash."

She felt Gregory press her fingers harder. "Gamborelli? Gamborelli was at the house?"

"Yes, he came to the house yesterday afternoon and threatened to kill me and—and Ambrose—" She choked on the name. "—if the diamonds were not returned. I was in the kitchen having tea. I didn't even hear them enter the house. They were suddenly just there in the middle of the living room."

"There was no sign of forced entry. Burnell and I checked."

"You and Chief Inspector Burnell were at the house?" she asked, surprised.

"Yes, I called Oliver when I didn't find you there."

"Ambrose said they likely had been watching the house and waited until they were sure I was alone."

Gregory gave her a pointed look. "Why didn't you ring me?"

"There was no time. Gamborelli was gone in a flash."

He could see that she was distressed enough as it was, so he didn't press his point. "Never mind. Go on about Gamborelli."

"There's not much else to say on that score. He said he would kill Ambrose and me if the diamonds were not returned by this evening. Gamborelli and his man had barely left, when Ambrose materialized. When I heard the door, I thought it was you. I told him about Gamborelli. He apologized for getting me mixed up in this mess and said he had come to take me to Gran's until everything settled down. I still don't understand how he knew about Swaley and Gran. I wanted to ring you to let you know, but Ambrose said the faster we left the better it would be."

When Gregory didn't say anything, Emmeline continued. "The rest of the story you pretty much know. We were nearing Barfrestone, when this car came up behind us and tried to run us off the road. He hit us hard…twice, I think. I'm not sure anymore. Everything is a bit muddled." She rubbed her temple. "Ambrose lost control of the car. It was dark. So very dark." Her voice fell to a whisper. "And the rain was coming down in torrents. It felt like we were plunging into a black hole. Then we stopped with a loud, jarring boom. The impact stunned me. I heard—"

She closed her eyes, trying to recall that dreadful scene. "I think…I heard a window crack and then Ambrose moan and the other car speeding away. When I looked over at Ambrose, I saw that he was—that he was dead."

Emmeline opened her eyes again. "I don't *remember* anything else after that."

"You managed to ring me on my mobile, while I was still with Burnell at the house. He called the local constabulary and they in turn rang the hospital. I raced down from London as quickly as the traffic would allow."

"And, of course, you rang Gran."

He smiled and ran a finger along her jaw. "Naturally, I rang Helen. It would be more than my life was worth, if she heard about the accident from someone else. Can you imagine?"

Emmeline giggled. "Ooh. It hurts when I laugh."

"Then don't. Just lie there quietly."

"But you make me laugh. I'm so glad you're here. I thought—I thought I would never see you again."

"Silly girl, don't you know that you can't get rid of me that easily?" He kissed her forehead. "Now, we have several things to discuss—"

Emmeline gripped his arm hard. "Wait. I've just remembered something Ambrose said."

"I'm listening, darling."

"He wanted me to tell you that you were right about the diamonds and Nick." She paused. "He said you would understand. He also said it was all about justice. 'An eye for an eye.' Do you understand what he meant?" He didn't respond immediately. "Gregory?"

His mouth was set in grim line and a shadow cast a pall over his cinnamon eyes. "Yes, I understand."

She tried to sit up, but he gently pushed her back down. "Gregory, do you know where the diamonds are?"

He debated how to answer this question and, in the end, decided that it was best to be honest with her. "Yes."

"I see. Did you tell Chief Inspector Burnell?"

Gregory remained silent.

"I take that as a no. Why? Two men have already been killed because of them."

"Emmy, there's a lot going on here that you do not understand."

"Then, tell me. So that I *can* understand. Don't think I'm going to run away from this story. What happened last night only makes me more determined."

Gregory sighed as if he was afraid that this would be her reaction. "It would be best if you stepped away from all this. Stay with Helen for a few weeks until it all blows over."

"You must be joking," she said incredulously.

"This is not a laughing matter. It's deadly serious, Emmy."

"You're telling *me* this."

"All right. All right." He threw his hands up in surrender. "Yes, I know where the diamonds are. For the moment, they are safe where they are."

"Which is where?"

"No, love, I'm not telling you that."

"Hmph." She stuck out her tongue at him.

"A very ladylike response, I must say. I didn't want to tell you my suspicions before because I wanted to protect you. However, rather than having you tearing about, stirring up a pot of trouble, I think the time has come for us to discuss the matter."

"How very magnanimous of you."

"Emmy, are you going to listen or not?"

"I'm listening."

"It really all started with you. I think you were right. I believe Lord Sedgwick is hiding something and is afraid you are getting too close. That's why he maneuvered your dismissal from the paper. He wanted to quash the story on the Ambrose Trent murder—well, the first Ambrose Trent murder anyway."

"Are you saying that you think that Lord Sedgwick killed Armitage?"

"Yes. He has a number of secrets that he wants to ensure remain buried. Forever. Secrets that can destroy his family's name, his reputation, his practice, in short everything he holds dear. Kenneth Armitage, the Ambrose Trent of Hyde Park fame, was blackmailing Sedgwick. I think he threatened to divulge his lordship's dirty linen, if Sedgwick objected to his marriage to Claire."

"Oh, my God. Poor Claire." Despite her row with Claire the other day, Emmeline felt a pang of sympathy for her former friend. "She loved him so much. You saw that for yourself. But what does this have to do with the real Ambrose Trent—if you can call him real. Why *was* he going about under an assumed name?"

"He's the one who put Armitage up to the whole charade."

"What? You mean he's the one who was really blackmailing Lord Sedgwick?"

"Got it in one."

"It doesn't make sense."

"Darling, it's too long of a story to get into here."

"I like long stories. Try me."

"No, I gave my word. Suffice it to say that Ambrose had good reason to want revenge on the Sedgwicks. You have to trust me. He was trying to right an old wrong. I won't say more than that."

"'An eye for an eye.'"

"Yes," Gregory said gravely. "I think Sedgwick found out who Ambrose really was. I believe Sedgwick is the one who tried to kill both of you last night."

"What?"

"Think about it, Emmy. Sedgwick was determined to prevent Claire from marrying Armitage, so he killed him, only to find out he wasn't the man he was really after and the blackmail was still continuing. Then you come along with your big story on Ambrose Trent and he's convinced you're in on the scheme. Another unexpected problem. When you persisted in pursuing the story after being sacked, he was desperate to get rid of you as well. What better way to kill two birds with one stone than an accident in the middle of storm on a quiet country road miles from London? Who would ever connect it to Lord Douglas Sedgwick?"

Emmeline nodded her head carefully as she mulled over his theory. "It makes sense. But I don't understand how the diamonds, Gamborelli, and the missing arms fit into the picture?"

"What if Sedgwick is the go-between?"

"Lord Douglas Sedgwick a traitor? The same Lord Sedgwick who waves the Union Jack at the drop of a hat and never tires of telling everyone he comes from one of the oldest of England's noble families? I can't believe it."

"Exactly, darling. Who would suspect such a man? A respected QC, a member of Parliament with access to all sorts of secrets that you and I don't have."

"Oh, Gregory. If you're right—"

"It would be one of the most embarrassing scandals in modern British history."

"We have to stop him."

"*We*? You are in a hospital bed. What do you think you're going to do? He's already tried to kill you."

She waved a hand in the air. "But he didn't succeed. I'm made of sterner stuff."

"There's also the little matter of Gamborelli having you in his sights."

"We'll figure something out. You just have to get me out of this hospital." Emmeline tried to throw off the covers, but was overcome by a wave of dizziness.

"Aha. That is out of the question. How do you intend to weave the mighty pen of the Fourth Estate if you're on the verge of swooning when you sit up in bed? No, you're not leaving this hospital until the doctor gives you the all-clear. And then—"

"But, Gregory—"

"—and then you're going straight to Helen's house to recuperate."

Emmeline crossed her arms over her chest. "You, Gregory Longdon, are an absolute beast."

"Thank you. I do my best to please," he said with a cheeky grin.

"Well, you've failed miserably. I'll make a deal with you."

He raised an eyebrow. "I do not make deals with invalids on Wednesdays. And as it's Wednesday today, you are out of luck."

This annoyed Emmeline even more. "I am *not* an invalid. Just shut up and listen to what I have to propose."

"Ah. Now, you'd like to propose. I don't accept proposals on Wednesdays either."

"Ugh," she growled and balled her fists at her sides. "I'm not so incapacitated that I can't punch you on the nose."

Gregory chuckled. He always enjoyed teasing her. She always rose to the bait.

"When I get out of this bed, I'm going to throttle you. Since you know I always keep my promises, you had better be prepared."

He only laughed harder. "Emmy, why don't you concentrate on getting well?"

"Aside from a little headache and some dizziness, I'm perfectly all right," she protested.

"And a concussion, and a two-day-old stab wound, and several bruises. Shall I go on?"

"No." She gave him a mutinous look. "But I'll be as right as rain by tomorrow. You'll see. Then we can go after Sedgwick together. You cannot leave me out of this."

Gregory bent down and kissed her tenderly on the lips. He smoothed a stray curl from her forehead. Emmeline smiled and reached up to touch his cheek, certain he had relented. He pressed her hand against his face and returned her smile. "The answer is no. You remain here until the doctor releases you and then you go to Helen's."

The smile vanished and she dropped her hand. "Beast."

"It seems to me we've just been through this. I'm a hardy soul. Insults simply bounce off."

"I'll be more use in London than holed up in the country. Gran will understand."

"Gran will understand what?"

Two pairs of eyes turned as Helen appeared in the doorway.

Gregory stood up. "Helen, talk to your granddaughter. She has this absurd notion that she will leave this hospital and return to London to confront a murderer."

Helen's brown gaze shifted from Gregory to Emmeline.

"She does, does she?" She placed her hands on her hips. "We'll see about that."

"Oh, Gran. Why do you always take his side in arguments? I'm your granddaughter."

"Because," Helen said as she sat down on the bed, "he's perfectly rational and you tend to leap without heeding the dangers staring you in the face."

"Gran."

"It's no good coming over all outraged. Just because I love you, doesn't mean I'm immune to your faults."

Emmeline sucked in her breath. "I never thought I would live to see the day when a blood relative of mine would engage in character assassination with a—" She flicked a disgusted glance at Gregory. "—with a beast."

Gregory and Helen shared a laugh. "On that happy note, I must be getting back to London to see Burnell. I leave you in capable hands. Goodbye, Helen. Lovely to see you again. Take care of this she-devil." He jerked his chin toward the bed as he shrugged into his Burberry. Then, he gave Helen a quick peck on the cheek.

It was unfair that such a beast should look so incredibly attractive, Emmeline thought.

"And me?"

Gregory quirked an eyebrow upward. "And you what?"

"No kind words. You're simply going to go back to London and abandon me here."

The corners of his mouth twitched. "Forgive me, darling." He bent down and kissed her cheek. "What I wanted to say—"

"Yes?" Emmeline looked up at him eagerly.

"What I wanted to say was, listen to your grandmother."

"Oh, go on, get out of here."

"Your wish is my command." In two strides, he was at the door.

"Gregory?"

He glanced over his shoulder. "Yes, love?"

"Thank you for coming. It meant—it meant a lot to me."

Gregory blew her a kiss. "It was nothing. Just get some rest."

"You will tell me how things progress with Sedgwick? By the way, why are you going to see Chief Inspector Burnell?"

"That's my cue to go. Goodbye, Emmy."

The door swung to and he was gone. Emmeline murmured to herself, "What have you discovered that you're not telling me?"

CHAPTER 25

Burnell yawned and took off his glasses. He pinched the bridge of his nose as he rubbed one of his bloodshot eyes with a knuckle. Every part of his body felt tired and his stomach was making subterranean noises. He was not quite in a state of complete exhaustion but neither was he as fresh as a daisy. His shirt was wrinkled, with the sleeves rolled up to his elbows. He had never made it home to his bed last night because he had raced down to Kent with Longdon to take the reins of the case from the local chaps. A case that left him with *another* body on his hands. The elusive Ambrose Trent himself.

The chief inspector shook his head. The closer he got to the truth, the farther it seemed to slip from his grasp. But the one bright spot in this jumble was when Gregory rang to say Miss Kirby would be all right. Thank God for miracles.

Burnell drummed his fingers on the report in front of him. Now to deal with Lord Sedgwick, who had led poor Sergeant Finch on a merry chase across London last night, in that filthy storm no less. His lordship thought he was being clever, but as the report revealed he was not clever enough. *They never learn*, the chief inspector thought.

Men like Sedgwick are so obsessed with their own self-importance they believe they can get away with anything. Even murder. But in the end, this arrogance always caused them to make a mistake. And that was when the chief inspector was right there, ready to pounce. There was a light tapping on his door.

"Come," Burnell bellowed.

Finch popped his head in. "Sir, Lord Sedgwick's solicitor is making loud squawking noises."

The chief inspector cracked a broad smile. "Is he? That's nice."

"He's demanding you either charge his client or let him go."

"A pushy sort of fellow, isn't he, Finch?"

The sergeant smothered a grin. "Yes, sir. A Mr. Hetherington-Soames. Very public school and old boy network."

"One of the hyphenated upper classes. How very grand. Oh, I do feel honored."

"There's more."

"I thought there might be." Burnell folded his hands on the desk and assumed a passive expression. "I'm all ears."

"He insists on speaking to Superintendent Fenton."

"I would have expected no less from someone called Hetherington-Soames. But as Mr. Acheson has already had a word with our dear superintendent about keeping his nose out of this case, I am not concerned. Next item."

"Finally, he said that if Sedgwick is not released *immediately*, he will personally see to it that your name is mud by this time tomorrow. He wanted me to underscore the fact that Sedgwick has a lot of friends in the press. Very adamant he was on this point."

"Thank you, Finch. The point is noted and disregarded. As you know, I don't take kindly to threats. They don't scare me. They only make me think someone has something to hide."

"Yes, sir. I was certain that would be your attitude. What would you like me to do about Sedgwick and Mr. Hetherington-Soames?"

"I think his lordship has stewed long enough, don't you? Perhaps we should go to have a cozy little chat with him."

"Right, sir. I'll have him brought to one of the interview rooms."

"Don't hurry on Lord Sedgwick's account. Remember the upper classes never do anything in a hurry."

Finch smiled again. "I'll keep that in mind, sir."

"See that you do."

ഐഔ

Far from his usual sartorial elegance, Lord Sedgwick was tieless. His white shirt was open at the neck and wrinkled. His face bore a night's growth of beard and his eyes felt gritty. He tapped his fingers impatiently on the table as he and his solicitor waited for Burnell and Finch to make an appearance.

"What does this Burnell think he's playing at, Alan?" Sedgwick demanded. "Doesn't he realize who he's dealing with? I can make life very ugly for him, if he's not careful."

Hetherington-Soames, a distinguished gentleman of sixty-odd years with steel-gray hair and shrewd slate-blue eyes, placed a hand on Sedgwick's arm in an effort to calm him down. "Doug, it won't help matters if you lose your temper. The chap is obviously trying to goad you into making a confession. I know his type. Probably has some grudge against his betters and is trying to make a point."

His lordship shook off his solicitor's hand. "Confession about what? Why has he brought me in? Do you know what this will do to my reputation? This is a gift for my enemies."

"Are you sure you have *no* idea what this is all about? Nothing you want to tell me? I'm your solicitor after all. What is said between us remains confidential."

Sedgwick's eyes narrowed as he sized up Hetherington-Soames. He opened his mouth to say something and then thought better of it. "There is nothing to tell. I'm just as much in the dark as you are."

The solicitor pushed his glasses up the bridge of his nose and nodded. "Very well. If you say so, I must take your word for it."

"How many years have we known each other?"

"Since we were at Eton together."

"And suddenly you're doubting my word? After all the business I've thrown in your direction."

"It's not that I don't appreciate it. I do, most sincerely."

"Well then?"

"I don't like being lied to, especially by an old friend."

Sedgwick was prevented from replying because the door opened and Burnell and Finch walked in.

"Ah, at last, the mighty Chief Inspector Burnell of the Met has deigned to make an appearance."

Before the chief inspector said anything, he pressed a button on the tape recorder in the middle of the table. "Twelve March 10 a.m. Chief Inspector Burnell and Sergeant Finch interview Lord Douglas Sedgwick. His solicitor Alan Hetherington-Soames is present." Burnell inclined his head to the two grim-faced men sitting across from him. "Good morning, Lord Sedgwick, Mr. Hetherington-Soames."

"Spare me your mock politeness, Burnell. What the devil is all this about?"

"My lord," the solicitor cautioned as he patted Sedgwick's arm. "Forgive my client's irritability, Chief Inspector, well justified though it may be. A man his position is not accustomed to spending a night in jail."

"Mr. Hetherington-Soames, I make no apologies. Your client has received the same treatment as anyone else under suspicion for committing a crime."

A feline smile crossed the solicitor's lips. "And what crime would that be?"

"Murder," Burnell said bluntly. "Two murders to be exact."

Sedgwick felt the blood drain from his face and a thin line of perspiration moisten his brow. He wiped the palms of his hands on his trousers and gripped his knees hard to retain an outward appearance of unruffled composure. His voice sounded remarkably steady, when he finally replied, "Murder? That's absolutely ridiculous. Who am I supposed to have killed?"

Burnell missed nothing. Sedgwick was clearly rattled. "Your future son-in-law, Ambrose Trent, or rather I should say the man you and everyone else mistakenly believed was Ambrose Trent."

"You're mad, Burnell. What reason would I have for murdering my daughter's fiancé?"

"Blackmail, Lord Sedgwick. That seems a pretty strong motive to me. The dead man was really Kenneth Armitage. A con man with a long history across the Continent of swindling women out of their fortunes and then leaving them at the altar."

"Chief Inspector, my client is a loving father and a well-respected barrister and member of Parliament. He would not risk his reputation and career by committing murder."

"Oh no, Mr. Hetherington-Soames? Not even if it was to protect his family's name and his career from being destroyed by a scandal that goes back decades?"

Finch thought that if his lordship's complexion turned any paler, he would be considered a ghost. His skin had taken on a chalky-gray hue and his eyes seemed to have sunk into his head.

The solicitor shot Sedgwick a questioning glance. His lordship swallowed once and licked his lips. "You're talking rubbish. Alan, can't you see that this is all part of a smear campaign hatched by my enemies to discredit me? Alan?"

Hetherington-Soames stared at his client for long moment without saying a word. He turned back to Burnell. "Go on, Chief Inspector."

"Armitage was really a puppet on a string."

"How so?"

"He was a front man for the real Ambrose Trent."

"So you're saying that this Trent fellow was blackmailing Lord Sedgwick through Armitage. Why?"

"Revenge. Pure and simple. Apparently, he wanted to get back at the Sedgwicks for something that had been done against his family during World War II."

Hetherington-Soames laughed. "Really, Chief Inspector, you are an amusing fellow. You can't expect us to believe that my client would murder a chap—albeit an unsavory sort from the sounds of it—for a perceived slight done decades ago. I really don't see how you can make such a charge stick. Now then, you mentioned something about two murders. Who else is Lord Sedgwick *supposed* to have killed?"

Burnell's fist was balled tightly in his lap and his jaw was set in a tight line. "Last night in a lonely part of Kent, someone forced a car carrying the real Ambrose Trent and Emmeline Kirby off the road. Unfortunately, Trent was killed. He was shot. Miss Kirby, however, survived and is in hospital with a concussion and assorted bruises."

Sedgwick slammed his palm against his thigh and murmured under his breath, "I knew that little Jewish bitch was working with him."

"Would you care to repeat that, Lord Sedgwick?" Burnell asked with exaggerated politeness.

"No," responded Hetherington-Soames. "My client has nothing more to say at this time. This is merely conjecture on your part, Chief Inspector. You have no proof to back up your wild theories. First of all, Lord Sedgwick was in London all of yesterday."

"That's right. I was in my chambers all night preparing for a very important case in two days' time. That is why it is imperative I be released at once."

"Your junior will have to carry on for you, Lord Sedgwick. I wouldn't make any future plans, if I were you."

"Why you impertinent bastard—"

"My lord, let me handle this. As I said before, Chief Inspector, where is the proof to connect my client to these *alleged* crimes?"

"There is nothing alleged about two bodies and an injured young woman. Your client has already lied. He was not in his chambers all night as he claims. Sergeant Finch saw him leave the building at seven o'clock and he followed Lord Sedgwick—"

"Of all the nerve. I'm a peer of the realm. How dare you spy on me?"

"—followed Lord Sedgwick," Burnell continued as if there had been no interruption. "who was aware he was being followed and so led Finch on wild goose chase across the city before managing to lose him in the Piccadilly Circus Underground station."

"Ah, I have no doubt that Sergeant Finch is a conscientious police officer." Hetherington-Soames bestowed a condescending smile upon the sergeant. "But if, as you admit, he did not actually witness my client attempt to run Trent's car off the road, then alas, you have no case against him."

Burnell's voice was very low. "Your client's car matches the description of the vehicle involved in last night's accident."

"Accident being the operative word. An unfortunate accident."

"Perhaps if you would allow me to continue, I could apprise you of the gravity of your client's situation."

The chief inspector tapped the manila folder in front of him. "This is a forensics report. I think you'll be fascinated by its contents. Shall we see?" He opened up the file. "I dispatched a team to Lord Sedgwick's home this morning and had his car impounded."

"You did what?" Sedgwick exploded with such force that he sent his chair tumbling backward.

"Sit down, Lord Sedgwick," Burnell ordered and watched two ugly crimson spots appear on his lordship's cheeks.

Sedgwick had never been so humiliated before in his life. "You'll pay for this, Burnell." His solicitor righted the chair and tugged at his sleeve, motioning with his eyes for Sedgwick to sit.

"The car was examined by the team. There is some damage to the driver's side headlamp and the front fender."

"In and of itself that is hardly conclusive," the solicitor pointed out.

"And silver paint matching your client's car is evident on Trent's rear fender."

"Again, Chief Inspector, there must be thousands of cars in London, in England in fact, that are identical to my client's. And as for the damage, well, I don't have to tell you I'm sure, about the traffic problem we have in London these days. It could have happened anywhere in the city, at any time I might add, and Lord Sedgwick may not have noticed the damage immediately."

"That of course is true, Mr. Hetherington-Soames. But I don't think there is another silver Mercedes in London that contains the murder weapon in the boot's wheel well."

The solicitor was visibly caught off guard by this bit of information. He cleared his throat and straightened his tie. "Chief Inspector, I would like to confer with my client. Alone. Lord Sedgwick has nothing more to say at the present time."

Burnell smiled. "I'm certain the two of you have quite a lot to talk about." He pushed himself to his feet. "Come on, Finch." He punched the button on the tape recorder and then leaned over the table. "You won't get away this, Lord Sedgwick. All your money and all your friends won't be able to help you. Murder is murder."

"Chief Inspector, I would watch my step if I were you. You could very easily find yourself before a review board for harassing a member of Parliament."

"Harassing?" Burnell made a show of looking around the tiny room. "I don't see anyone being harassed, do you, Finch?"

"No, sir. I do not."

"Sorry, Mr. Hetherington-Soames. I'm afraid you don't have witnesses to substantiate your claim and, as you are well aware, hearsay evidence is not accepted in a court of law."

Burnell turned his back and ushered Finch out of the room, leaving solicitor and client open-mouthed.

The minute the door was closed Hetherington-Soames rounded on Sedgwick. "Start talking, Doug. I want the truth. *Now.* Otherwise, I'm going to walk out of this room and you can go to blazes for all I care."

CHAPTER 26

Burnell and Finch found Gregory sitting in the chief inspector's chair with his hands propped behind his head and his feet up on the desk.

"Who the devil let you into my office, Longdon?" Burnell slapped at Gregory's legs. "Go on. Get up."

"Certainly, Oliver. You only had to ask nicely. I was keeping it warm for you."

His smile infuriated the chief inspector, who grunted in response.

"Lovely to see you too, Finch," Gregory said as he and the sergeant settled into the chairs opposite Burnell.

"How's Miss Kirby doing?" the chief inspector asked, concern etched in every line of his round face.

"The doctor said that she'll be fine. She was awake when I left her. Emmy will probably have to spend another night in hospital and then she's going to her grandmother's until she's fully recovered."

Burnell's thin white eyebrows lifted in surprise. "Miss Kirby agreed to this arrangement?"

Gregory smiled. "She has no choice in the matter. Helen, her grandmother, is the most tender and loving soul on earth, but she's also a general. What she says is law."

The three men exchanged a chuckle. "At the risk of being rude, Miss Kirby has never struck me as a submissive woman.

Quite the contrary. She is very independent and strong-willed. I don't envy her grandmother."

"Don't worry about Helen. She raised Emmy and knows how to handle her. However, you're right. Emmy was ready to leave the hospital with me this morning. That is until she nearly fainted when she tried to get out of bed. She does not want to be left out of things. She *demanded* to be kept abreast of what's happening with the case. As she will be out of harm's way, it would be unfair to keep her in the dark."

"Yes, it would," the chief inspector agreed, "especially because a lot of the evidence that we have is thanks to her dogged efforts to find the truth about Ambrose Trent."

"Oliver, I certainly hope you haven't forgotten my contributions."

"Hmph. It seems to me that your 'contributions' fall into a gray area that borders perilously close to the illegal. And they were extracted with great reluctance, only *after* they came to light."

"Better later than never, I always say."

This elicited another "Hmph" from the chief inspector.

"Come now, Oliver. A chap must remain circumspect in times like these. How are things progressing? Have you collared your man?" Gregory saw Burnell and Finch exchange a look. "Something *has* happened then."

The chief inspector leaned forward and put a hand on Gregory's forearm. "This does not go beyond these four walls. Understood, Longdon? It is highly irregular and more than my career is worth. The only reason I'm going to tell you is because of Miss Kirby."

Gregory tapped the side of his nose. "You can trust me."

"Ha. I doubt *that* very much. However, I will take a chance because you may be many things, but a cold-blooded murderer is not one of them."

"Oliver, I never knew you had such a way with words. You really know how to make a chap feel wanted."

"Longdon, you will never be wanted around here, except in a jail cell, where you belong."

Gregory waggled his forefinger. "Promises, promises.

You'd have to catch me first. And, as I'm a law-abiding citizen, I'm afraid I will have to dash your hopes and dreams on that score."

"Enough of this piffle, Longdon. Do you want hear the latest developments or not?"

"I'm all aflutter with anticipation."

Finch rolled his eyes to show it was beyond him why the chief inspector put up with Longdon.

"We arrested Lord Sedgwick last night."

Gregory rested his chin on his hand. "Do tell. I want all the juicy details."

Over the next ten minutes, Finch explained about how he had followed Sedgwick from his chambers and all across London. Then Burnell picked up the thread by discussing the forensics report about the car and the gun. "The bullets from Armitage and Trent match. I haven't been able to connect Sedgwick to Nick Martin's murder. But we're working on it."

Gregory leaned back in his chair and remained quiet as he mulled over everything he had just heard.

"Well, Longdon? No insightful comments? No pithy words of wisdom?"

"Oliver, I tell you, it all seems to fit together, but—"

"But what?" Finch prompted.

"Much as I'd like Sedgwick to be the killer—there's no one more deserving of the villain's role in this drama of ours—I can't help wondering whether we've got the wrong end of the stick."

Burnell pounded his fist on the desk. "What? This after you practically shoved it down my throat that Sedgwick was our man."

"Yes, yes, I know," Gregory said soothingly, "It's just that—we all despise Sedgwick for the devious bastard that he is. However, we can't deny the fact that he is an extremely intelligent and wily man. After all, he wouldn't have gotten as far as he has in life if he wasn't."

The chief inspector nodded his head warily. "His family's name and money greased the wheels a bit, but go on."

"I've been sitting here trying to fathom why such a cunning chap would suddenly go against his nature and use his own car to commit the crime, let alone hide the murder weapon in it. One other thing that seems a bit odd is that Sergeant Finch chased Sedgwick *on foot* and through the Underground. Where was his lordship's car that entire time? You must agree that it simply doesn't make sense." Gregory looked from Burnell to Finch. "Does it, chaps?"

The chief inspector stroked his beard meditatively.

Finch was the first one to break the silence. "Sir, if Sedgwick is not the murderer, that means—"

"That the real killer is having a jolly good laugh at our expense."

"Someone like Gamborelli, perhaps?" Gregory asked.

"It's possible. We can't overlook anyone or make any assumptions. You can see where that has gotten us so far. Finch, keep digging until you find out where *exactly* Sedgwick was the night of Armitage's murder. I know we couldn't discover his alibi the first time we checked, but he had to have been somewhere. And find out where the devil he was for those two hours last night when you lost track of him. Also get on to Mr. Acheson. Maybe MI5 can help us out with this one."

"Right, sir. At once." The sergeant quickly left the room.

Burnell turned his blue gaze on Gregory.

"No need for thanks, Oliver. I'm glad I could be of assistance to Scotland Yard. Always a pleasure. Any time you feel the need to go over the particulars of a case, feel free to give me a ring."

"It's Chief Inspector Burnell and you've just complicated my life no end."

Gregory smoothed the corners of his mustache and smiled, knowing his eyes were filled with mischief. "If I weren't around, *Oliver*, imagine how very dull your life would be."

"Longdon, I ought to—" Whatever he had intended to say was cut off by the shrill peal of the telephone. "Hold that thought. I'm not finished with you yet. Burnell," he barked into the receiver. "What?" His face reddened and his eyes bulged. "Would you care to repeat that? I don't think I heard you properly."

Gregory frowned. "What is it?" he mouthed silently.

The chief inspector flapped his hand at him. "When? I see. What reason did he give for telling us this now?" He sighed. "No. I'm on my way downstairs." He replaced the receiver in its cradle and stared at Gregory.

"Don't keep me in suspense, Oliver? What's happened?"

"I knew this case was going to be trouble." Burnell shook his head wearily. He suddenly felt very old and tired. "What's happened is that Lord Sedgwick has just confessed to the murders of Armitage and Trent."

❧❧❧

The news exploded virtually the minute it was known. It was the lead story in all the papers the next morning, while the BBC and Sky News had been airing segments on Lord Sedgwick's bombshell confession since the previous evening. It had even sent ripples through the foreign press, which had picked up the story because of Sedgwick's prominence on the world stage.

The throbbing in his temples only seemed to intensify as Burnell looked out his office window at the horde of reporters and camera crews camped out on the street below. "I should never have gotten out of bed this morning," he muttered under his breath. "Wait a minute. I never made it *to* my bed last night. Bloody Sedgwick." He wanted to throttle his lordship with his bare hands.

The chief inspector went to his desk and violently yanked open the top drawer. He tapped out two aspirins from the bottle he kept there and swallowed them down with his coffee, which had gone cold by this time. Naturally. Nothing seemed to be going right lately.

There was a knock at his door. Burnell grunted. *Now what?* "Come in."

"Sorry, sir," Finch said as he entered. He stifled a sneeze. "Sorry," he mumbled again. Poor chap. He had caught a cold as a result of his nocturnal wanderings after Sedgwick. Finch looked as miserable as the chief inspector felt.

"What is it, Finch?"

"Superintendent Fenton suggested that as this is your *special* case—he made sure to underscore *your* case—you should go outside and make a statement to the press. He left the impression that it was more an order than a suggestion."

The corner of Burnell's mouth lifted in a half-smile. "Typical, isn't it, of our fearless leader? Normally, he relishes the opportunity to appear before the cameras in his exquisitely tailored Savile Row suit. However, as this business is a bit unsavory, to say the least, he is quite willing to step out of the limelight and throw me to the lions. Thank you very much, Superintendent bloody Fenton." The chief inspector lifted his coffee cup in mock toast to his superior. "There is no loyalty left in this world of ours, Finch. Nowadays, it's everyone out for himself or herself."

"Sadly, that's very true, sir." Finch sniffled and he sneezed again. "Except that there is one person who still knows the meaning of loyalty."

"You mean aside from you and me?"

The sergeant smiled. "Yes, sir, aside from us. That would be Miss Kirby. She's always been fiercely loyal to her friends and—Longdon."

Burnell dropped his head between his hands. "Longdon. I wish that man never darkened my doorstep." He looked up again. "But yes. Miss Kirby is among that rare breed these days who knows the meaning of loyalty—and love, I believe."

The sergeant nodded.

"Unfortunately, Finch, that's what's going to get her into trouble. Well, already has gotten her into trouble too many times to count. Let's hope there never comes a day when we're not there to protect her."

The sergeant arched his eyebrow knowingly. "From danger or from Longdon?"

"Aren't they one in the same thing, Finch?"

"Is that a nice thing to say, Oliver?"

Burnell grunted. "Speak of the devil." He leaned back in

his chair and cast a glance toward the door. "Longdon, how do you always manage to get in here? Are you bribing someone?"

"Oliver, I'm shocked that you would suggest such a thing. I would never dirty my hands in such a sordid manner."

"No, only by stealing jewels and driving chief inspectors mad."

Gregory clucked his tongue as he walked over to the desk. He put the package he was carrying under his arm down and gracefully draped his body into the chair. "May I sit?"

"You're already sitting."

"Oh, so I am." Gregory flashed him a smile. "Funny how that happened."

Burnell sighed. He jerked his head toward the door. "Go on, Finch. Tell Fenton I'll be down in half an hour to make a brief, *very brief*, statement to the press."

"Very good, sir."

The sergeant had his hand on the doorknob when Burnell halted him. "Finch, any progress on Sedgwick's alibis?"

"No. I spoke to Mr. Acheson and he promised to have a discreet nose round. He said he would ring me this afternoon."

"I suppose that's the best we can do for time being. All right. Thanks."

Finch nodded and quietly closed the door behind him.

The chief inspector rested his head against the back of his chair. "So, Longdon, to what do I owe this return engagement of yours?"

"I was wondering what Sedgwick had to say for himself. What made him decide to confess knowing all the consequences that would follow?"

"Apparently, the burden of keeping all the lies had become too much for him. He said that it was a father's and husband's duty to protect his family. He knew Armitage was a scoundrel of the lowest order and couldn't bear the thought of such a man marrying his darling Claire."

"I see. And what did his lordship have to say about Ambrose?"

"Well, naturally, he *had* to kill Trent. He was the mastermind behind the entire scheme. Once he was out of the way all his troubles would be solved. But then, the horror of what he had done became too much for him so he decided to come clean."

"Uh. Huh. Confession is good for the soul?"

"Something like that."

"Oliver, you don't believe all that rubbish, do you?"

"It's not what I believe, Longdon. It's the story that the evidence has to tell. At the moment, the evidence seems to be pointing directly at Lord Sedgwick. Until something surfaces to the contrary, I have no other choice but to keep him locked up. However, he will likely be out soon. His solicitor is trying to arrange bail as we speak."

Gregory tapped his fingers on his package. "May I see Lord Sedgwick?"

Burnell planted his feet on the floor with a heavy thud and leaned forward. "Have you lost your mind? What do you think would happen to me if word got out that I allowed a known jewel thief to visit a suspected murderer?"

Gregory looked at a spot somewhere over Burnell's shoulder. "*Alleged* jewel thief. Remember it's alleged jewel thief. It was merely a thought. I have a few questions for his lordship."

"You talk to him without his solicitor present and you'll be accused of being a police agent, which could bollox the whole case." Burnell pointed at Gregory's fingers. "What *is* that incessant drumming? And what is that parcel?"

"What? Oh, you mean this?" He lifted the package, which was wrapped in heavy brown paper. "It's a book. I thought that if I got in to see Sedgwick, I'might bring him something to read. After all, all those long hours in his jail cell with nothing to do but stare at the ceiling must be terribly dull."

"Something to read for Lord Sedgwick?" Burnell asked incredulously. "You have taken leave of your senses."

"You can examine the book, if you like. I promise there are no files hidden in the binding. If you don't trust my word, take a look. I have nothing to hide and I know you're dying to satisfy your curiosity."

The chief inspector's blue eyes searched Gregory's face,

which held an inscrutable expression. What was the man up to? For Longdon was always up to *something*. It was like an incurable disease.

In the end, Burnell pulled over the package and carefully tore open the paper wrapping. "Why, it's a—"

"Book. As you may recall I said that. You should really learn to trust your fellow man now and then, Oliver."

"I don't understand, Longdon. What are you up to?" Burnell turned the leather-bound book over and flicked through a few pages. It was obviously a first edition and in mint condition.

Gregory put a hand to his chest theatrically. "Up to? Me? I don't know what you mean. I happen to be an avid fan of James Bond. May I have my book back?"

The chief inspector scratched his head. He turned the book over again, before reluctantly relinquishing it to Gregory. "I don't know what you have up your sleeve, but I suggest that you abandon any nefarious plots."

"Really, Oliver. I think you have been watching too many old movies and have become paranoid in your old age."

"We'll see. Now, get out of my office. Unlike some people who shall remain nameless—" Burnell gave Gregory a pointed look. "—I have work to do."

☙℧☙

Gregory was still chuckling to himself as he walked out of Scotland Yard and into the bright March sunshine. He shouldn't really tease Burnell so mercilessly, but the chief inspector made it too irresistible not to.

His attention was drawn to the mass of reporters gathered outside the building, waiting for any morsel of news. He shouldn't have exited on Victoria Street, although he imagined that the Dacre Street side was not much better. Ah, well. He had strong elbows. He would just have to muscle his way through the throng. Suddenly, the crowd surged forward toward a taxi that had pulled up to the curb. From his vantage point, Gregory couldn't see who had elicited such a response.

However, it provided a perfect distraction that would allow him to slip away unmolested. He scooted round the rear of the inquisitive group and had taken only a few steps when he heard a familiar voice. "Do you mind? No, I have no comment. Please let me pass."

Gregory turned back to see Claire, all golden and flustered, trying to get out of the taxi. He pushed his way through until he was by her side and grabbed her elbow. "Claire, are you all right?"

Claire's green eyes, so much like her father's, widened in surprise. "Gregory? What are you doing here?"

"Never mind. Follow me." With great difficulty, he managed to clear a path for them through the crush of reporters. Gregory didn't stop until they were safely inside the building.

Claire brushed back a stray strand of her long blonde hair that had come loose. She tried to catch her breath, as she glanced outside. "They're beasts. All of them. They take pleasure in other people's suffering. My car's at the garage for repairs. Otherwise, I wouldn't have taken a taxi. I don't know what I would have done, if you hadn't come to my rescue." She tilted her head slightly to give him a watery smile. "My knight in shining armor."

"It's a bit tarnished after tangling with that lot. Are you all right?"

Claire patted herself. "Yes, I think so." Impulsively, she threw her arms around his neck and whispered in his ear, "Thank you."

"Don't mention it." He patted her shoulder soothingly. As he pulled away, the book dropped to the floor.

"Oh, sorry. My fault." Claire was quicker than he was. She bent down and scooped it up. "James Bond? Is this a secret vice, Gregory?"

He smiled. "Actually, I popped over to give it to a friend of mine. I thought he might like it. But unfortunately, he's rather busy at the moment so I'll have to come back another time. Another friend of mine, Nick Martin, was a huge James Bond fan and recommended this book highly."

Claire listened politely, but her mind was clearly somewhere else. "I see." She bit her thumb. "I suppose you know why I'm here."

"I can guess. Your father?"

"The whole thing has been a nightmare. First Ambrose." Her voice caught in her throat. "Now finding out that Dad— that Dad—" A sob wracked her slender frame.

"There. There." He patted her arm. "I'm sure everything will work out in the end. The truth always finds a way to come to light."

Claire looked up at him with her tear-stained face. "Do you really think so?"

"Yes, I do."

"It's been worst for Mum. She's been a nervous wreck since last night. She wanted to come down today, but I persuaded her not to until—" She waved a hand toward the press on the other side of the door. "—until the initial brouhaha settles down."

"Very wise. Can I give you a lift anywhere?"

Claire wiped her tears with the back of her hand and squared her shoulders. "No, thanks. I promised Mum that I would see Dad and tell her how he's bearing up."

"All right. Keep your chin up." He gave her elbow a squeeze. "I'll be off." He started to walk away.

"Gregory, wait."

He turned on his heel. "Yes?"

"It's awfully decent of you to be so kind to me, after what's happened with Emmeline. I suppose you heard about our row the other day."

"I did, yes."

"It would be only natural for you take her side in the matter, seeing as the two of you are...well, you know."

"I haven't taken any sides. It's between you and Emmeline."

"I wouldn't blame you if you did. How is she by the way?" Claire asked tentatively.

Gregory frowned as he remembered Emmeline looking very small against the sterile sheets of the hospital bed. "She's fine. She's gone to spend some time with her grandmother."

Claire's eyes widened in surprise. "Did she? I hope there's nothing wrong with Helen."

"No, nothing like that. Emmeline has been working herself too hard lately and, what with being sacked, Helen thought it might be a good idea for her to get away from London for a few days. Fill her lungs with some country air, and all that."

"That sounds like Helen. At least Emmeline's being looked after."

"Have no fear with Helen hovering about. Now, I must dash. It was nice to see you, Claire." He gave her a quick peck on the cheek and was gone.

CHAPTER 27

Emmeline had been comfortably ensconced at her grandmother's graceful Tudor-style home for one day and already she was chafing to get back to London. It wasn't that she didn't want to spend time with Gran. Helen was the person she loved most in the whole world. Gran had raised her here after her parents died. Emmeline had fond memories of helping Gran with the baking or gardening or going on long, rambling walks through the woods.

Above all, she remembered the winter afternoons spent snuggled against Gran in front of a crackling fire as they devoured Agatha Christie novels and spy thrillers or poured over the images in a book about Renoir or Canova. Emmeline's love affair with art began on those afternoons long ago. She also had Gran to thank for introducing her to the beauty and elegance of ballet.

At this moment though, Emmeline wished she were back in London. She had been following the coverage on Lord Sedgwick's confession and she wanted to be in the thick of things.

Gregory had rung several times to check on her and to keep her informed about the latest developments in the case, but it was not same as being there on the spot. One had to rely on the impressions of others, which were highly subjective. No, she was not satisfied with her banishment in the country. It left a lot to be desired.

"If you scrunch your forehead any harder, young lady, you will have a relapse and have to go right back into hospital."

Helen was standing above her.

"What? Oh, sorry, Gran. I didn't hear you come in."

"The way the wheels were turning in that brain of yours, I'm not surprised. Emmy, you're here to rest. Forget about London."

A streak of black fur came bounding into the room and straight onto Emmeline's lap. "Down MacTavish." But Helen's Scottish terrier ignored his mistress and immediately proceeded to lick Emmeline's face. "You naughty boy. Emmy's sick. She does not need you slobbering all over her."

MacTavish halted for a second and cocked his head at Helen in askance.

"You know very well what I'm saying, you little devil." Helen wagged a finger at him. "Down, now."

Emmeline laughed as the little dog daintily hopped off the sofa and curled up at her feet. "Really, Gran. He wasn't doing anything."

MacTavish barked his agreement.

"I see that I have been cast as the villain and am clearly outnumbered. So I will go to the kitchen and start making some lunch for us." Helen stood and bent down to kiss the top of her granddaughter's head. "I love you, my precious girl. I just want you to get well." She caressed Emmeline's cheek. "I've been quite worried about what's been happening to you over last few days."

Emmeline squeezed her grandmother's hand and kissed her palm. "I know, Gran. I love you too. I'm the luckiest woman in the world because I have you as a grandmother."

"Oh, piffle. Now, I better start on that lunch before we both end up blubbering here in the living room. And you—" She pointed at MacTavish, who barked again. "—the four-legged bane of my existence, you watch over Emmy and see that she doesn't get into any trouble. Understood?" He barked and emitted a low growl to show that he was worthy of her confidence. "Good."

Emmeline giggled. "Ooh, my side still hurts when I laugh."

"Shall I get you something, love?"

"No, Gran. I'll be all right. What more could I want? I have MacTavish to protect me."

Helen gave the dog a doubtful glance. "I don't know about that. But at least he's a loyal little ruffian. Aren't you?" She bent down scratched behind his ears. "Can you imagine the havoc on the Ark, if Noah had picked two of *him*? It doesn't bear thinking about."

MacTavish got up and chased his tail twice before settling back at Emmeline's feet.

"He knows you've just insulted him."

"It serves him right for taking sides against me. Emmy, why don't you lie back and have a little nap before lunch?" Helen eased the pillows behind her granddaughter's head. "Close your eyes and forget about Lord Sedgwick and Claire's fiancé and the all the rest of that nasty business."

"Message received and understood." Emmeline gave Helen a crisp salute and dutifully closed her eyes. She had to admit that she was very tired. Perhaps a nap would help to put things into perspective.

৩৩৩

Half an hour later Emmeline awoke with such a start that she upset MacTavish, who jumped up onto her lap. "Sorry, old chap." She gently took his face between her hands and kissed his wet nose. "I didn't mean to scare you."

Helen came bustling into the room, drying her hands on a towel. "Emmy, are you all right? I heard you call out."

"I'm fine, Gran. It's just—"

"Just what? Shall I ring the doctor?"

"No, nothing like that. Honestly. I feel fine. I had a...a bad dream. I think."

"What do you mean *you think*?" Helen felt her forehead. "You don't have a fever."

Emmeline shooed her away. "I already told you. Physically, I'm fine. But something's...wrong. I remember thinking that in my dream and then I suddenly woke up. I think my brain is trying to tell me something. Something I've missed." She squeezed her head between her hands. "I simply don't know what it is."

Helen pulled her hands away and gently pushed Emmeline's shoulders back down. "Never mind. If it's important, it will come back to you. It's not good for you to overexert yourself."

Emmeline would not be put off. She scrambled up on her elbows. "I was thinking about Lord Sedgwick and how he killed those two men to protect Claire."

"Yes, yes. Well, to a certain extent, I can understand and sympathize with the man. It is difficult for any parent to sit by idly and watch as his or her child make a mistake. Parents instinctively want to shelter their child from all bad things. However, I don't think I would go as far as to murder another human being unless, of course, your life was in danger. Then heaven help that person."

Emmeline laughed. "Gran, my hero."

Helen laughed, too, and gave a dainty curtsy. "Oh, go on. I'll be back in a tick. I just want to make sure lunch doesn't burn. It will probably be ready in about ten minutes."

"Hmm. Smells delicious, as usual. I can hardly wait."

"Good. Then I expect you to eat. You look like you've lost weight again."

Emmeline sighed. It was the same story every time she came down to Kent. "No, Gran. I have not. It's simply your imagination."

"Hmph. We'll see about that."

Emmeline settled back and stared at the ceiling. She could hear her grandmother moving about in the kitchen. It bothered her. What was it that she had dreamed? It was on the edge of consciousness, a hair's breadth out of reach. If only she could remember. MacTavish chose this moment to start walking all over her. "Ooh," she whispered. "Gran's right. You are a devil." He cocked his head and gave her a wounded look. "But a lovable one. Despite what Gran says, I think if you and your double had been on the Ark, you would have been the life of the party."

MacTavish barked.

The fog suddenly cleared. "The Ark. Of course. Why didn't I see it earlier? Everyone has two. I've been so very wrong about everything. I just hope it's not too late. Gran," Emmeline yelled and leaped off the sofa. "Gran."

"For heaven's sake, what is it now? And *what* are you doing up?"

"Gran, I have to go back to London. At once."

"I beg your pardon? I don't think I heard you properly. I thought you said you were going back to London."

"I did. Can I borrow your car?"

Helen's brown eyes narrowed and she put her hands on her hips. "No, you certainly may not. You are in no condition to be driving for two hours. Have you forgotten that you have a concussion?"

"Then will you give me a lift to the train station? Either way, I'm going back to London. I'll just nip upstairs to get my bag. I'll be ready to go in ten minutes." With that, she hurried out of the room.

Helen looked down at MacTavish. "My granddaughter is stark raving mad." The dog barked and wagged his tail. "Oh, so now, you're trying to get into my good graces again. You fickle creature. Come on."

MacTavish barked again and followed closely on her heels.

CHAPTER 28

The train pulled into Charing Cross at four-thirty. Emmeline had tried unsuccessfully several times to ring Gregory on his mobile. She didn't want to leave a message. She tried to call Chief Inspector Burnell, but was told he was tied up. Emmeline stressed that she had some vital information about the Sedgwick case and asked that Burnell return her call as soon as possible.

She was able to hail a taxi almost immediately and they were soon wending their way through the afternoon traffic. Twenty minutes later, they were pulling up to the curb in front of Lord and Lady Sedgwick's Lowndes Square mansion. She paid the driver and hurried up the stairs.

The butler opened the door virtually the instant she rang the bell.

"Hello, Albert. Is Lady Sedgwick at home?" Emmeline asked breathlessly. "It's rather urgent."

"Yes, Lady Sedgwick is at home. If you'll just wait here a moment, Miss Kirby, I'll let her ladyship know you're here."

"Of course. Thank you, Albert."

He inclined his head and noiselessly disappeared up the stairs.

Emmeline paced restlessly in the hall while she waited for the butler to return. She was not looking forward to this interview.

Albert returned after a few moments. "Lady Sedgwick is

in the library. She said that you may go straight up."

"Thanks, Albert. I know the way. No need for you to show me up."

He sniffed and stepped aside to allow her to pass. "Very good, miss."

At the top of the stairs, she turned right. She tapped lightly on the library door. A muffled "Come in." came from the other side.

Emmeline turned the knob slowly and quietly slipped into the elegant room. She had always loved the library. There was something very reassuring about the rows upon rows of leather-bound volumes in the floor-to-ceiling sunken bookshelves. Lady Sedgwick was standing at the window that overlooked the garden. She had her back toward the door. "Lady Sedgwick, it's me, Emmeline." She didn't know why she was whispering. "Lady Sedgwick?"

A mournful sigh escaped Vanessa's lips and her shoulders drooped forward. Without turning around, she said, "I knew you would come. Sooner or later, I knew you would come."

Emmeline didn't need to see her ladyship's face to know she was crying.

Emmeline took half a step forward and hesitated.

"Where are my manners? Sit down. Please," Vanessa implored as she turned away from the window and gestured toward the two deep-moss-green armchairs by the fireplace.

Emmeline crossed the room and waited until Vanessa had lowered herself onto one of the chairs. Then she sat down uneasily on the edge of her seat. An uncomfortable silence settled in the short space between them. Her ladyship was cradling a silver-framed photo against her chest.

Emmeline's eyes searched Vanessa's face. The tears and tension of the last week had taken a toll on her natural beauty. The lines on either side of her mouth looked deeper and the fine spray of wrinkles surrounding her lovely brown eyes seemed to have multiplied.

"May I see?" Emmeline asked softly and held out her hand.

Vanessa stared at her for a moment, as if she didn't understand the question and then she loosened her grip. She gave it to Emmeline. It was a photo of Vanessa, Lord Sedgwick, Claire and another man Emmeline didn't know. "That was taken about ten years ago in Lake Como."

"Of course. I've been to Lake Como. It's beautiful there. It must have been taken when Claire was at university. I remember she wore her hair in a short bob that year. Who's this man?"

Vanessa smiled fondly. "Oh, that's my brother Alex. He's in the army and was stationed out in Italy for several years. He managed to get a week's leave. His wife had died six months earlier and he was still at loose ends, so he joined us in Como. The trip did wonders for him."

"Family is the best medicine." Emmeline glanced at the photo again. "You all looked so happy."

Her ladyship's voiced cracked. "Oh, we were. Alex and his wife were never able to have children, so they doted on Claire. She was like a daughter to them. Claire adored them, too. She's especially close with Alex, always has been. But—" Vanessa choked back a sob. "—things change very quickly in this world of ours. I wish we could turn back the clock to that summer. Things were much simpler then."

They were both quiet again, each lost in her own thoughts. Finally, Emmeline tore her gaze from the photo and gathered her courage. "You said you know why I'm here."

"Yes," Vanessa whispered. "You came because of Doug."

Emmeline nodded, not trusting her voice. She cleared her throat. "I'm sorry, Lady Sedgwick."

Vanessa smiled through the tears that were again trickling down her cheeks. She reached out and squeezed Emmeline's hand. "You were always a thoughtful and sensitive girl. I was so happy when Claire found such a wonderful friend. And Maggie, too."

Emmeline didn't know how to respond. Tears stung her eyelids. She looked down at Lady Sedgwick's hand covering her own.

"You realize that he did it for me, for us, for our family. Doug always took his role as protector seriously. I've been sick with worry since he was arrested last night. And then when he confessed—" Vanessa swallowed the lump that had suddenly formed in her throat.

"Lord Sedgwick confessed because he knows you killed Kenneth Armitage, the man who posed as Ambrose Trent, the man who was Claire's fiancé," Emmeline said softly. "Did you also try to kill the real Ambrose Trent and me the other night? It's all right. You can tell me. I won't hold a grudge. I realize you were only trying to protect Claire. That's what every parent does."

"I—I—" Vanessa's voice was a dry croak.

"Mum, what's going on here?"

They both looked up to find Claire standing in the doorway.

❦❧❦

"Sir, this just came in from Mr. Acheson."

"I hope it's good news, Finch."

"That depends on what you consider good news."

Burnell raised an eyebrow and waggled his fingers for the file. He felt a bit self-conscious when he had to slip his glasses on to read the report. "He was with the prime minister. Why the bloody hell didn't the fool tell us that? What about the night Armitage was murdered?"

"Continue reading. It's all in there. Mr. Acheson was very thorough."

The chief inspector was silent for a few minutes as he skimmed the rest of the report. He slammed the file shut, when he came to the last paragraph and took off his glasses. "Damn and blast. We've been blind, Finch. Perhaps I ought to retire this very instant to a nice little cottage in the country and grow turnips."

The sergeant stifled a smile. "I can't really picture you as a gardener, sir."

"Well, I suppose not. So perhaps I had better stick to this job. How could we have been so blind?"

"I don't think that we can really blame ourselves. She deceived a lot of people."

"I don't care about the others. I care about me." Burnell poked his chest with his thumb. "Get your jacket, Finch. A certain lady has a lot of explaining to do. And a word of advice, never get involved with the idle rich. It can only lead to trouble."

"Yes, sir. I will bear that in mind. Oh, I nearly forgot. A messenger just dropped off this package." Finch handed it to the chief inspector.

"What is it?"

"I couldn't say, sir, but it's from Longdon."

"Longdon? I don't have time for his games now. I have a murderer to deal with. Leave it here on my desk. I'll open it later. No doubt it's one his little jokes."

⌘

Claire pushed the door closed and leaned against it. In her stylishly cut beige suit and with her golden hair cascading to her shoulders, she looked like a model posing for a *Vogue* advertisement. "Mum, what's going on here?" she repeated. "*Emmeline*? I'm surprised to see you. I thought Gregory said you were down in the country."

"Hello, Claire," Emmeline replied stiffly. "I was down in Kent, but I came back this afternoon. Gregory doesn't know I'm back yet."

Vanessa stood and opened her arms. "Darling, come join us. Emmeline and I were having a nice little chat." When her daughter didn't move, she asked nervously, "Did you see Dad? Is he all right?"

Claire's green gaze shifted between her mother and Emmeline. "It didn't sound like a nice chat."

"Lady Sedgwick, perhaps I should go. You need some time with Claire to talk about everything." Emmeline stood and slung her handbag over her shoulder, before lightly touching Vanessa's arm. "If you like, I can ring Chief Inspector Burnell. You have nothing to fear from him. I assure you. He's very professional and understanding. He'll be discreet."

Lady Sedgwick folded Emmeline in her arms as if she were another daughter. "Thank you, my dear." She kissed her cheek lightly.

"How *very* touching." Claire clapped her hands. "Always know just the right thing to say, don't you, Emmeline?"

The hard edge to Claire's voice startled both Vanessa and Emmeline.

"Darling, is something wrong?" Vanessa asked.

Before her daughter could say anything, Emmeline answered, "I'm afraid we had a rather nasty row the other day, Lady Sedgwick. This is the first time that Claire and I have seen one another since then."

"Oh, I see." Vanessa looked at her daughter. "I hope the two of you can work out whatever it is."

"No, Mum, we can't."

"Claire, what a terrible thing to say. How do you know, if you don't try? Such a friendship as the two of you and Maggie have is rare and too important to throw away simply because ill-chosen words were exchanged in the heat of the moment. I'm sure you both regret it now."

Emmeline looked at her feet and then cast a glance at Claire. "Your mother's right. Shall we start again? Life is too short and anger takes up too much energy."

Claire tossed her golden head back and began laughing. "Oh, Emmeline, you are amusing. Your life doesn't seem to be short enough."

Emmeline was stunned. "What?"

"Darling, what's gotten into you tonight? How can you speak that way to your friend?"

Claire ignored her mother. Her eyes were like icy green daggers. "Always meddling, aren't you, Emmeline? Time and time again, you stick your bloody Jewish nose into things that are none of your concern. Dad was right. You can never trust Jews. At least Maggie is quiet and docile. But you—" She shook her head disapprovingly as she walked to the middle of the room.

Emmeline sucked in her breath, shocked at the vehemence with which these words were spoken. She shivered involuntarily. Unconsciously, she took a step backwards as she clutched her handbag to her side.

"Why can't you ever leave things alone?" Claire pulled out a gun from her handbag. "And another thing, you Jews seem to have nine lives. Why can't you stay dead? Just when I think you're out of my hair, there you are popping up again. I gave you a chance that day outside the tea room. I warned you, but you didn't heed the message. You just kept digging. Then at the Tower Hill station, you refused to take the hint again. You couldn't leave well enough alone, could you?"

All at once, something clicked inside Emmeline's head as she recalled what Maggie had said that day a week ago. Had it only been a week? It felt like ages.

'I'm meeting Claire tomorrow for lunch and I'll broach the subject then. She was supposed to join us now, but she rang a little while ago to say she had a million and one things to do for the wedding.'

"It was you." Emmeline's eyes widened in horror as the truth finally dawned on her. "Not your mother. Not your father. It was you. You saw me speaking with Armitage outside the tea room and assumed we were working together." Her finger trembled slightly as she pointed at Claire. "That's why you rang Maggie and cried off joining us for tea. You're the one who tried to run down Gregory and me. It was a silver Mercedes. *Just like yours.* You're Gamborelli's girlfriend, aren't you?"

"Got it in one, Miss Clever Clogs," Claire sneered.

"Of course," Emmeline murmured more to herself than anyone in particular, as she tried to work out the sequence of events. "You lured Armitage out to Hyde Park that night and killed him."

Claire curtsied. "He made it so easy. By that time, the fool had fallen in love with me."

Vanessa's legs turned to water and she had to grip the chair to steady herself. "Claire, I—"

"Please, Mum," Claire put up a hand. "Spare me the speeches. Renato and I were married at a lovely little chapel onshore at one of the cruise stops. There's nothing you or Dad can do about it."

"Oh, my God." Vanessa collapsed onto the chair and buried her face in her hands. She moaned as she rocked back and forth. When she lifted her face, it was moist with tears. "I thought he tried to hurt you and you killed him in self-defense. That's why I took the gun."

Claire gave her mother a pitying look. "So that's how the gun disappeared from my room. I was wondering what happened to it. I was frantic the morning after his body was discovered, especially with the police prowling into every nook and cranny. And my dear old Mum had it the whole time. Dad must have found the gun and assumed Mum did it. That's why I found it in the glove box of his car."

She shook her head and laughed. "Then he decided to become all noble and confess to protect her. How sweet. Life is funny, isn't it, Emmeline?" She pointed the gun at Emmeline. "I said *isn't it?*"

Emmeline swallowed down her fear. She had to keep Claire talking. She needed time to figure a way out of this nightmare. "Absolutely hilarious. Now, tell me more about your grand plot with Gamborelli. Who was the mastermind, you or him? I assume you put him in contact with your uncle about the weapons."

Poor Vanessa trembled as she looked from her daughter to Emmeline. "Weapons? Alex? Whatever do you mean?"

"Lady Sedgwick, I'm afraid Claire has been a very busy girl these past few months. Not only was she planning to marry Gamborelli, but she introduced him to your brother, who must have become dissatisfied with the army and was seeking to get his own back for some reason. They are all involved in a scheme to sell British weapons on the Black Market."

Vanessa covered her mouth with her hand. The strangled cry that came from her throat was that of a wounded animal in its death throes.

"After Uncle Alex dedicated his life to the army, they denied him a promotion. Can you imagine how humiliating that was for such a proud man? Well, that was simply not on, so I

put Uncle Alex in touch with Renato. I left it to them work out
the details of their arrangement."

"Are you proud of that, Claire? You and your uncle betrayed your country and you stand there gloating about it."

Claire yawned exaggeratedly. "I can do without your
moralizing tone, Emmeline. It is too, too boring. Renato and I
planned everything down to the last detail. The arms dealing
was—" She waved a hand in the air. "—merely an entertaining
sideline that helped Uncle Alex. I owed him that much. All
along our real objective was the diamonds. Renato's cousin,
Leonardo Notarbartolo, was the only one to get arrested for the
Antwerp diamond heist. However, recently he got word to Renato about where he had hidden the jewels. Very decent of
Leonardo. He believed that Renato could safeguard them until
he was released from prison. Blood being thicker than water
and all that. Instead, he provided us with a very tidy little nest
egg. It's amazing how gullible we humans can be."

"Amazing." Emmeline took a fraction of a step back toward the fireplace. If she could get a hold of the poker, maybe
they had a chance of getting out of here with their lives. It all
depended on whether she could distract Claire sufficiently to
knock the gun from her hand. "Go on. I'm fascinated by your
story."

Claire's smile did not touch her eyes. "You have a morbid
sense of curiosity. But then, I suppose you would like to know
why you're going to die."

A shiver slithered down Emmeline's spine, but she remained silent.

"Naturally, Renato and I hopped on a plane immediately.
The precious jewels were exactly where Leonardo had said
they would be. They were simply sitting there, waiting to be
liberated. We couldn't return to England by plane because
there would be too many questions asked at the airport, especially with all the tedious security measures in place these
days. So we settled on a leisurely Mediterranean cruise, where
Renato had arranged to sell the diamonds to a dealer from Amsterdam.

"Armitage was lurking about the first day of the journey.

What a fool. He thought he was pulling the wool over my eyes with a so-called whirlwind romance, when the whole time Renato and I knew exactly who he was. We were laughing at his every bumbling move." Her green eyes narrowed suddenly and an ugly glint entered them. "Only it wasn't so funny when the diamonds went missing. Understandably, the dealer was not very happy to say the least.

"At the time, we still believed Armitage was Ambrose Trent. I accepted his marriage proposal because I was certain he had stolen the diamonds from me. I was going to retrieve them and then kill him. His death was always part of the plan," she said matter-of-factly, "because he had been blackmailing Dad. Although Dad and I have never gotten on, I couldn't allow our family to be ruined for something that happened during World War II. Grandad had every right to keep those diamonds the Jew brought over from Belgium. He was a Sedgwick, after all. We Sedgwicks go back 400 years. Grandad knew how to put the money to good use. What did that poor Jew know?"

Emmeline's fists curled into tight balls at her side. Anger had started to displace the fear that had gripped her in a vice for the last ten minutes. "I don't understand. What does your grandfather have to do with the diamonds?"

Claire took a step closer and waved the gun menacingly. "Oh, Emmeline, that was not very convincing. I wish you would stop playing dumb. It really doesn't suit you. You know very well what diamonds I mean."

"You're entitled to believe whatever you wish, but I'm totally in the dark."

Claire snorted and started to pace the length of the room. "Fine. I could care less either way. Your time on this earth is fast running out. Now, let's see. Where was I? Oh, yes. It was only after Armitage was dead and the blackmail intensified that I realized he wasn't the real Trent. Real Trent? That's a laugh. Where did your cousin come up with such a ridiculous name?"

"Cousin?" Emmeline stared at her in confusion. Her head throbbed mercilessly. Perhaps it was the concussion and she was losing her sense of focus. "What do you mean, cousin?"

"Your little innocent act is getting rather old, Emmeline. You know perfectly well that I'm referring to your partner in crime *and* greed, Jonathan Steinfeld. The chap who went around calling himself Ambrose Trent."

"I have no idea what you're on about. That man was *not* my cousin. The first time I ever laid eyes on him was the day before yesterday."

Claire sighed. "Have it your own way. I saw him with you in the corridor at the courthouse. The day we had our row. The day *you* humiliated Dad with your disgusting public display. I knew then that you had been working with Steinfeld all along. That's why I followed you to see what else you were up to."

"You stabbed me." Emmeline's voice was low and hoarse.

"You were trouble and I had to silence you. I must admit, though, my anger got the better of me and I wasn't thinking clearly when I did it. Renato was terribly annoyed with me when I told him. It was too public. I was very nearly caught. I saw Steinfeld come to your rescue just as my taxi was pulling away. Once again, you were snatched from the jaws of death. This was becoming too much even for you, Emmeline. There had to be a way to get rid of the two you. *Fast.* I knew if I threatened your life, Steinfeld would come running. And that's exactly what he did. I searched his house twice, but the diamonds weren't there. Renato and Vincenzo couldn't find them in your house either. They weren't in Steinfeld's car. So that only leaves *you.*"

Claire halted in her perambulations. There was a soft click when she took off the safety catch and leveled the gun at a spot between Emmeline's eyes. "Where are my diamonds? I'm not going to ask a second time."

⁊ა⁊ა

Gregory had followed Claire since she left Scotland Yard that afternoon. The minute he had seen her arrive in the taxi, something that had been niggling at the back of his brain for the past few days suddenly screamed at him. The car that had tried to run Emmeline down outside the tea room was a silver Mercedes. *Just like the one Claire and her father drive.* Claire must have seen Emmeline talking with Armitage. That had to be it. Claire also must have been the one who tried to kill Ambrose and Emmeline the other night in Kent. She must have borrowed her father's car, since hers was at the garage. Lord Sedgwick must have realized this and decided to confess to protect his daughter.

Gregory had been fairly certain that his theory was correct, but during his little conversation with Claire at the station he had decided to test her. When he casually mentioned Nick's name, she unexpectedly let her guard down and for a fraction of a second he saw a flash of fear in those cool green eyes of hers. Then the mask fell back into place.

Gregory snapped his mobile shut and glanced at his watch, as dusk slowly enveloped him in its charcoal embrace. Claire had been inside her parents' house for half an hour. He was parked at a safe distance, although his view of the front door of the graceful, white stucco mansion in Lowndes Square was gradually being obscured by smoky wisps of fog. He didn't want her to slip past him, so he got out of the car and hovered in the shadows being cast by the bare tree branches in the square. Gregory leaned one shoulder against the wrought iron railing and crossed his arms over his chest as he waited patiently for his quarry to reappear. He wanted Claire to lead him to Gamborelli. He wanted both of them. For Ambrose's— no Jonathan's, he corrected himself—sake. For Jonathan's great-grandfather and his grandfather. He wanted to right that old wrong. There was no one else left except Emmeline and, thank God, she was safely tucked away in Kent with Helen. One less thing for him to worry about at the moment.

The fog hissed mockingly in his ear as a taxi pulled up outside the Sedgwick house. "Bloody hell," Gregory muttered under his breath as Lord Sedgwick alighted and settled the fare. "The man is going to ruin everything." Gregory stepped out of the shadows to waylay Sedgwick before he could give his daughter a chance to elude justice again.

Although it was muted by the fog, Gregory heard the soft click a second before the cold muzzle of a gun was pressed against the back of his neck. "I suggest you remain where you are, Longdon. Better to live another day than to die a hero, wouldn't you agree?"

CHAPTER 29

Lord Sedgwick quietly let himself into the house. There was no one about in the hall. Then, the low murmur of voices floated down to him. He couldn't make out what was being said, but one voice in particular rose above the others. Strident, angry. Claire. He had to stop her. He bounded up the stairs two at a time. Once he reached the landing, he hesitated for only a second before opening the library door.

All three women were startled when he burst into the room. Claire stared at her father with disdain, bordering on hatred. "So the great Lord Sedgwick has returned to the roost. How did it feel in jail, Dad? Pick up any gossip from your fellow convicts." Her green gaze, the mirror image of her father's, dripped ice.

"It's over, Claire. You can't run anymore. Give me the gun." His lordship took half a step forward and extended a hand toward his daughter.

Claire threw her head back and laughed. "Really, Dad. Don't be so melodramatic. I'm not one of your lackeys you can order about. But you've never realized that, have you? No, the great Lord Douglas Sedgwick just wanted his daughter to look pretty and make all the right, polite noises. Something he could pull out for the guests and the press to give the impression of a nice family life. And then once I had played my part, I was shunted away and ignored. Well, you can't ignore me anymore can you, Dad?"

"Claire, how dare you speak to your father that way?" Vanessa was incensed. "I will not tolerate it."

Lord Sedgwick went to his wife's side and put an arm around her shoulders, which were trembling. "There, there, old girl. Never mind. It's all over. No need for you to get upset."

"Oh, Doug." She leaned into his body and turned her tear-stained face to look up at her husband. "You can't imagine the horrible things she's been telling us."

"I think I can." He spoke to his wife, but he looked straight at Claire.

"Where did we go wrong, Doug? Where?" Vanessa's voice cracked and she rested her head against Sedgwick's chest.

He kissed the top of her head and whispered softly, "We loved her too much and gave her anything she desired. That was our mistake."

"How very touching, Dad." Claire clapped her hands slowly. "I didn't know you had it in you. Now if you've quite finished being soppy, I've more important things to attend to."

She turned back to Emmeline, but her attention had been distracted just long enough for Emmeline to grab hold of the poker. With one swift upward swing, the poker made contact with Claire's knuckles with a satisfying crack. The gun arced over the chair and landed somewhere on the carpet.

A guttural cry of pain mingled with shock escaped from Claire's throat. Blood trickled onto the carpet and her hand dangled limply as if broken. "You," she said through clenched teeth. Beads of perspiration appeared on her upper lip. "That was your last mistake. They're never going to recognize your body when Renato's men are finished with you. That's *if* your body is ever found."

Emmeline didn't wait for Claire to say anything else. She launched herself, shoulder first, straight at Claire. They crashed to the ground with a resounding thud.

Vanessa screamed, "Doug, stop them. Please."

While Claire lay winded from Emmeline's weight on her, Emmeline desperately fumbled around for the gun. Where was the bloody thing? It had to be here somewhere. Claire suddenly regained her breath and became like a wild animal. She clawed and scratched at Emmeline, as they rolled around on the ground.

"Where are my diamonds, you Jewish bitch? I—want— my—diamonds." Claire managed to get her hands around Emmeline's throat and banged her head against the carpet. A wave of nausea roiled Emmeline's stomach and the room began to swim. This was definitely not good for her concussion. Perhaps it would have been a better idea if she had stayed with Gran after all, she thought. Then mercifully, everything went black.

"Oh, Emmeline." Claire got to her feet unsteadily, but she shot her parents a malevolent smile before turning back to Emmeline. "You've robbed me of so many things. So many. But you're not going escape what you deserve. Not this time." She picked up the gun with her undamaged hand and aimed it at Emmeline's chest. "Goodbye, *old friend.*"

"No, Claire," Sedgwick shouted. "Don't."

✖✖✖

"You'll understand that I have to search you," the voice hissed in his ear.

"Naturally," Gregory replied calmly, well as calmly as was reasonably possible when a gun was pressed to one's head. "I quite understand. I would do the same if I were in your place, Gamborelli. It *is* Renato Gamborelli, isn't it?"

He felt rather than saw the other man smile.

"Ah, Longdon, I see what they say about you is correct."

"I'm glad to hear that I stack up to all your expectations. I'd be happy to give you an autograph. That is, if you've finished."

Gamborelli spun him around, but the fog and shadows blurred his features. "No weapon."

"Sorry to disappoint you, old chap. I could have told you that from the beginning. I never carry a gun. They're nasty things that can go off and leave uninvited holes in one's anatomy. Now, did you want anything specifically or were you simply passing?"

The gun found an uncomfortable spot against his ribs. "Longdon, I'm not in the mood for your nonsense." Gamborelli grabbed the lapels of Gregory's Burberry and pulled him so that their faces were only inches from one another. "I want the diamonds."

"Diamonds? Is *that* what all this fuss is about?"

Gamborelli's response was to jab the gun deeper into Gregory's side.

"Well, I haven't got them."

"Then perhaps, we should join the ladies and ask Miss Kirby where they are?"

Gregory flicked a piece of imaginary lint off Gamborelli's shoulder and smiled. "I'm certain Emmeline would love to see you again, old chap. But alas, you're out of luck. I'm afraid she's not in London. She'll be sorry that she missed you."

Gamborelli's lips twisted into his trademark lupine smile. "Ah, but you're wrong, Longdon. The delightful Miss Kirby returned late this afternoon and is, at this very moment, inside there." He pointed at the Sedgwick house.

Gregory swore under his breath. He should have expected this. Why was Emmeline so stubborn? How could Helen have allowed her to leave?

"I see Miss Kirby doesn't keep you informed about all her movements."

"Apparently not," Gregory mumbled. "I'll have to have a little talk with her about that." His jaw set in a tight line. "Not that it will do much good."

"I wouldn't want to think that I came between two lovers. You see, I'm a romantic at heart. Shall we go across the street? I've kept Claire waiting far too long as it is. She's probably getting anxious and when she gets anxious she becomes a bit...reckless. Perhaps after you and Miss Kirby tell us where the diamonds are, you can kiss and make up. If, that is, there's enough time before you die." With that, Gamborelli gave Gregory an unceremonious shove. "Move."

Their footsteps echoed loudly against the slick pavement as they walked the hundred yards to the Sedgwick house. A taxi suddenly materialized out of the vaporous swirl and half a second later was swallowed up again as it rolled on by. The fog distorted sight and sound, and the very notion of time. The hairs on the back of Gregory's neck prickled. The stillness was unnerving, claustrophobic, suffocating. A thousand different things raced through his mind. However, the overarching thought was how to get Emmeline and himself out of the house alive. If he managed that feat—which appeared doubtful, judging by the grim determination etched on Gamborelli's features—he would give Emmeline the thrashing of her life for being so headstrong.

They walked up the steps and halted in front of the door. Gregory patted his pockets. "I seem to have forgotten my key, old chap. Would you be kind enough to oblige?"

"Your jokes are wearing thin. I suggest you curb your tongue unless you'd like a bullet between your eyes right now."

Gregory cocked his head to one side and appeared to give this serious consideration. "Wouldn't that be rather messy? This is a new suit, after all. Besides you wouldn't get the diamonds that way."

Gamborelli slipped a key into the lock and turned the knob. "Enough. Get in." He jerked the gun impatiently. Once they were in the hall, he said, "I give you fair warning. The first sign of any heroics on your part and I shoot Miss Kirby. I have no qualms about doing so. Do we understand each other?"

"Perfectly," Gregory replied grimly and allowed himself to be led by the elbow up the staircase.

The sound of scuffling mingled with angry voices grew louder and louder with each step. Then everything suddenly went very quiet. They had just reached the top of the landing when a gunshot shattered the silence. Gamborelli stiffened and dug his fingers deep into Gregory's upper arm, which made him wince. When a woman started screaming hysterically, Gregory elbowed Gamborelli in the ribs sending him tumbling backward down the staircase.

Heedless of the danger lurking on the other side of the door, Gregory rushed toward the library. He prayed he was not too late. He was stunned by the scene being played out before his eyes. Lady Sedgwick was cradling her husband in her arms. She was rocking back and forth, murmuring incoherently. An ugly, dark stain was slowly soaking through what had been Lord Sedgwick's crisp, white shirt. His eyes were closed. Gregory couldn't tell whether the man was dead or simply unconscious. But that was the least of his concerns at the moment.

The air crackled with tension. Claire hovered over her parents, one hand dangling oddly at her side while the other was held aloft, trembling slightly as she continued to point a gun at her father. From this angle, Gregory could only see her profile. Her cheeks were flushed a feverish crimson hue. She hadn't heard him enter the room. He had to get the gun away from her. But where the devil was Emmeline? This silent question was answered by a low moaning coming from the vicinity of the floor next to one of the armchairs. Bloody hell. Claire had hurt Emmeline, too.

Claire seemed to snap out of her trance and turned the gun on Emmeline, whose dark eyes flickered open just as the safety catch clicked off. "Goodbye, Emmeline."

A jolt of pure adrenaline coursed through Emmeline's veins in that instant and another part of her brain took over as she stared up at the barrel of the gun. She quickly rolled over and kicked Claire's feet out from under her. Gregory seemed to appear from out of thin air. He scooped up the gun and drew Emmeline to a sitting position in one seamless movement. "Are you all right?" he asked anxiously. His worried eyes searched her face.

She nodded slowly. He gave her shoulders a reassuring squeeze.

"Oh. Except for my head," she whispered hoarsely, as she buried her hands in her curls to stop the dizziness.

"It serves you right, darling. Perhaps the next time you'll listen to your elders, who are much wiser. But now is not the appropriate moment for chastisement. There will be plenty of time later."

Emmeline's response was to stick her tongue out at him.

"As for you," Gregory said with disgust, pointing the gun at Claire, "get up. I have a feeling that Chief Inspector Burnell is quite eager to have a little chat with you."

Claire held her broken hand in her good one. Her body shook with rage and undisguised hatred. Then the corners of her mouth twitched into a smile as something over his shoulder caught her eye. "I wouldn't count on that, Gregory. I think you'll find Renato has other plans for you and Emmeline. Right, *amore mio?*"

Gregory was trying to support Emmeline, but the hairs prickling the back of his neck told him Gamborelli was looming nearby. "Longdon, first I would like to repay you for your kindness on the stairs."

The next instant, Gregory doubled over in pain after Gamborelli delivered a vicious kick to his kidney

Emmeline gasped. "*Gregory.*" She eased him against the floor and shakily got to her feet.

She glared up into Gamborelli's arrogant face. "Animal," she spat. "You're nothing but a thug and a bully in designer clothes. There was no call for that." She poked the Mafia boss in the chest with her forefinger, ignoring the gun pointed at her. At six foot two, Gamborelli—who had men killed without batting an eye and whose very name sent the fear of God into those who crossed him—backed away from Emmeline, who was a full head shorter. She advanced on Gamborelli like a bulldog, anger driving all notions of fear out of her mind. She poked him again. "What? Nothing to say for yourself, Mr. Mafioso?"

"Steady on, old thing," Gregory said as he carefully stood up. "Gamborelli, I'd cut my losses if I were you. Before you get on Emmy's bad side."

Gamborelli looked at Gregory and then back at Emmeline. His dark eyes narrowed and he took a firmer grip on the gun. "*Basta,*" he shouted. "Enough. I've had enough of the two of you." He reached out a long arm and easily grabbed Emmeline, pulling her against his chest so that she faced Gregory. He placed the gun to her temple. "Now, where are the diamonds, Longdon?"

"And if I don't feel like giving them to you?"

Emmeline stared wildly at Gregory, beseeching him not to anger Gamborelli further.

Gamborelli's warm breath ruffled the top of her hair as he threw his head back and laughed. "Poor, Miss Kirby. It's unfortunate that you will have to die because you gave your heart to such a greedy man."

"Go ahead and shoot her," Gregory replied nonchalantly. Emmeline's eyes grew as large as saucers. "You'll never get the diamonds if you do. I already told you I don't have them and neither does Emmeline. The diamonds are with a friend for safe-keeping. So you see, Gamborelli, if you kill either one of us, you'd never see those pesky diamonds again. But I leave the choice entirely up to you." He casually hitched a hip on the arm of the chair and flashed one of those smiles calculated to infuriate.

Emmeline held her breath. Gregory was playing a dangerous game with Gamborelli. She watched him closely for a hint of what he had up his sleeve, but Gregory's face was blank. It was unnerving that he appeared to be so calm. She just hoped that he didn't overplay his hand.

Gamborelli gave a little salute. "We seem to have reached an impasse." He let go of Emmeline and she ran to Gregory's side.

"Is that it? You're just going to let it go like that, Renato?" Claire screamed. They had all forgotten about her.

A flash of annoyance crossed Gamborelli's face. "*Cara*, what would you have me do?"

"You're bloody useless. After everything that I went through to get those diamonds. I *earned* those diamonds. No one is going to take them from me. Do you understand?"

Gamborelli's jaw set in a tight line. He was fast losing control over his temper. "You forget yourself, Claire. Those diamonds are *mine* by right. My cousin entrusted them to me. You have absolutely no claim upon them. None whatsoever. In fact, I think it would be best if we ended our...how should I put this politely?...our relationship. It was amusing for a time, but it has run its course."

Claire gasped. "Why you egotistical bastard. It was all just a game from the start."

"Come now. Don't play the little ingénue. We are both adults. It was merely physical attraction. We enjoyed each other for a time, but such things cannot last in the long run, *cara*," Gamborelli said matter-of-factly.

"You're my bloody husband, for Christ's sake."

"A mistake that can be corrected with the assistance of a good lawyer."

All the blood drained from her cheeks and her fist clenched at her side. "You can't just toss me away like an old shoe. I'm Claire Sedgwick."

"Please, Claire, stop this. You're embarrassing yourself," Gamborelli replied with loathing.

A guttural sound emanated from deep within Claire's throat as she flew at him in a blind rage, her good hand raised like a claw. He slapped her across the mouth, before she even had a chance to take a swing at him. Claire cried out in pain as a thin trickle of blood appeared at the corner of her mouth.

"*Basta*. Get out of my sight. You make me sick." Gamborelli turned his back and stepped around Claire, who was trembling in shame and anger. He jerked the gun at Gregory and Emmeline. "We've wasted enough time here tonight with these hysterics. I don't care how you do it, but you will get me the diamonds. *Now*. Or I—"

The sniper's bullet shattered the window and tore through Gamborelli's right temple. He crumpled to the floor in a heap. His lifeless brown eyes stared up at Claire, mocking her even in death.

CHAPTER 30

Claire swayed and then collapsed to the floor screaming. "Renato? *Renato?*" She shook him and slapped his face, but there was no response. Gamborelli would never speak to her again. "He can't be dead. I love him. He can't be dead. He's my husband. He can't be dead," she repeated over and over, her voice thick with tears.

Emmeline buried her head against Gregory's neck. It was too awful to watch.

"It's all right, Emmy." He held her close and kissed the top of her head. "It's over now. Hush, love, no one can hurt you anymore."

What happened next became a blur. Chief Inspector Burnell and Sergeant Finch burst into the room, guns drawn. Philip was hard on their heels. Heavy footsteps and shouts could be heard down below and on the staircase as Special Branch and Metropolitan Police Hostage Unit officers thundered into the house. Finch rushed over to Lord and Lady Sedgwick. His lordship had lost a lot of blood, but miraculously he was still alive. Vanessa was shivering and clearly in severe shock. The sergeant called for an ambulance.

"Ah, look, Emmy, the cavalry has arrived at last," Gregory said wryly. "You were cutting it rather fine, weren't you, Oliver?"

"If it weren't for Miss Kirby, we'd have contemplated leaving you in God's hands, Longdon," Burnell replied as he and Philip bent down beside Gamborelli's body.

Gregory clucked his tongue. "Not very sporting, I must say. Especially in view of the fact that you would never have caught Gamborelli, if it hadn't been for me. By the way, you'll find that he's quite dead."

The chief inspector and Philip rolled their eyes and shot exasperated looks at Gregory. Claire was still clinging to Gamborelli's arm.

"Finch," Burnell called to the sergeant who left the paramedics to render aid to Lord and Lady Sedgwick. "Get a WPC and take Miss Sedgwick down to the ambulance. She needs medical attention. Her hand's broken and she's in shock."

"Yes, sir." Finch came over and gently took Claire by the shoulders. "Come, Miss Sedgwick. Why don't we go outside?"

Claire lifted her tear-stained face. Her green eyes stared at him uncomprehendingly. "But I can't leave. My husband needs me."

"It's all right, Miss Sedgwick," the sergeant whispered. "Chief Inspector Burnell will take care of him. I promise you. Now, come with me." He smiled encouragingly.

Claire blinked and gazed at his outstretched hand for several seconds, before finally placing her good one in his. She halted at the door and took one last glance over her shoulder at the prone body on the floor.

"Come, Miss Sedgwick," Finch quietly prompted. "There's nothing more you can do here."

"Thank God, for that," Burnell muttered under his breath after Finch escorted Claire from the room.

Burnell and Philip got to their feet.

"Emmeline, are you all right?" Philip asked.

She was still curled against Gregory's chest, but she turned and sat up. "Yes. Except my head hurts."

"Which is not surprising, miss, as you have a concussion and should not have gone off gallivanting on your own," Gregory said as he gave her a severe look. "I just hope you have not done yourself a permanent injury with tonight's little adventure."

"I was not gallivanting, as you put it. I was following through on a theory. Lord Sedgwick's confession bothered me and the more I thought about it, the more it didn't ring true. And then, when Gran mentioned Noah and the Ark everything suddenly clicked into place."

The three men looked at her quizzically. "Noah and the Ark? What does the Bible have to do with this?" Gregory asked.

"Noah had two of everything on the Ark. That's what got me thinking. Everyone thought Lord Sedgwick confessed to protect Claire. But everyone has *two parents*, so what if it wasn't Lord Sedgwick who killed Armitage and Ambrose Trent as everyone believed, but Lady Vanessa?"

"But it wasn't Lady Vanessa," Gregory pointed out.

"N—no, well—" Emmeline stammered and felt her cheeks flame. "I admit I was a little off the track there. However, Lord Sedgwick initially confessed because he *thought* Lady Vanessa had killed Armitage and wanted to protect her. In the end, he confessed because he realized it could only have been Claire because she had borrowed his car."

The three men glanced at one another and smothered their smiles.

"Pity, though, you didn't think to inform anyone else about your theory. It could have averted tonight's escapade," Gregory said with a wave of his hand about the library.

"Ah, but you're wrong there. I did try to ring you *and* Chief Inspector Burnell, but I couldn't reach you. So I—"

"So once again, you ventured forth like a one-man band, heedless of the dangers involved," Gregory finished for her.

"That's unfair. Tell him, Chief Inspector."

"Miss Kirby, I'm afraid in this instance—I can't believe I'm going to say this—I agree with Longdon."

"Philip?" Emmeline turned to her friend, her dark eyes pleading for support.

"Much as I love you, Emmeline." Philip took her small hands in his and brushed her knuckles with a kiss. "I must say it was rather reckless to go in alone."

She pulled her hands back and crossed her arms over her

chest. "Ooh. Men. If Maggie were here, she'd be in my corner."

"But she's not here, darling. It's only us inferior men," Gregory said as he patted her shoulder.

"More's the pity," Emmeline mumbled. Then, her face brightened. "If I was so reckless, how is it that I managed to wangle the whole sordid story out of Claire?"

"Miss Kirby, I'm afraid hearsay evidence is not accepted in a court of law."

"It's not hearsay evidence. I can testify I heard her say it without articulating whether it's true or not. Lady Vanessa was a witness, too. She can back me up. And if that is not enough—" Emmeline bent down and picked up her handbag. She rummaged around for a minute. "Ah, here it is. I have the whole thing on tape. I managed to turn it on without Claire noticing." She flashed them a triumphant smile as she pulled out a small tape recorder. "Shall we take a little listen?"

Emmeline rewound the tape and pressed the *PLAY* button. Claire's voice rang out loud and clear. "I was going to retrieve the diamonds and then kill Armitage. His death was always part of the plan."

There was a soft click as Emmeline turned it off. "Heard enough, gentlemen? I assure you the rest of it is just as juicy. It's all there. Every dirty detail of how Claire and Gamborelli connived to get hold of the diamonds, the murders of Armitage and Trent, the arms dealing. Everything." She tapped the tape recorder with a finger. "Now, *who* was being reckless?" she asked with a lift of her eyebrow.

Burnell reached out a hand and smiled. "I'll take that, if I may, Miss Kirby. I can't deny it is the solid evidence we will need against Miss Sedgwick. Thank you. But—"

"But? I never liked that word," she murmured.

"Emmy, it's not polite to interrupt Oliver when he's speaking," Gregory chided.

Burnell gave him a pointed look. "Chief Inspector Burnell. How many times must I remind you?"

"As you wish, *Oliver*."

"Never mind. It's a lost cause." The chief inspector

sighed. "As I was saying, Miss Kirby, the Metropolitan Police greatly appreciate what you've done. You've helped the case enormously. However, in future, we would appreciate it, even more, if you wouldn't dash off on your own. Please."

Emmeline's cheeks flushed again and she looked up at him from under her eyelashes. "I'm sorry, Chief Inspector. I promise to be more prudent from now on."

Gregory snorted. "Darling, I really don't think you should go around making promises you can't keep."

They all laughed at Emmeline's expense as her blush deepened to rosy coral and she gave Gregory's arm a punch.

"Ouch that hurt." He made a show of rubbing the spot.

"Good. You deserve it. You're a beast."

"Despite your decisively combative tone, my love, I shall take you home and make sure that you're tucked up safely in your bed. Otherwise, Helen would never forgive me."

"You are not getting anywhere near my bed."

"I assure you my intentions are strictly honorable. My only concern is for your health and safety. Truly." He took two fingers and crossed his heart. "I'll even swear to it on a Bible, if you like."

"Ha. I wouldn't put too much stock in that. Since when did you find religion?"

"God spoke to me in a dream and said that my mission in life is to watch over a troublesome brunette. That's proving rather difficult of late because you seem to be colluding with the Devil."

Emmeline gave his arm another punch. This one was harder than the first. Gregory stood and put out his hand for her. "Yes, definitely in league with the Devil. Come, darling. Chief Inspector Burnell, Acheson, if there's nothing further I think it's time I take Emmy home."

He pulled her to her feet. She swayed slightly for a second. He put his arm around her waist to steady her.

"Thanks," she mumbled. Her head was throbbing again.

"Gentlemen." Gregory nodded to Burnell and Philip and guided Emmeline toward the door.

"Just a minute, Longdon," Burnell called. "There's one piece of unfinished business."

"Is there, Oliver? What could that be?"

"It's the small matter of the diamonds. *Where* are they?"

"Yes, Longdon," Philip said as he slipped his hands into his pockets and took a step forward. "I hope you weren't thinking of absconding with them."

"Me?" Gregory put a hand to his chest in mock innocence. "Such a thought never even crossed my mind. I'm a law abiding citizen."

"There are two schools of thought on that," Burnell replied.

"Oliver, I'm shocked that you would even suggest such a thing. Why, it's…it's dishonest."

"That's never stopped you before. Now, where are the diamonds?" Burnell snapped.

"Gregory, perhaps you should turn them over to the chief inspector," Emmeline urged.

"But, darling, I don't have them."

"What?" Burnell exploded. "You're the only one who could have them."

Gregory clucked his tongue. "Oliver, you should really try to rein in that temper of yours. It's not good for your blood pressure."

"Never mind my blood pressure. If you don't turn over those diamonds, I will have you arrested. And it will give me tremendous pleasure to do so."

"Gregory, please," Emmeline implored. "They're not worth a jail sentence."

He patted her shoulder reassuringly. "Emmy, don't fret. No one's going to prison."

"You will be in the next ten seconds, Longdon."

"But, Oliver, it's morally unjust to jail an innocent man."

Burnell snorted. "You were born guilty. The diamonds."

"You haven't been listening. I already told you. I don't have them."

"Then who does?"

"You do, of course."

Three pairs of eyes turned toward the chief inspector as Finch walked back into the room. "What do you mean *I* have the diamonds?" Burnell asked incredulously.

"Exactly that. As a law abiding citizen—I did mention that point a few moments ago—I knew it was my civic duty to turn over those evil diamonds to the police. So I did."

"Longdon, that's an outrageous lie. You *know* you never gave me the diamonds."

"Not personally. That's true. You were so preoccupied this afternoon with Lord Sedgwick that you practically ejected me from your office, remember? Well, I didn't want to disturb such a great man at work. Therefore, I had them delivered."

"Had them delivered? You expect us to believe that you sent $100 million in diamonds through the post."

"Not through the post. By messenger. Safer that way."

"By messenger? Do you believe this load of rubbish, Finch?"

"No, sir." The sergeant shook his head as he positioned himself in front of the door to prevent Gregory from leaving the room.

Emmeline looked anxiously from Burnell to Philip. Gregory, however, remained unperturbed. He flashed a smile at the chief inspector. "I know for a fact that the package was delivered to Scotland Yard this afternoon, Oliver. Presumably into your hot little hands."

"That's preposterous. I never received your fictitious package—"

"Hang on a minute, sir," Finch piped in. "There was that package that arrived just before we left headquarters. Remember?"

Burnell's blue eyes blinked at his sergeant and he was silent for a long moment. "Yes," he murmured as he pictured himself tossing the brown paper package onto his desk. "Yes, I remember."

"Oliver, it's rather late. I'd like to take Emmy home. I promise to come visit you tomorrow and we can have nice long chat. All right?"

"No, it's not all right. I'm not letting you out of my sight until this matter is resolved. We're going to the Yard right now."

Gregory shrugged and sighed as if all the burdens of the world rested on his shoulders. "If you insist. I'm sorry, love. You see how things are. Oliver, perhaps someone can take Emmy home."

"I'll be glad to, sir," Finch offered.

"No," Emmeline said. "No one is taking me anywhere. I want to see this thing through to the bitter end."

"Thank you, darling." Gregory smiled down at her. "I'm glad to have your unstinting support."

"I wouldn't go that far."

"Well, it will be nice to have you along, in any case. But are you sure you're up to it?" His eyes searched her face for any signs of pain.

"I'm fine."

"Then it's all settled. Oliver, will you lead the way? I will follow you to the ends of the earth."

Burnell rolled his eyes. "Get moving, Longdon. Mr. Acheson, it would ease my mind, if you rode in Longdon's car."

"Certainly, Chief Inspector," Philip agreed as his cool blue gaze wearily turned to Gregory.

"Really, Oliver. I don't need a chaperone. I'm a big boy."

"It'll ease my mind, Longdon."

Gregory shook his head. "What is this world coming to, when two friends can no longer trust one another? I'm truly hurt."

Half an hour later, the expectant little group trouped into the chief inspector's office. The package was lying on the desk in exactly the spot where Burnell had left it. Gregory held out a chair for Emmeline. "Darling, I think you ought to sit down. This shouldn't take a minute. Then I'll drive you home."

Burnell extended a hand toward the chair. "Please, Miss Kirby."

"Thank you." Emmeline eased herself onto the edge of the seat. She was too nervous to lean back.

"Now then, Longdon," the chief inspector said as he

snatched up the package and began tearing at the paper, "this had better not be one of your jokes."

Gregory simply smiled, as he stood behind Emmeline's chair with a hand resting lightly on her shoulder.

Burnell's blue eyes narrowed when he removed the last of the brown paper. It was a book. "*Diamonds Are Forever*? James Bond. This *is* one of your cheap jokes, Longdon, and it's not very amusing, as usual."

"I regret to contradict you, Oliver. It's not cheap at all. In fact, you'll find that it's a first edition and I gather it will fetch around £3,700."

"That's all very well and good, but—"

"Not only that," Gregory continued. "This volume is extra special."

"Extra special how? It looks like an ordinary book to me. A pricey one, but a book nevertheless."

"May I?" Gregory extended a hand for the book. The chief inspector hesitated. "Come, come, Oliver. I'm in the nerve the center of Scotland Yard. Where can I run? If I make it through the gauntlet of you, Finch, and Acheson, there are a dozen constables out there who can apprehend me." He waved his hand in the direction of the door.

Philip cleared his throat. "He's right, Burnell. He has no chance to escape."

"Oh, very well." The chief inspector grudgingly handed the book over to Gregory.

"Thanks, old chap. As I was saying, gentlemen, this edition has a little something that other James Bond books do not." Gregory walked around the chair and placed the book in the center of the desk. Emmeline held her breath. She gazed up at his handsome profile and prayed this was not some trick to make Burnell look foolish.

"My late friend Nick Martin was one of the cleverest men who walked this earth. One would never have thought so to look at him. Most people overlooked him in a crowd, but that was part of his genius. Hide in plain sight. Unfortunately, he and Ambrose crossed paths with Gamborelli and Claire and they paid for that with their lives."

"Yes, yes. We know all of this. Get on with it."

Gregory pulled out a pocket knife and brandished it in the air with a conjurer's flourish. "Patience, Oliver. All good things come to those who wait."

Burnell and Finch exchanged weary glances, as they watched Gregory take the point of the blade and carefully make an incision along the book's spine. A tightly rolled handkerchief popped out. Gregory smiled at his audience. "And just as I suspected, there we have $100 million in diamonds stolen from the Antwerp Diamond Centre."

No one spoke. Philip and Burnell stared at Gregory open-mouthed as he calmly took the chair beside Emmeline. With a trembling hand, she reached out and unwrapped the handkerchief. The diamonds spilled out across the desk. A shimmering sea of fiery brilliance. Beautiful, bewitching. It was easy to see why some men would kill for them.

Epilogue

Helen was in the kitchen fussing over the tea, while Emmeline and Gregory chatted in the living room. Emmeline was under strict orders not move from the sofa on pain of death. Her grandmother left MacTavish behind to reinforce this directive. However, after a few minutes of running around the sofa, the dog curled up on the floor at Emmeline's feet and promptly fell asleep. He woke up when Helen came bustling into the room with the tea tray and then sheepishly scurried to his basket in the kitchen.

"You call yourself a guard dog," Helen called over her shoulder in mock anger as Gregory took the tray from her and placed it on the coffee table. They heard two barks from the kitchen in response.

They all laughed as Helen settled herself beside her granddaughter. "What an ego that little devil has. Now, my dears—" She rubbed her hands together. "—let's have some tea and you can tell me about all the trouble you've been getting up into London."

"Oh, Gran," Emmeline said. "We helped to solve three murders and recovered $100 million in diamonds."

"That's all very well and good, Emmy, but you nearly got yourself killed *twice*. No, three times when you include your mad dash back to London yesterday afternoon."

"Don't be so melodramatic, Gran. I'm fine," Emmeline mumbled.

"That's only because Gregory was there—*again*, I might add." She gave her granddaughter a pointed look, which brought a pink flush to Emmeline's cheeks.

"Really, Helen, it was nothing. All in the line of duty," Gregory chimed in as he grinned at Emmeline, who rolled her eyes.

Helen patted his knee. "I hope you're never put in a dangerous situation like that again because my granddaughter takes it into her head to play an avenging crusader."

"Oh, Gran," Emmeline murmured as she tucked her legs under her and took a sip of tea.

Helen handed a cup to Gregory and cut a slice of poppy seed cake for him. Then she poured a cup for herself and settled back against the sofa. "Now then, I'm all ears. Don't leave out any of the juicy details," she said with a child's eagerness for a good yarn.

"It all started when I bumped into a man named Kenneth Armitage. He was a con man, but I didn't know that at the time," Emmeline said as she recalled that day only a week earlier, when she went to meet Maggie at Miss Charlotte's Tea Room. She described the episode when the car tried to run her and Gregory down and then discovering that Claire's fiancé was not the real Ambrose Trent, but this man Armitage. "You see it turns out that the real Ambrose Trent was a good friend of Gregory's. So the instant he saw the photo of Claire's fiancé, he knew something was amiss."

Helen put her cup down and inched to the edge of the sofa. "Really? How fascinating. This is more intriguing than I thought."

"There are more twists in the tale, Gran. Some things *I* still don't know, but *he* does." Emmeline pointed an accusatory finger at Gregory.

Her grandmother grabbed her finger. "It's not polite to point, Emmy. Perhaps you could put her out of her misery, Gregory, before the curiosity kills her."

Gregory laughed and picked up the thread. He revealed that Ambrose Trent's true identity was Jonathan Steinfeld and how Lord Gerald Sedgwick stole the diamonds Jonathan's great-grandfather brought over from Belgium during World War II. He told them the heartbreaking story of how Jonathan's grandfather subsequently tried to recover the diamonds with the help of Emmeline's grandfather, but was cheated once again. Then he detailed how Lord Douglas Sedgwick, in turn, played his part to hurt the Steinfeld family. And finally, they all knew first-hand the deadly lengths Claire had been willing to go to get what she wanted.

"In the end, you can't really blame poor Jonathan for his vendetta against the Sedgwicks. Each succeeding generation did something to destroy his family."

Emmeline sat up suddenly. "Of course, it all makes sense now. 'An eye for eye.' That's what Ambrose, I mean Jonathan, said to me that night. He stole the diamonds from Claire to compensate for the diamonds that her grandfather had stolen from his family."

Gregory nodded. "You're right, darling. This whole thing was about revenge *and* justice. Sadly, the poor chap had to pay for it with his life. At least Claire will go to prison for a very long time for the hand she had in all this."

Helen shook her head. "Yes, that's *some* justice after all. But it's terribly sad to die so young."

"I wish he had told me about the family relationship. That's how he knew all about Gran and why he was taking me to her that night." Emmeline was quiet for a moment. "I would have liked to have gotten to know him. He seemed like a nice bloke," she said wistfully.

"I remember him as a small boy and his father and mother, too. He was a little older than you, Emmy, but he wasn't too proud to play with you. Such a lovely boy. The families lost touch, though. Now, I understand why." Helen shook her head again. "What a tragedy."

"Yes." Gregory nodded thoughtfully as he took a sip of tea. "I wish I had done more. Perhaps if I—"

"Nonsense," Helen interrupted. "Don't second guess yourself. There are some things beyond our control. But don't you dare blame yourself for this mess. It was none of your doing, dear boy."

His good humor restored, Gregory flashed one his cheeky smiles. "Ah, Helen, that's why you'll always be the love of my life." He reached across for her hand and brushed his lips across her knuckles.

Helen blushed and burst into a fit of giggles. "You're shameless, but don't stop."

They both laughed at this remark, while Emmeline shook her head in disapproval. "You shouldn't encourage him, Gran. It will only swell his head."

Helen gave her a sidelong glance. "Is that jealousy I hear talking?"

"You must be joking. There's absolutely nothing for me to be jealous about."

"Really?"

"Yes, really."

Helen winked at Gregory and gave him a conspiratorial smile. "Well, I have a thousand things to do in town this afternoon, so I must be off. I'm assuming that the two of you can manage here on your own."

"Of course, we can. Isn't that right, Emmy?" Gregory asked.

Emmeline ignored him and turned to her grandmother. "When did this list of a thousand things come up? You didn't mention anything this morning."

Helen spread her hands and shrugged her shoulders. "You know how it is, darling."

Emmeline narrowed her dark eyes. "No, I don't know how it is. Why don't you explain it to me?"

Her grandmother glanced at her watch. "Is that the time? I'm late." She leaned over and gave Emmeline a quick peck on the cheek. "See you later. Make sure you behave this afternoon. Don't give poor Gregory too much trouble."

"What?" Emmeline was outraged. "Me give *him* trouble. It's more the other way around."

"Now, now, Emmy." Gregory sighed melodramatically. "Don't worry, Helen. I've learned to live with this kind of abuse." Emmeline made a face at him. He wagged a finger at her. "And that, too."

Helen ruffled his hair affectionately and gave him another wink. "I'm off. The two of you will have to sort this out for yourselves. I'm leaving MacTavish here."

"That improves things enormously," Emmeline said.

MacTavish barked to register his offense at this remark.

Ten minutes later, they heard Helen's car pulling away from the drive. Emmeline and Gregory were alone.

Gregory slipped onto the sofa beside her. "So here we are."

"Yes, here we are." Emmeline didn't know why, but she suddenly felt very shy. Damn, how did he always manage do this to her? She was *usually* a perfectly sane, intelligent woman.

What she needed was something to distract her mind. As if Gregory could read her thoughts, he leaned over and brushed her lips softly with his own. That was *not* what Emmeline had in mind. It only served to muddle things even more.

"Gregory, I—"

"Shh." He smothered whatever she had been about to say with another kiss.

Emmeline pushed him away and cleared her throat. Her mind went blank when she looked into his cinnamon-brown eyes. It would be so easy to give in. Having him around again made her want to. Very much. She lifted her hand to touch his face, but then let it drop into her lap. Something held her back. Would she *ever* be able to forgive him for abandoning her two years ago?

The thought of the baby she had lost—their baby—came to mind just then. The overwhelming sadness and emptiness of that ache made her sigh. Gregory was back. For now. But would he stay? Could she trust him? She didn't know any of the answers. And she was afraid to give her heart away again.

Gregory saw a range of emotions flit across her face and he shivered involuntarily. Someone had just walked over his grave. He was suddenly overcome by the suffocating fear that the dark secrets of his past were about to catch up with him and he would lose Emmeline—*forever*. He couldn't allow that to happen. He wouldn't.

Fate, though, had other plans. And very soon, the day would come to settle old accounts. Could Emmeline and Gregory escape this trial unscathed? Or would it be *murder*?

About the Author

Daniella Bernett is a member of the Mystery Writers of America NY Chapter. She graduated summa cum laude with a B.S. in Journalism from St. John's University. *Lead Me Into Danger* is the first novel in the Emmeline Kirby-Gregory Longdon mystery series. She also is the author of two poetry collections, *Timeless Allure* and *Silken Reflections*. In her professional life, she is the research manager for a nationally prominent engineering, architectural and construction management firm. Daniella is currently working on Emmeline and Gregory's next adventure.

Visit www.daniellabernett.com or follow her on Facebook at https://www.facebook.com/profile.php?id=100008802318282 Or on Goodreads https://www.goodreads.com/user/show/40690254-daniella-bernett.

CPSIA information can be obtained
at www.ICGtesting.com
Printed in the USA
FSOW04n2047030217

303GFS